PENGUIN CRIME FICTION

ON THE OTHER HAND, DEATH

Richard Stevenson is a professional writer living in Massachusetts. He is the author of *Death Trick*, the first Donald Strachey Murder Mystery.

ON THE
OTHER
HAND,
DEATH

RICHARD
STEVENSON

PENGUIN BOOKS

This book is fiction. All of the characters are made up. Any resemblance to real public officials or private citizens in Albany, New York, or elsewhere, is coincidental.

PENGUIN BOOKS
Viking Penguin Inc., 40 West 23rd Street,
New York, New York 10010, U.S.A.
Penguin Books Ltd, Harmondsworth, Middlesex, England
Penguin Books Australia Ltd, Ringwood, Victoria, Australia
Penguin Books Canada Limited, 2801 John Street,
Markham, Ontario, Canada L3R 1B4
Penguin Books (N.Z.) Ltd, 182–190 Wairau Road,
Auckland 10, New Zealand

First published in the United States of America by St. Martin's Press 1984
Published in Penguin Books 1985

LIBRARY OF CONGRESS CATALOGING IN PUBLICATION DATA
Stevenson, Richard.
  On the other hand, death.
  I. Title.
[PS3569.T4567O5 1985]   813'.54   85-9416
ISBN 0 14 00.8319 7

Printed in the United States of America by
George Banta Company Inc., Harrisonburg, Virginia
Set in Caledonia

For Andy, Madilyn, Sally, Jack,
Jim, John, Bob and Don: Tenastelign
    and for Barbara Joslyn

On the Other Hand, Death

1.

Trefusis was going on about a case of "Mandelstam" or "Handel-schism," which made no sense.

"Hang on a minute," I yelled into the mouthpiece. "I can't make out what you're saying."

"I'll hold, of course, Mr. Strachey."

I set the sweat-slick receiver on my desk, reached around, and whacked the top of the clanking and gurgling air conditioner with a slat from the wooden swivel chair that had collapsed back in January. The only effect was a slight shift by the machine in its rotten moorings. The 200-pound Airtemp now threatened to plummet out the window onto Central Avenue two stories below, crushing the shins of the winos who lounged in my entryway. I reached down and yanked out the plug. A distant thunk was followed by a diminishing whine, a sputtering sound, and then hot wet silence.

"Sorry," I said into the phone again, "but I couldn't hear you over the racket my pilot was making up on the helipad. You were saying . . ."

"What I've got for you," Crane Trefusis went on, holding no interest in self-deprecating humor, "is a case of vandalism. Now before you tune out, Mr. Strachey, I'd like you to hear my pitch, because, believe me, this is not your usual run-of-the-mill type of vandalism. It will interest you. I don't want to go into it over the phone, so I'd appreciate your stopping by the office, if you don't mind, where I can lay it all out for you." A little pause. "Under certain conditions our fee could go as high as ten."

Ten. Ten hundred? No, Trefusis would call that a thousand. Or "one."

I hedged anyway. "I've never handled a case of vandalism," I told him. "But with the scale your outfit operates on, I'd expect you to use the term to describe the firebombing of Dresden. Are you sure you wouldn't be better off using an agency with more resources than I've got? Helicopter jokes aside, Mr. Trefusis, I'm just me and a couple of friends who help me out once in a while whenever they haven't got something better to do, like reading Proust in Tagalog or sponsoring disco benefits for the Eritrean Liberation Front. You might want to shop around."

Trefusis was unfazed by either false modesty or fact. "I'm told you're a very solid type," he said, "and the word that comes back to me is that you are definitely the man for this job, Mr. Strachey. I feel strongly that this situation is rather . . . well, special. And when you hear about it I'm confident you'll agree. Can you drop by around four? I can fit you in then."

I hesitated. I'd never met Trefusis, but I'd read a lot in the *Times Union* about both him and his company, and I wasn't overwhelmed with warmth for either. The origins of Millpond Plaza's capital were reported to be murky and its operating methods, under Trefusis, harsh. I was curious, though, about what made a vandalism case "special" for me, and of course there was the "ten." On the one hand this, on the other hand that.

I said, "I doubt that this is a job for me, Mr. Trefusis, but I'll drive out there and you can fill me in. I'm not promising that I'll want to handle it, though. Just so you understand that."

"That's a fair enough arrangement, Mr. Strachey. I'll look forward to seeing you at four."

Arrangement? What arrangement?

I phoned Timmy at his office and said, "It's hot."

"Say, look, I've got important business to transact for the people of the State of New York. If you want to report heat, call the weather bureau. Is this a crank call?"

"I'm cranky and this is a call, so describe it however you want. Anyway, this is a semi-official crank call. What do you know about Crane Trefusis? Anything good?"

"No."

"Bad, then."

"When the Millpond company wants to build a shopping mall, it gets built. Cows, chickens, ducks, geese, grass, people—they'd all better scurry. Millpond is slick, fast, fat, and vicious. Crane Trefusis is their point man. He makes it happen. Something's holding him up on the new project Millpond's planning for west Albany, but I'd guess not for long."

"I've read all that in the papers. Any problems with the law?"

"Probably, but not with the people who enforce the law. Millpond makes friends, one way or another, in the places where friends count. Why are you asking me these easy questions?"

"Trefusis has a job for me, he says. A case of vandalism."

"To solve it or initiate it?"

"I'll find out in a couple of hours when I meet him. I doubt whether we'll find a way to do business, so it shouldn't take long. See you at the apartment around six?"

"Sure. Or six-thirty. Oh—seven, better make it seven. Yeah, seven or so."

What was this? "Or how about eight? Or nine? Or eleven-thirty-five? Aren't you going to the center to meet

Fenton McWhirter? The reception's at seven. What's up?"

"Guess who's in Albany that I'm having a drink with?"

"Happy Rockefeller."

"Uhn-uhn."

"Averell Harriman?"

"Not even close." I could tell he was grinning. "It's Boyd. Boyd's in town."

So. "Oh-ho! Boyd-boy. The return of the native."

"Yep."

"He just called you up and said let's have a drink? Just like that? No intermediaries making preliminary inquiries to find out if you carried a pistol?"

"Ten years is a long time, Don. Wounds heal. He said he *was* a little worried that I might hang up on him. But he took a chance, and he was right. I felt nothing. It might as well have been my Uncle Fergus calling."

"Yeah, well, my regards to Aunt Nell. And to Boyd-boy, even though I've never had the pleasure. So I'll see you later—where? Up the avenue?"

"No, no, I'll meet you at the center for the McWhirter thing. I mean, for chrissakes, Don, we're just having a *drink*."

He said drink as if I had moronically failed to understand that the word really stood for bran muffin. I said, "I'm just giving you a hard time because my brain is melting like frogurt in this heat. In fact, I wish you and Boyd a moderately happy reunion. See you later, lover."

"Moderately happy sounds about right, with the emphasis on the first part. See you at the center. Watch your step with Crane Trefusis, unless you're planning on getting heavily into S and M."

"No chance. You can take the boy out of the presbytery, but you can't take the Presbyterian out of the boy. You'd know about that."

He laughed and hung up.

So. Boyd-boy was back. So? So nothing. Maybe. On the one hand this, on the other hand that.

Droplets of sweat dribbled off my chin onto the copy of *Memoirs of Hadrian* I'd been reading since midmorning. I stripped off my sodden T-shirt, used it to wipe up the lunch-hour sub bun crumbs from my desk, and flung the reeking shmateh into the wastebasket.

I checked my watch. Still time for two or three more chapters of Hadrian before I stopped by the apartment for a quick shower and drove out to Trefusis's office. I opened the book and looked at a page, which contained a picture of Boyd—or, more precisely, a picture of what I imagined the famously azure-eyed diving coach looked like. I refocused and he was gone. I laughed, restrainedly, then reached down and jammed the balky air conditioner's plug back into the wall socket. Something popped. A plume of smoke erupted, and the lights went out from Ontario Street to Northern Boulevard.

I drove home.

2.

At four o'clock, Albany still lay blistering under a savage August sun, but the headquarters of Millpond Plaza Associates remained untouched by mere climate. From the outside, the five-story cube of black glass on outer Western Avenue was as austere and inward-looking as the company's two dozen or so suburban shopping malls. Past the revolving door I half expected to find crowds of young matrons toting G. Fox shopping bags and glassy-eyed kids in game arcades, but the airport-departure-gate-functional lobby was deserted except for a uniformed security guard hunched uncomfortably on a high stool. Bouncy music came out of holes in the ceiling, with no consumers to dance to it.

The temperature in the building couldn't have been above sixty and there was a faint odor of synthetic carpeting and cleaning fluids, as in the loan office at a branch bank or the cabin of a DC-10. Coming in from the steaming heat in chinos and a light cotton sport shirt, I wanted to wrap myself in a blanket. Getting on the elevator, I sneezed.

On the more expensively done up and equally well refrigerated fifth floor Crane Trefusis's secretary was seated in a funnel of brightness behind a kidney-shaped slab of white marble. The sleek blonde was groomed as elegantly as a transvestite I knew who once worked briefly behind the LeVonne Beauty Products counter at Macy's, and she wore a big amber bow around her neck, like a TV anchorwoman.

She flashed a rictus of corporate welcome. "Hi, I'm Marlene Compton. May we help you?"

I didn't know whether the "we" was corporate, imperial, or referred to the small television camera mounted halfway up the polished black granite wall and aimed at me. "Donald Strachey to see Crane Trefusis. He phoned." I sneezed again.

The woman mentioned amiably that her sister-in-law was bothered by the August pollen too, then conversed briefly on an intercom.

"Mr. Trefusis will be able to see you right away," she said, smiling, as if I'd petitioned for this audience, then ushered me past an unmarked white metal door.

Trefusis's office was a long rectangle of rusts and buff with track lighting and *Star Trek* furniture upholstered in orange velvet. The sunlight was molasses-colored pouring through the tinted floor-to-ceiling windows; and Trefusis, moving around from behind his desk with a kind of pained jauntiness, like an athletic man with a bad back, or chronic hemorrhoids, sported deep brown aviator shades. I was afraid he might stumble over something, but he seemed to know his way around the office.

"Good to meet you, Mr. Strachey," he said with a restrained but not uncordial smile. "Your reputation precedes you." His cool hand gave mine a tight squeeze.

"Thank you. Yours too."

He removed the shades and gave me a drolly appraising look. "Sit down and we'll get to know one another," he said, moving back behind the desk. "I'm really quite grateful for your taking the trouble to drive out here. I picked up the impression during our phone conversation that you're somewhat reluctant to work for Millpond— that we are not one of your favorite capitalistic enterprises. Or am I reading something into your manner and tone that wasn't there?"

He was unexpectedly un-ogre-ish and benign-looking, short and compact in a well-cut chocolate brown silk suit and pale orange tie, with thinning red hair streaked with gray, and sun-bleached eyebrows. His bright china blue eyes were the only objects of their color in the room, which might have meant nothing, or could as easily have been some goofy device with a vaguely manipulative purpose he'd picked up in Robert J. Ringer. I decided that if I ever again visited Trefusis's office I'd bring along six old ladies with aqua anklets and blue hair, just for fun, to see if it affected his powers.

I said, "No, I'm not sure I do want to take on this job for you, Mr. Trefusis—whatever it is. But you asked me to hear you out, and it's no trouble for me to do that much. What's the problem?"

An amiably sly look. "I'm guessing that it was partly your curiosity that brought you out here, Mr. Strachey, am I right? Plus, of course, the large fee I mentioned must also have tempted you enormously," he added, the creep. "But *I'm* curious too. I'm told you've done work in recent years for other large Albany corporations. Naturally I've gone into that. You evidently are not anti-business to the point of turning away a fat fee when one is offered. I'm sure you could not do that constantly and survive. So, tell me. What exactly is it about Millpond—about me—that makes you so unenthusiastic? I'd really like to know. Be candid."

I'd been in his office for two minutes and the man almost, but not quite, had me feeling sorry for him. I said, "I've been reading in the papers about the way Millpond keeps pushing people around and ripping up the countryside in order to build the kind of shopping malls we've already got enough of. That's really about all there is to it, Mr. Trefusis. See my problem? I'm one of those eco-freaks. If I worked for you, it'd be a sort of conflict of interest."

Having heard all this before, he laughed lightly, knowingly. "Well, maybe one day we can have a drink and I can convince you that, on balance, our way of doing business ultimately benefits everyone, ecologically minded Americans like yourself included. Ever been to the GUM department store in Moscow, Mr. Strachey? It's a memorably depressing experience. A Soviet citizen once visited our mall in East Greenbush and told me confidentially he thought he had died and gone to heaven. I was impressed by that too."

"You miss the point. It's not retail outlets run by the Bureau of Mines I advocate, Mr. Trefusis. It's a sense of proportion."

"That's a nice catchy phrase. How about a 'Sense of Proportion Liberation Front'? You should put it on a bumper sticker." He waited for me to chuckle along with him.

I said, "You're planning a five-department-store mall in one of the few unspoiled areas left in west Albany, when we've already got Stuyvesant, Latham Circle, Colonie, Mohawk, Pyramid's mammoth going up in Guilderland, and dozens of other smaller shopping centers all over the place. Who needs another one?"

"The hundreds of thousands of people who will shop there need it, Mr. Strachey. They need it and they want it."

"Has there been a referendum? I hadn't heard."

He grinned. "They'll vote when the mall opens, my friend. With their K-cars and Toyotas."

I couldn't argue with that, and I hated his being right. And the smaller shopping centers that would turn into plywood-covered eyesores surrounded by twelve acres of littered tarmac when Millpond opened its new mall were of no importance to anyone except the several hundred people who worked in them or lived around them. The throngs en route to Millpond's consumers' utopia could carefully avert their eyes.

I said, "On the phone you mentioned a case of vandalism. I guess that's a subject you'd know something about."

The anomalous blue eyes hardened for just an instant, but he caught himself—We Do What Works. "I think you'll find, Mr. Strachey, that in this instance Millpond is on the side of the angels. *Your* angels," he added brightly. Then, like a TV anchorperson shifting abruptly from a story on the White House Easter egg hunt to a subway station decapitation, Trefusis looked suddenly, and a little phonily, grave. He said, "Now I'm going to show you something that will make you angry, Mr. Strachey." He shoved a file folder across his Maserati of a desk. "Open it," he said darkly.

I opened it. Trefusis watched me while I leafed through a series of eight-by-ten color photographs. They showed, from various angles, a large well-kept white Victorian farmhouse. The place was surrounded by flowers and flowering shrubs and trees, and was abutted by a smaller white carriage house on which three slogans had been crudely spray-painted in large red letters. One said, DIKES GET OUT; another, LEZIES SUCKS; the third, LEAVE OR DIE! Additionally, a row of pink, white, and deep red hollyhocks along the side of the building had been slashed and mangled.

I closed the folder and slid it back toward him. I said, "Whose house?"

"The owner's name is Dorothy Fisher. Her friend's name is Edith Stout. The house is on Moon Road, off Central Avenue, in west Albany."

Now it was starting to come clear. "I met Dorothy Fisher once," I said. "But I didn't know where she lived."

"It's a vicious act," Trefusis said, shaking his head in disgust. "I hate this kind of intolerance."

"Right. Intolerance is no good. When did this happen?"

"Last night, late."

"You called it a case of vandalism. It's more than that. There's a death threat involved. 'Leave or die!'"

"I don't take that entirely seriously," he said, looking thoughtful. "My guess is, someone's just trying to frighten the . . . ladies. Wouldn't you say?"

"Could be. And you want me to find out who. Is that it?"

He nodded. "Yes. I do. I'll pay you five now and the other five after an arrest has been made. I'm sure your customary fee is a good deal less than that, but I want to be certain that this business is taken care of quickly, and I also want to demonstrate just how important the matter is to me."

Crane Trefusis, humanitarian. I said, "I guess you know that I know *why* this is so important to you, Mr. Trefusis."

A little snort of laughter. "No, I hadn't really supposed, Mr. Strachey, that you were just back from a month at the seashore." He looked mildly insulted. "No, I had no illusions about that. No, indeed."

I'd read about it in the *Times Union*. Millpond had received the necessary environmental and zoning approvals for its proposed west Albany mall and had put together its land package—with one critical exception. There was a lone holdout among the landowners. A Mrs. Dorothy Fisher, whose eight acres were smack in the center of the site, was refusing to sell. She loved her old family home, she said, and planned on living in it until she died. Mrs. Fisher was sixty-eight years old but came from a hearty strain and expected to be around for another twenty or twenty-five years. Millpond had offered her three times the market value of the property, then four times, then five. But money was not the point, Mrs. Fisher insisted. No deal. Millpond was reported to be deeply frustrated and becoming desperate as its delaying costs accelerated.

"So you want to earn Mrs. Fisher's goodwill," I said. "Smite the vicious homophobes and loosen the old dyke up a little so that she'll be more inclined to look favorably on your next offer."

He nodded, poker-faced.

"And by hiring a gay detective to do the job, you further encourage Mrs. Fisher and her friends to concede that Millpond is in the vanguard of enlightened social thought, and to wonder how could she possibly continue to be so stubborn and unreasonable. Why should she refuse to do business with such a nice right-thinking guy like you?"

He looked neither embarrassed nor smirky, nor did he cackle maniacally. He just shrugged. "I see it as a potential happy coincidence of interests," he said mildly. "And if Mrs. Fisher still refused to deal with us after we'd paid you to clear up this unfortunate business for her, then that would in all probability be the end of it. She would in no way be legally obligated to us."

"That's correct."

"I'm prepared to take my chances," he said, smiling faintly. "I've been meeting the public for a good number of years, Mr. Strachey, and I think I know something about human nature. But if I'm wrong—and somehow Mrs. Fisher's gratitude did not extend to accepting our more than generous offer—well, we'd still have the satisfaction of knowing that, whatever the cost, whatever the outcome, Millpond just went ahead and did what was right."

I said, "What a crock."

A faint crooked smile. "You're such a skeptic, Mr. Strachey. I suppose that results from your constantly coming into contact with the seamier side of life. Your outlook, I'm afraid, had become just a little bit distorted, if I may say so."

His statement was not meant to be, so far as I could tell, ironical. I said, "You've got a forty-million-dollar project riding on this."

He threw up his hands in a what-choice-have-I-got gesture and made a face.

Irritated, with Trefusis and with myself, and knowing full well how this loony discussion was going to conclude, I said, "Why don't you just let the Albany cops handle it? They have detectives on their force who will look into the matter for a good bit less than 'ten,' and I happen to know there are several who will investigate a crime for no fee at all."

"Of course they've been notified already," he said, shaking his head doubtfully. "But I want Speedy Gonzales on this one, Mr. Strachey. Someone who can clear it up in a few days. And, as you pointed out, there is the additional advantage for me of your having entree with Mrs.

Fisher and her friends. I've gotten the impression that relations between Albany's finest and the gay community are not what you would call cordial."

"Not cordial, no."

"So there you are."

"Have you told Mrs. Fisher you were planning on hiring me to do this?"

"I . . . left a message."

"She refused to speak with you today, right?"

"When I phoned her about your possible involvement, yes. I'm afraid so."

"Do you know why?"

"Of course. Mrs. Fisher naturally assumes that Millpond is responsible for the vandalism."

"The vandalism and the threat. Are you responsible?"

"No," he said matter-of-factly.

I waited for a barrage of offended posturings, but the simple denial was all Trefusis had to offer on the subject. A blunt and honorable man of his word.

Timmy, who works for politicians and knows a rat's nest when he sees one, would have advised that I politely thank Trefusis for his confidence in me and then swiftly flee the premises. But once I'd seen those photos I knew I was going to become involved in the case in one way or another. And, of course, Trefusis was hardly going to miss the "ten"—which I could always split with Dot Fisher after encouraging her, if she needed encouragement, to refuse Trefusis's final offer. I could also urge Dot to suggest to Trefusis that he take the money he would have paid for her property and donate it instead to the Gay Rights National Lobby, now that he was such an ardent and established benefactor of the cause.

Knowing too that none of it was going to work out anywhere near as simply as that, I still went ahead and said, "Fine. I'll take the case."

The brightness of his china blues intensified a degree

or two. "I'm pleased," he said, nodding once. "A meeting of minds. I thought we might come to an arrangement, Mr. Strachey, and we have succeeded. Let me write you a check for the five," he said, placidly smiling now and removing a cream-colored checkbook from his inside breast pocket. "Or would you prefer cash?"

"A check will be fine," I said, remembering the reports of Millpond's vaguely tainted capital. What was I getting myself into?

"And I've got one other thing for you, Mr. Strachey." He reached for a file folder on a shelf behind his desk.

"What's that?" I asked.

He said, "A list of suspects."

3.

I turned onto Fuller Road and headed toward Central. Bright heat undulated across the concrete pavement and traffic swam through it like schools of bluefish. I stopped at a gas station phone booth, took a deep breath, and went inside. I phoned Timmy and told him it might be nine o'clock before I'd be able to meet him.

"Let me guess. You're having a drink with . . . Buster Crabbe."

"No, that's you, as I recall. I'm on my way out to Dot Fisher's." I described my meeting with Crane Trefusis.

"Dot's a real sweet lady," he said, "and I hope you catch the dementos who did it, even if Millpond shares the credit. Dot's a friend of Fenton McWhirter, did you know that? In fact, I think he's staying with her while he's in Albany."

"Dot gets around for such a late bloomer."

"You've met her, haven't you?"

"Once, briefly, at the demonstration after the baths were raided."

"She caused quite a sensation that day. The cops and the TV people thought she was somebody's grandmother. Of course, she is. So, where do you begin? If, by some crazy chance, Millpond is not behind what's happening out there, who might be?"

"Trefusis thoughtfully provided me with a list of suspects," I said, moving the door of the airless phone booth back and forth like a fan. "There are two other families on Moon Road with a strong interest in seeing Dot deal. It turns out Millpond has *optioned* their properties but won't buy outright until Dot's been lined up too. Both parties are hot to sell and don't like it at all that Dot is standing in the way of their windfall. They're very mad, maybe mad enough to provide Dot with some rude encouragement. That's where I begin."

"Millpond has set it all up with their characteristic finesse," Timmy said. "This way they let someone else do their dirty work without lifting a finger."

"I think I'll keep an open mind for a day or two on who lifted which finger for what purpose. Like you said, Citizen Crane is a fairly complicated guy. He tries to come across as Mister Hardnosed-but-Open-and-Direct, yet the whole time I was with him I felt as though I was in the presence of a rather extensive rain forest. I don't envy anyone who has to navigate his mind regularly."

"Better take along a machete on this one."

"My Swiss Army knife will have to do. And my heat-addled brain. See you around nine, then?"

"Oh . . . yeah. Around nine. For sure."

"Swell. See you."

For sure? In the six years I'd known him I'd never heard him use that phrase. Only twenty-year-olds said that. Where had he picked it up? From a twenty-year-old? Or from someone who spent a lot of time hanging around twenty-year-olds? The hell with it, I thought. Timmy and I were solid, a twosome. The heat was cooking my few million remaining brain cells, that's all it was. Marrakech-on-the-Mohawk. Ouagadougou-on-the-Hudson. For sure.

The two other homes on Moon Road were of more modest proportions, so Dot Fisher's farmhouse was not hard to pick out.

The first place I passed was an old two-story frame box with flaking tarpaper shingles. The place listed crazily to the southwest, and a newer freshly painted side porch sat partially detached from the sinking house, like a dinghy by a shipwreck. It was easy to see why the owners of this one wanted badly to take Millpond's money and run with it.

The second house, another fifty yards down the narrow rutted road, was a two-tone beige and electric blue 1950s ranch. It had a big picture window with a lamp in the middle, a double garage, and a long, fat Plymouth Fury wagon with a smashed taillight parked in the driveway. There was a green plastic worm with wheels and a seat lying on its side on the recently mowed lawn, and off to the left of the property, in an area where the underbrush had been cut away, a '68 T-bird was up on cinder blocks. As at the first house, I saw no sign of life.

Banging on ahead over the potholes, I passed a Channel 12 TV van lurching and swaying back toward Central Avenue. I guessed I had just missed a media event and had mixed feelings about what the report, once broadcast, was going to mean.

Moon Road dead-ended just beyond the Fisher house, so I bypassed Dot's driveway with two cars already in it and parked by a scraggly stand of sun-scorched sumac trees where the pavement ended. A newly bulldozed dirt track ran off to the left. The foliage along it was wilting under fine brown dust. I could hear the roar of the traffic on the interstate a hundred yards or so beyond the trees, though not the heavy equipment building the new interchange—more canny planning by Millpond. It was after four on a Friday now and work had stopped for the weekend. I walked back toward the house.

As I moved up the fieldstone walkway past long, tall clumps of purple-pink phlox, a young man emerged from behind the house carrying an aluminum ladder. I recognized his face from news photos in *The Native* and *Gay Community News*, and I cut across the lawn under a big spreading oak tree to meet him. He was moving purposefully toward the carriage house, which still had the ugly slogans sprayed all over its side, like a Manhattan subway car lost upstate.

I called, "Hello . . . Fenton McWhirter?"

He turned abruptly and looked at me uncertainly for a few seconds, then set the ladder down and extended his hand. "Yes, how do you do? Are you a reporter?"

"No. Don Strachey. I'm a private investigator. That looks like a real job in this heat. Will the graffiti wash off, or will you have to paint over it?"

Looking harried and put out, he spoke to me impatiently in a raspy baritone. "Mrs. Fisher isn't sure whether or not she wants to talk to you, you know? You're the guy Crane Trefusis said he was sending out here?"

"I'm the guy, but I'd probably have come anyway. Try not to think of me as Trefusis's agent. It's true he's paying me, but what the hell."

He peered at me as if I might not be the most mentally stable person he'd met that day. In ragged cutoffs and a sweat-stained T-shirt, he was in his early thirties, slender but solid, with the sort of lean, exaggeratedly de-

fined musculature and bone structure I'd always associated more with Renaissance anatomical studies than with
real people. The lips of his wide mouth were severely
ridged rather than rounded, a feature I'd always found
erotic, but the mess of teeth beyond them was badly in
need of tidying up. His strong face was all angles and
planes, with a thick stubble of dirty blond hair that might
have been meant as a beard, or could have been the result
of his not having had the time, or the interest, to shave for
a few days, or could as well have been the way movement
people on the West Coast were wearing their faces these
days and the fad would reach Albany in 1990. His deep-
set gray eyes were smallish and bloodshot, and they
looked at me with no pleasure.

"This Trefusis asshole sent a crew over earlier to re-
paint the barn," McWhirter said sourly. "Dot told them to
fuck off. But she says she knows you, or heard of you or
something, and she's surprised you're working for Millpond."

"That makes two of us," I said. "Life gets complicated
sometimes. On the one hand this, on the other hand
that."

He peered at me stonily. "You sound to me like a
rather indecisive person to be doing the kind of work you
claim you do. I can't actually see how you're going to be
any help around here. Dot and Edith need protection, not
a lot of bullshit existential angst."

"Maybe I won't be much help," I said, seized by a fit
of free-floating perversity. "Or maybe I will." I wished
somebody would offer me a cold Molson's.

McWhirter was supposed to burst into laughter at this
point, and I'd laugh too, and we'd immediately become
great pals. But he didn't laugh. He just shook his head
incredulously and made a little astonished sound with his
breath, like "eeesh." Revolution was a serious business. I
hadn't made a hit.

"What do you mean, 'protection'?" I said, trying to meet him on his own terms, of which I'd run into worse. "Has something else happened since last night? Have there been more threats?"

His look hardened and he was about to reply, when another figure appeared from around the back corner of the house carrying a gallon can of paint and two brushes.

"Peter, come over here and meet the gay James Bond," McWhirter said loudly. "He says he's going to catch the assholes who are after Dot—except he's also on *their payroll*. He's a little confused, but he says not to worry."

I recognized Peter Greco, McWhirter's lover, an Albany native who'd been in California or on the road with McWhirter since I'd come to Albany eight years earlier, so we hadn't met. He was short and fragile-looking in jeans and no shirt, with shiny olive skin and a frail boy's thin arms. He had an open, quietly cheerful face, curly black hair on his head and chest, and placid dark eyes. I'd always thought poets were supposed to be pimpled and funny-looking, but I'd read some of Greco's verses and he, unhappily, was no Auden, so maybe that explained it.

"Hi," he said, smiling easily despite McWhirter's sarcastic, and possibly accurate, introduction. "You're a gay detective? I don't think I've ever met one before."

"Of course you have," McWhirter put in emphatically. "You just didn't *know* they were gay. That's the whole *point*."

"I'm Don Strachey," I said, offering my hand. There was a brief tussle of fingers and thumbs while we found the old movement handclasp of the '60s. "I am a private investigator, yes, and more or less coincidentally gay, and it's also true that I'm being paid by Millpond. But I'll be working for Dot, if she's agreeable. I'd have done that anyway."

"Why don't you come in and talk to her?" Greco said,

cheerfully accepting me at my word. Was he an instant judge of good character, or a dangerously vulnerable naif? "Dot won't admit it," he said, "but she's really pretty upset, and she can use all the help and support she can get right now. And Edith's not making things any easier."

I thought at first that "Edith" might be a pet name for McWhirter, but then I remembered.

I said, "Fine, I'd like to talk with Dot. When did you two arrive? Were you here last night when it happened?"

"No, we just got into town this morning, but we were here when the letter arrived. It really shook poor old Edith up. At first Dot wasn't even going to show it to her."

"What letter was that? Trefusis didn't mention a letter."

McWhirter snapped, "Why should he? He *wrote* it, didn't he? Or his Mafia goons did. Or maybe you wrote it yourself, Strachey. I've heard all about this Trefusis gangster, and I wouldn't trust anybody who had *anything* to do with him."

Greco and I went on with our exchange of information while McWhirter stood there adding to the humidity. "It was in the mailbox when Dot went out around three this afternoon," Greco said. "Dot called the police right away, and they said they'd send a detective out, but he hasn't shown up yet. It's just a plain piece of notebook paper with printing that says, 'You're next. You got three days. Saturday you die.' It was addressed to both Edith and Dot."

I said, "Today's Friday. The letter arrived in the regular mail?"

Greco nodded. "It was postmarked Wednesday in Albany. Whoever sent it must have thought it would be delivered the next day."

"Could be," I said. "Somebody who doesn't patronize

the Postal Service regularly and doesn't know how slow it can be. Or someone who can't add, or use a calendar."

"I am going to demand," McWhirter said, eyes flashing, "that the police provide round-the-clock protection for Dot and Edith. And if those assholes aren't out here within half an hour, I am notifying the media and driving straight in to city hall and the mayor's office. It's been two fucking hours since Dot called them!"

"Ask nicely and the Albany cops might be helpful," I said. "Demand anything of them and they'll vanish without a trace. Or worse. They're a sensitive lot." McWhirter glowered. "As for the mayor," I went on, enjoying myself a little, "I'm fairly certain it's already past his bedtime. Not that he's all that alert and responsive during his waking hours. I'm not saying, Fenton, that municipal government in Albany functions exactly the same way it does in, say, Buenos Aires. It's more benign here—slower and sleepier than in the tropics. But don't get your hopes up. To a very large extent, if you're gay in Albany you're on your own. I'm a little surprised at your expectations. Surely you must have run onto similar situations elsewhere."

McWhirter scowled at me with disgust, as if I were a prince of the local machine instead of one of its taxpaying reluctant benefactors. "And people like you just sit around and take it," he said acidly, then abruptly picked up his ladder and stalked off muttering.

Greco frowned after him for a moment, then shrugged and smiled, his most natural expression. I thought it would be nice to go lie down with him in some shady spot. He said, "Poor Fenton. He's having a hard enough time getting the campaign off the ground, and then when he comes here he runs into this awful mess. It's been a rough year for him, believe me."

He set down the paint cans and brushes and we

walked toward the back of the house past a bed of nasturtiums that looked like cool, soft fire. I said, "There's been no mass of recruits signing on for the gay national strike?"

A weary laugh. "No, no masses. If the GNS is going to work there'll have to be millions, of course. But so far the people who've pledged to come out of the closet and join the strike can only be numbered in the hundreds. Or maybe tens," he added, shaking his head dolefully. "We've only been to nine cities so far, and we've got almost another year—ten and a half months—to get people committed. But so far it's been pretty discouraging. A joke, really. I mean, it's partly because it's summer, don't you think? People are more interested now in cultivating their tans than they are in social justice. Maybe in the fall . . ." He turned to me with a tentative smile. "So, how do you think we'll do at the center in Albany tonight?"

"Hard to say," I lied, having a good idea of what was going to happen. Which was too bad, because McWhirter's notion of a national coming-out day as the first event of a week-long gay national strike seemed to me a wonderful piece of whimsy—which, if it ever somehow actually happened, could make a real difference in the way American homosexuals were thought of and treated.

McWhirter, I'd read in the gay papers, envisioned gay air traffic controllers, executives, busboys, priests, construction workers, doctors, data analysts, White House staffers, Congressmen, newsboys, waitresses, housewives, firemen, FBI agents—the whole lot of us suddenly declaring ourselves and walking off our jobs and letting the straight majority try to keep the country running on their own for a week. It was a bold, wacky, irresistible idea.

But a lot of people were resisting the GNS anyway. The big national gay organizations estimated—correctly, I guessed—that too few people would participate and the thing would end up an embarrassment to the movement. This was also a self-fulfilling prophecy: McWhirter was receiving no financial support from the big outfits. His waspish personality was said to be putting off a number of would-be supporters too. Another good idea done in by its originator's poor social skills.

The gay press was covering McWhirter's campaign sporadically and offering wistful and qualifiedly encouraging editorials. Notice by the straight press had been even more fitful, and the tone of the few stories printed or broadcast had ranged from the tittering to the maliciously bug-eyed.

Albany would not, I thought, be the place where the GNS campaign took off. Of the sixteen people likely to show up at the Gay Community Center that night to hear McWhirter's plea for support, three would tiptoe upstairs midway in the presentation and play Monopoly. Of the six who would sign on at the end of McWhirter's description of how we would shut the country down for a week, three would be full-time recipients of public assistance. The outlook in Albany was not promising.

"Well," Greco said, putting the best face on it, "even if we don't do terribly well at the center tonight, we'll be leafleting the bars afterwards. I remember when I lived here that on Friday nights the bars are full of state workers. Imagine what it would be like if all the gay people in the South Mall walked out for a week. What a glorious mess that would be!"

"Right. The state bureaucracy would become sluggish and disorganized."

He stopped by the back door of the house and looked at me uncertainly, examined my face, then suddenly shook with bright laughter. "Well," he said, "you know what I mean." He laughed again, and his hand came up and gently brushed my cheek, a gesture as natural and

uncomplicated for Greco as a happy child's reaching out
spontaneously to touch a sibling. Greco, waiflike and vulnerable, was not a type I usually went for. But on the
other hand . . . Maybe it was the heat.

Inside the big pine-paneled kitchen of the farmhouse, Dot
Fisher was slumped against a doorjamb and speaking wearily into a wall phone. One hand pressed the receiver
hard against her ear under a short, damp thicket of frizzy
gray-black hair, and the other arm rested on the little
crockpot of a belly that protruded from her otherwise wiry
frame. Wet half-moons stained the sides of the white cotton sleeveless shift she wore, and her long, sun-reddened
face, deeply etched with age and the things she knew, was
screwed up now in a grimace of barely controlled frustration, and gleamed with sweat. She forced a distracted
smile in our direction and waggled a finger urgently at the
refrigerator.

Greco and I helped ourselves to the iced mint tea and
sat at a cherrywood table by the window overlooking the
farm pond while Dot finished up her conversation. "Well,
not at all. Thank *you* for *your* time," she told whoever was
at the other end of the line—a reporter, it sounded like—
and then collapsed in a chair across from us, where she
began to fan her face with a Burpee seed catalog.

"Oh, what a day this has been!" she croaked. "And this
heat! Good heavens, the least these awful people could
have done was wait until October to . . . to do whatever
they're trying to do to us. Speaking of which— I suppose
you're Donald Strachey, aren't you? Mr. Johnny-on-the-
spot from Millpond." Her look was not friendly.

"Yes, ma'am. We met last year around this time. Under similarly depressing circumstances."

"Mm-hmm." She examined me coolly. "Depressing is
certainly the word for it. And *confusing*," she added
pointedly.

"I really think Don is going to be helpful," Greco put in, grinning a little zanily. "He cares a lot about you, Dot, and he can work twenty-four hours a day to find out what's going on and put a stop to it. I mean, you know, the police will go through the motions and all, but to have an experienced private investigator on your side, even if he's employed by— Well, it can't hurt, can it? If you're going to stay here and not give in—"

"What do you mean, *if* I'm going to stay and not give in?"

Greco shrugged, grinned tentatively. "Naturally I meant *since* you're not going to give in."

"You'd *better* mean it."

I said, "I'm glad to see how determined you are, Mrs. Fisher. Most people in your position would have locked up the house and booked passage on a three-month cruise through the Norwegian fjords. Or sold out to Millpond and headed for Fort Lauderdale. And I know you know how formidable an outfit Millpond can be. Treacherous even. You've got lot of guts."

"You really needn't explain the obvious to me, young man," she said evenly. "And don't waste your breath trying to flatter me either." Her brown eyes had softened, though, and she looked as if something had suddenly struck her funny and she was trying hard not to smile. "And I might add, you'd better not let *Edith* hear you say that word, Mr. Strachey—"

"Don."

"Well, Don," she said, "however brief your visit on Moon Road might turn out to be, you're going to have to remember that Edith cannot *stand* that word."

"Which word? Fjords? Fort Lauderdale?"

"Oh, no!" She found a way to laugh now, shakily, despite herself. "No, no. Peter, you say it."

"Guts," Greco whispered. "Edith hates the word 'guts.' She also, unfortunately, can't stand the word 'rot.'"

"One time a whole lot of years ago," Dot said, looking relieved to be distracted for the moment, "Edie and I were at a teachers' convention in Buffalo, and I mentioned during dinner that I thought the wine tasted like rotgut. Well, Edie just stood right up and marched out of the room! Oh what a brouhaha that was between us. I haven't said either word in front of her since that evening, and that's been twenty years ago if it's a day."

Greco and I laughed, but Dot's mood had shifted abruptly back, and she was watching me levelly again, somberly. "Now then," she said. "Let's do get to the point of all this, Mr. Strachey—Don. You're not exactly in my home on a social call, are you? Crane Trefusis phoned earlier and told Peter that he was sending you over to help us out. That struck me as *extremely* peculiar. *Is* that correct? That you are working for Millpond?"

"It is. On this case, yes."

"Mm-hmm. Well. You know, I'll bet, just what my opinion of Crane Trefusis is, don't you? That he's a . . . a crock of rotgut." She shot a quick look down the hallway again.

"He mentioned it. Or words to that effect."

"However," she went on, watching me even more closely now, "I called up a mutual friend of yours and mine this afternoon, Lew Morton, and Lew told me emphatically that I could trust you. He said even if you were being paid by Millpond you'd be a good man to have helping us out, and that you would know what you were doing. I didn't like the sound of that, but I trust Lew's judgment about people. So, Mister-Private-Eye-with-the-Morals-of-Rhett-Butler—and the mustache—tell me then. *Do* you know what you're doing?"

I said, "No."

Greco laughed and Dot looked startled.

"All right then," she said, reassured slightly by

Greco's good humor. "Let me put it this way. Do you plan to *figure out* what you're doing?"

"That's the plan," I said.

"And you're on our side in this great war with Mill-pond?"

"Absolutely. Trefusis is paying me to catch the vandals. We can both imagine what his motives are in hiring me instead of someone else, but forget that. I'll just do the job, and after that I bow out."

She considered this carefully for a long moment, then said, "And you understand that I am *not* selling this house under *any* circumstances?" Her face was set now, her dark eyes bright with emotion.

I said, "That's clear by now."

"Oh, all right then." She sighed, the apprehension about me fading but the fear still in her eyes. "In fact, thank you. Yes, thank you very much. I'm a tough old bird, any of my former students will tell you quick enough. Yes, I've always been a very strong person. But I'm frightened. Today I'm just scared to death. And I just want you to . . . I just hope you can help get us out of this . . . this phantasmagoria!"

"That's what I want to do."

"It has *not* been pleasant. Oh, no, not pleasant. First today it was those asinine words on the barn. And then *this* infernal nonsense arrived."

She picked up the Burpee seed catalog she'd used as a fan, slid an envelope from between the pages, and handed it to me. I opened it, lifted out the single sheet of paper by a corner, flipped it open, and read: "You're next. You got three days. Saturday you die!"

It was hard to tell whether the printing had been done by the same hand responsible for the carriage house graffiti, which had been hurriedly and sloppily spray-painted. There were similarities in the way the *Y*'s and

G's slanted, but an expert would come up with a more reliable opinion than mine. Maybe the police would provide a graphologist and fingerprint person. I knew they did that sometimes.

I asked Dot to describe one more time the events of the past eighteen hours. She groaned, decided she'd better have a Schlitz, brought me and Greco each a can too, then sped through it.

Dot and Edith had gone to bed at eleven-thirty the night before, watched *Nightline*, then slept soundly with the air conditioner running. They were not awakened by any sounds during the night. At seven in the morning Dot went out to pick up the *Times Union* from the roadside box and saw the graffiti. She informed Edith, who promptly went back to bed with a headache. Dot phoned the police, who arrived around eight-thirty.

At eight-fifty the two patrolmen departed, having expressed sympathy and stated that a police detective would arrive later in the morning. None had. At nine-forty-five, Dot, frustrated and "hopping mad," phoned Crane Trefusis and told him what she thought of "his cruel prank." Trefusis denied all. He sent a PR lackey out to the house to recoil in horror and further plead Millpond's innocence, and a photographer to record the crime on film. These were the pictures I'd seen.

McWhirter and Greco arrived from New York City around eleven in their car, the old green Fiat I'd seen in the driveway alongside Dot's Ford Fiesta. McWhirter went straight for the phone book and began calling newspapers and radio and TV stations. A Millpond paint crew showed up at noon. Dot would have let them do the job, but McWhirter explained that none of the television people had arrived yet—"You get more air time with a good visual," he correctly pointed out—so the Millpond crew was sent away.

Trefusis called back in the early afternoon—probably just after he'd phoned me—and told Peter I might be showing up to help out. Dot refused to speak with Trefusis. At three, the threatening letter was discovered in the mailbox. Dot phoned the Albany Police Department once again and was promised assistance. As yet, none was forthcoming. A television news crew showed up an hour or so later, and soon after that I arrived.

"Fenton wasn't too happy to see Don," Peter told Dot. "He's convinced Don must be a spy or something for Millpond. Part of the pressure they're putting on you."

"That's understandable," I said. "Trefusis is one of Albany's most accomplished sneaks. I would have been just as suspicious of me myself."

"Fenton heard all about that Crane Trefusis from me," Dot said, getting the same nauseated look on her face that Trefusis's name tended to inspire in a lot of people, as if a dog under the table had silently farted. "Someday I'll tell you stories about that man that will just curl your hair!"

I looked over at Greco's curly hair and wondered if he'd already heard them. For the second time in an hour I wanted to reach over and take his head very carefully in my hands.

A door opened somewhere in the front reaches of the house, and a warbly nasal voice, like a flute with a piece of straw stuck in it, wafted down the hallway. "Dor-o-thy? Are you back there, Dor-o-thy?"

"Yes, we're back here, hon. In the kitchen."

A short plump woman in a floral print dress ambled into the room. She had an abstracted, vaguely wounded look, as if preoccupied with a deep pain that had begun a long time ago, or maybe her feet hurt. Her prominent jaw was set like a pink Maginot Line, and she had snow white hair done in a beauty parlor wave. She smelled of lilac water, face powder, and old bureau drawers. Through white plastic-framed glasses, her cool blue eyes gave me a weary baleful look. I was another sign of the trouble.

"Edith, this is Mr. Strachey," Dot said loudly. "He's a detective."

Edith squinted at me, looking lost, as I stood up.

"He's a *detective*, Edie. A detective—Donald *Strachey*."

"H. P. Lovecraft? Why, I thought he was dead!"

"*Strachey*. Donald *Strachey*, Edie. A detective who's going to catch the people who wrote on the barn!"

"Yes, yes, someone wrote on the barn, you already told me about that, Dorothy. I know all about that. Has anyone watered the peonies, Dorothy? This weather . . . my word!"

"Fenton and Peter watered them a little while ago, hon."

"The petunias in the window box look about ready to expire. And, my stars, I know just how they feel. Are you a gardener, Archie?"

She seemed to be addressing me. I said, "No, I'm not, Mrs. Stout. When I was a boy in New Jersey I once caused a single onion to sprout for my Cub Scout agrarian badge, but that's about the extent of it."

"We tried brussels sprouts too one year," Edith said sadly. "But the coons filched them."

"Oh. Sorry."

Something crossed her mind and, suddenly alert, she gave me the fish-eye. "I suppose you're one of Dorothy's gay-lib friends. Is that it? March up and down the street, make a commotion, get us all into this trouble?"

"I guess I am," I said. "But I don't think I'll march today, Mrs. Stout. Not in this weather."

"That is *not* what I *meant*," she said, glaring, "and you know it." She sniffed and gave Dot a why-do-you-do-this-to-me look. "I guess I'll just wander out and rest my feet

by the pond for a spell. You young people enjoy your-
selves. Are you coming out, Dorothy?"

"After a bit, hon. When it cools down a bit we can go
for a stroll. And I think I'll take a quick dip in the pond
later."

"Oh, that would be lovely," Edith said, forgetting the
trouble again. "I'll fix some cucumber sandwiches and
lemonade. This weather! My land, when will we get some
relief!"

When Edith had gone, Dot smiled weakly. "Edie's
hearing isn't what it once was. I guess you could tell. And,
yes, she's fretful too, and forgetful and . . . every once in
a while, thank the Lord, Edith is cheery and sweet and
sharp as a tack. Just the way she used to be. But, oh dear,
the years certainly are taking their toll. Not that that isn't
to be expected. Edith's seven years older than I am, Don,
did you know that? Edie will be seventy-six next month."

I wanted to say she didn't seem it, but she did. Older,
in fact. Edith appeared sturdy enough, her health generally sound. But her mind was on its way out, well ahead of
the rest of her. I wondered who this would happen to
first—Timmy or me?

The telephone rang, and Dot sprang up to answer it.
She was as light on her feet as Edith was heavy, as alert as
Edith was vague and uncertain.

As Dot listened to the caller, I watched the color drain
from her face. Abruptly, she slammed the receiver down.
The blood returned to her cheeks and neck in a rush as
she looked at me, stricken, and said, "Now they're *phoning* us with their horrible threats! Now this is the absolute
limit!"

4.   "Tomorrow you die!" was what the voice on the phone had said in a harsh whisper. Dot wasn't certain whether it had been a man or a woman speaking.

I summoned McWhirter and Greco, who had just finished up the paint-over job.

"I'm calling the police again," McWhirter said, livid, and grabbed up the phone.

I said, "Good idea."

Dot sat down and shakily drank from her can of beer. While McWhirter explained to the police desk officer how he was an unwitting agent of heterosexist oppression, I asked Dot about the other families who lived on Moon Road, the ones on Crane Trefusis's list of suspects.

"I do feel sorry for them," she said, trying hard to smile and focus on something other than her fear. "We don't see much of one another, of course, but both the Deems and Wilsons seem like awfully nice people—or at least Kay Wilson does—and I do wish there was some way for them to get their money without my having to sell out to those thieves from Millpond."

She sipped at the beer, glanced once at the phone, which suddenly had become a menacing object for her, then made herself go on.

"Kay Wilson used to come up and draw water from our spring and we'd chat, but she hasn't been by since last month, when I told her we definitely weren't going to sell. And Joey Deem doesn't come by to mow the lawn anymore. It's upsetting. And I feel terribly guilty sometimes, but . . . *really*. This is my *home*. I suppose I *could* pick up and start over. But after thirty-eight years in one place . . . well, it's hard to tell where this house ends and I begin. It would be like cutting off an arm and a leg.

"And Edith! Oh, my. She's been with me since her Bert died in sixty-eight, and what a trial it would be for her to pull up stakes. A trial for *both* of us. I'd probably try to drag her off to Laguna Beach or P-town, or some other reservation for old dykes, and, oh, Lord, she'd just be fit to be tied! In case you didn't notice," she added with a little laugh, "Edith's a conservative and I'm a liberal."

I said, "I caught that."

"Well, let me tell you, young man. When I came out in seventy-nine, Edith nearly had a fit. I marched in the gay-pride parade in New York that year—that's where I met Fenton and Peter—and Edith almost drove the both of us right into the booby hatch with her fussing and carrying on. Finally she did ride along with me on the bus down to the city. But then, wouldn't you know, when the parade started up Fifth Avenue, Edith just stomped over and walked up the sidewalk alongside the parade! Her legs were better then, but she still had a devil of a time keeping up. Mad as a wet hen she was, fretting the whole time that one of the girls in our bridge club might see me on TV.

"Not that it would have mattered to *me*. In fact, later that summer was when I finally came out with the girls. Now *there's* a story I'll tell you someday, and you won't know whether to laugh or cry. There were eight of us in the bridge club back then, and now we're just five. That's a good number for poker"—she laughed—"but not worth a tinker's damn for bridge."

"It sounds pretty awkward."

"I guess that's one reason I'd like to hang on to this old house. It's like a true friend that doesn't judge us."

"You'll keep it. You'll get through this."

"Will we?" Her brown eyes were dull with exhaustion and defeat. "Sometimes I'm not so sure. After a while you just begin to run out of steam." She heaved a deep sigh and began to fan her face with the Burpee catalog. "Well, Don, I guess there's no shortage of steam today, is there?"

I agreed that there was not. McWhirter came back from the phone, announced that he had dealt persuasively with the Albany Police Department, and said he was going to paint the rest of the barn while he awaited their arrival and their apologies for being tardy.

I said, "I'll look forward to that too."

Greco followed McWhirter outside, and I asked Dot for quick sketches of her neighbors on Moon Road, which she provided. One of them, Bill Wilson, who at the height of an argument over the Millpond situation had called Dot "a stubborn old bag" and kicked the fender of her Fiesta, sounded like a man especially worth getting to know. Though I planned on calling on all the rest of them too.

Dot adamantly refused my suggestion that she and Edith spend the next few days in a motel. Who would water the peonies? Nor would she consent to phoning any of her or Edith's children or grandchildren, all of them spread about the Sunbelt, where she and Edith visited each February. Dot said her friend Lew Morton was coming over to spend the evening, and Peter Greco had promised to return to the house by midnight with or without McWhirter, who had set a goal of recruiting at least a hundred gay national strikers that night as he moved through the Central Avenue bars and discos. The man was from Mars, but I figured Albany could stand it for a day or two. In its history as a state capital, the town had seen stranger sights.

As I bumped back up Moon Road, I passed an un-marked blue Dodge with a familiar face at the wheel heading toward Dot's. Detective Lieutenant Ned Bow-man was busy avoiding potholes, but he glanced my way as he careened past. He must have recognized me, as his eyebrows did the little dip-glide-swoop dance of horror my presence always triggered, and which over the years I'd come to look forward to in a small way.

I pulled up in front of the Deem house. The old Fury was still in the driveway, and now a cream-colored Toyota sedan was parked beside it, fresh heat undulating off its muffler. Above the house, the sun was a great white blot against the western sky. I checked my watch. It was just six-ten.

"Good evening. I'm Donald Strachey and I'm working for Millpond Plaza Associates. Are you Mrs. Deem?"

"Oh. Yes, I'm Sandra Deem. You're from Millpond? Oh, gee. Why don't you come in, Mr. Strachey? Jerry's in the shower but he'll be out in a minute." Her voice was muted, insubstantial, as if it came from a high place where the air was too thin.

"Thank you. It's hot out here."

"Oh, isn't it awful? Gosh, nobody called us from Millpond today. Is there anything new? We haven't heard from Mr. Trefusis at all for a couple weeks."

As I stepped into the living room, Mrs. Deem looked tentatively hopeful. She was thirty-seven-ish, with pale skin, a plain round freckled face, and black rings of sweat around dull hazel eyes. She wore tan bermuda shorts, a sleeveless white cotton blouse, and rubber thongs on small feet. She smelled heavily of Ban.

I said, "As a matter of fact, there have been some developments. But none that will be helpful for you and your husband, I'm afraid. A problem's come up. Somebody is harassing and threatening Mrs. Fisher and Mrs. Stout."

Her eyes narrowed and she thought this over. She brushed her hand across her own cheek the way Peter Greco had touched mine earlier. "Why don't you sit down, Mr. Strachey," she said after a moment, and directed me to a long high-backed couch covered with pictures of "colonial" scenes. A picture of a blond haloed Jesus hung above it.

"What is this person actually doing to harass Mrs. Fisher?" she said. "Whoever's doing it. Gosh, that's an awful thing."

I stepped over the blocks and dolls and stuffed animals on the gold-colored shag rug and seated myself behind a coffee table. "Nasty slogans were painted on the carriage house last night. A letter and a phone call came today threatening death if Dot and Edith didn't leave. You're right. It's upsetting for both of them."

A toddler toddled into the room from the kitchen. "Hi-ee," she said, checking me out with big inquisitive blue eyes.

"Hi," I said. "What's your name?"

Mrs. Deem breathed, "Heather, you go out and play now. We'll have supper in a couple minutes. Go on."

"By-eee." Heather spun around several times, pretending to be dizzy, then went out and played.

"That must be real scary," Mrs. Deem said, and perched on the edge of an easy chair that matched the early American couch. "Gosh, I just don't approve of that at all. Scaring a couple of old people like that." She was speaking to me but she also seemed distracted by a thought, as if she might have knowledge of the subject she wished she didn't have, or an opinion on it that was forming itself in a troubling way.

"No one knows, of course, whether the threats are serious," I said. "But that's part of the problem in a thing like this. The not knowing. I've been hired by Millpond to track down whoever's responsible."

"Oh, I see." She looked even more worried. Then she remembered something and stood up. "Why don't you come out to the kitchen, Mr. Strachey, if that's okay? Do you mind? I'm getting supper and we can talk in the kitchen. Jerry will be out any minute. I want him to hear about this too."

I followed her and took a seat by the Formica table. A little color Sony was on the counter. Dick Block and the anchor news team were chattily rattling off brief accounts of the day's convenience-store holdups and double suicides.

Sandra Deem dumped half a bottle of something Kelly green over a bowl of chopped-up iceberg lettuce and said, "Do you think somebody around *here* is doing these things to Mrs. Fisher? Is that why you're here? I mean, why are you asking us about it?"

"We have to assume that's a possibility, Mrs. Deem. The three parties with something to gain by Mrs. Fisher's being scared off are your family, the Wilsons, and of course Millpond, my employer. So I have to ask you if there's anyone in your household—or maybe some sympathetic friend of yours or your husband's—who you think might be mad enough to break the law in this way."

Her face tightened, and she stood there blinking at me with the half-empty bottle of green glop poised above the salad bowl. "No," she said after a moment. "No, I really don't think so. Not something as mean as that. No, I can't think of *anybody* who would do such an un-Christian thing." Her voice gained an approximation of fervor as she spoke, but there was apprehension in her eyes.

The man who padded barefoot into the kitchen, looking startled when he saw me there, was around my age, forty-three, paunchy in a fresh white Fruit of the Loom T-shirt and pale green slacks, and smelling of chemical substances meant to be cosmetic. He had thinning sandy hair, alert wide eyes the color of his pants, and the expression on his pleasant boyish face was one of mild perplexity.

"Hi, I'm Don Strachey from Millpond Plaza Associates," I said, getting up, and sounding to myself like a character on *Dynasty*.

"Glad to meet you. I'm Jerry Deem."

We shook hands. His eyes never left mine. He was looking for something in them, but I didn't know what. What the hell I was doing at his kitchen table, I guessed.

"I'm sorry to bother you at this time of day, but I'd like to talk with you for a few minutes about some trouble that's come up over at Dot Fisher's place."

"Oh?" He looked puzzled but not overly concerned. "Well, why don't we go out and sit on the—"

"Shhh, listen!" Mrs. Deem interrupted. "It's on the news. Oh, gosh."

We all looked at the little Sony, and Deem turned up the sound.

First we saw the graffiti on the carriage house while Dick Block's voice intoned something about "the latest alleged incident of harassment to the gay community." The "gay community," we soon saw, was Dot, seated on the stone terrace behind her house. She was being questioned by a young woman wearing the obligatory TV newswoman's scarf around her neck, even in the heat, like a drag queen trying to cover up his Adam's apple.

"And what were your thoughts," the reporter was saying grimly, "when you came out this morning and saw the words painted on your pretty barn, Mrs. Fisher?"

"Well," Dot replied, a little uncertainly, "my thoughts were . . . what I guess you would call . . . unhappy."

The reporter paused, squinting uncomprehendingly, as if Dot had just recited in Urdu. She said, "Unhappy?"

"Yes," Dot said. "Unhappy. Wouldn't *you* be?"

The newswoman, her mascara looking dangerously moist, was growing fidgety. She said, "You must have been . . . upset."

Dot nodded. "Yes. I was. Though these things don't

bowl you over the way they once did. I've seen a good bit of nastiness on the way to where I am now. And you learn to take a lot of it. Though only up to a point," she added emphatically.

Instead of asking about the point at which Dot was not going to lie down and take "it" anymore, the reporter continued to probe into Dot's "feelings." Dot was unaccustomed, however, to the requirements of video journalism and refused to tremble or burst into tears or turn herself into a rising fireball. Finally, the woman asked Dot who she thought might be responsible for the threats, to which Dot replied, "I'd rather not say. I'll discuss that with the police. If they ever get out here."

Throughout all this, Sandra Deem stood with her arms folded and saying from time to time, "Oh, gosh! That's awful, just awful." Jerry Deem stared at the set transfixed, not speaking or moving at all.

McWhirter appeared next. He discoursed briefly—the report must have been heavily edited—on the deficiencies of the "hopelessly homophobic" Albany Police Department, and then launched into a pitch for next June's national coming-out day and the gay national strike. He mentioned the meeting at the center that night and the bar tour that would follow. The report closed with a shot of McWhirter and Greco watering Dot's peonies—Edith was nowhere to be seen—and then a pan to the side of the carriage house while the reporter's voice said that the Albany police had told Channel 12 they planned a thorough investigation of the incident. The Millpond situation was noted briefly, and Crane Trefusis was quoted as being "sickened" by the incident.

"Isn't that awful, Jerry?" Sandra Deem said, watching her husband. "Who would do a thing like that to a couple of old ladies? Even with their lifestyle?"

Deem was still gazing fixedly at the TV set, which was

now singing a song about how "If it's not your mo-ther, it must be How-ard Johnson's."

"I was hoping," I said, "that one of you here, Mr. Deem, might have some idea of who's been harassing Mrs. Fisher. Later today she and Mrs. Stout also received a letter and then a phone call threatening them with death if they didn't get out of the neighborhood. It's all turning into a fairly serious and frightening business for them."

Deem slowly raised his head and peered at me again. "Oh, no," he said when my words had registered. He shook his head. "No, I really can't imagine who around here would behave in such an un-Christian way. Do you suspect *us*? Is that why you're here?" He suddenly looked hurt, incredulous.

"I don't suspect anybody," I said. "It seemed like a logical idea, though, to talk to the people with something to gain from Mrs. Fisher's selling out. Of course, you're one of them. Are there other members of your household besides the three of you? Dot Fisher mentioned you had a son."

"You're really looking in the wrong place," Deem said, shaking his head, seeming more relaxed now, and faintly amused at the thought. "Heck, it's true we've been pretty disappointed with Mrs. Fisher for making things a little bit tough for us. It's not that we really *need* the money, actually. I mean, we're above water. I'm a provider. It's just that selling to Millpond would be a real *opportunity* for us. Know what I mean? To get ahead. But this stuff on the news—wow! No, Sandra and I just weren't brought up that way."

Mrs. Deem was back at the stove now, dropping pink franks into a pot of boiling water. She giggled nervously and said, "Like Jerry says, we *could* use the money. Right, Jer? Steak would be nice for a change. Or even hamburger," she added, and giggled again.

I took it this was all for her husband's benefit, but he let it go by.

I said, "What sort of work do you do, Mr. Deem?"

"I'm an accountant," he said, watching me carefully again.

"Where?"

"Where do I work?"

"Yes. Where are you an accountant?"

"Murchison Building Supply. In Colonie. I just got home from the office a little bit ago."

We were still standing in the dining alcove. No one had invited me to sit down again since Deem had entered the room. The boiling hot dogs smelled like boiling hot dogs but they reminded me that I was hungry.

The screen door banged open and Heather reappeared. "Hi-ee."

"Hi, honey," Sandra Deem said. "Getting hungry?"

"Yep. We're having hog-ogs for supper," she said to me proudly. Then, to her father: "Where's Joey?"

Deem didn't answer for a second or two. Then he said, "At work. Joey's at work, sweetheart. He'll be home later."

"Joey's your son?" I said.

"Yes. That's right. Joey's working over at the Freezer Fresh for the summer. He turned sixteen in June and just got his driver's license, and Joey's saving up for a new transmission for that eyesore out in the yard. Teenagers. Boy, what a handful they are."

I nodded knowingly. Raising adolescents was a topic of which I knew nothing, though a brief affair I'd once had with an eighteen-year-old suggested to me that "handful" was hardly the word for it.

Sandra Deem was grim-faced again as she set the table without looking at any of us. We were all pirouetting awkwardly as Mrs. Deem reached around us trying to get the plates and utensils into place.

Deem said, "Well, gee. I'm sorry we couldn't help you out, Mr. Strachey. It's our suppertime now, but if we think of anybody who might be mixed up in this thing down at Mrs. Fisher's we'll be sure to let you know."

"I'd appreciate it," I said and handed him my card. "Just give me a call."

"Will do. And you have Mr. Trefusis give *us* a call. I mean, if Mrs. Fisher changes her mind. I mean—with all this trouble she's having—maybe it would make sense for her to make the move. You know, cut her losses while she can. I guess she's kind of stubborn though, isn't she?"

"What she is is gutsy," I said, and automatically looked over my shoulder for Edith.

"Are you going to talk to the Wilsons?" Mrs. Deem asked as her husband led me to the front door. "Maybe it's nervy of me to put my two cents in, but . . . well, to tell you the truth, I wouldn't put *anything* past *them.*"

"Oh, yeah," Deem said, liking the sound of that. "Yeah, check out the Wilsons. Gosh, they're about as trashy a family as you'll ever run across. It's hard to tell what kind of funny business they might pull. Don't mention we said it, but that's a good idea Sandy had there. You check out the Wilsons."

"I plan to stop by there now."

"Swell idea. Well, nice meeting you. Sorry we couldn't help out."

"Thanks anyway. See you again."

"Oh. Yeah. Well, that would be nice."

"Bye," Sandra Deem called from the kitchen.

"By-eee," another voice added.

In the car, I got out my notebook and wrote: "1. Joey Deem."

*   *   *

I guessed her age to be between twenty-five and seventy. Phosphorescent blond wig, the last beehive north of Little Rock, and beneath the mountain of shimmering hair, active black eyes in a wide mottled face that still held suggestions of the youthful pretty face under the mask that age had grown there. She was grandly voluptuous in a white halter above the waist, a vast lumpy pudding below. Her tight powder blue shorts had worked up into her crotch, and as I approached the porch, where she occupied a sagging plastic chaise, she laid her *National Enquirer* demurely across her lap.

"If you're lookin' for Bill," she said, giving me a whatthe-hell's-this-one-want look, "he's down to the plant. Won't be back till later."

"I'm Don Strachey from Millpond Plaza Associates," I said. "Are you Mrs. Wilson?"

She perked up at the sound of Millpond and set her can of Pabst on the concrete floor as her eyes widened. "Yeah, I'm Kay Wilson. You work for Crane Trefusis?"

"Right now I do, yes."

She struggled upright with one hand, adjusted her wig with the other, and, offering a toothy grin, motioned for me to sit in the lawn chair next to her. Her opinion of me had risen.

"Now, that Crane, he's quite a guy, ain't he? *Quite . . . a . . . guy.* Bill and I had Crane over for a drink on the Fourth of July, he tell you that, Bob? Crane's wife was feeling poorly and couldn't make it, but Crane, he came. Sat right where you're sitting. Drank Chivas Regal with a chunk of lemon. Say now, what's your pleasure, Bob?"

"It's Don. Don Strachey. A cold beer would be great."

"Hot enough for ya?" she said, winking, and commanding her inertia-prone lower body to raise her more willing upper body off the chaise, like an elephant trainer urging the mammoth beneath her into motion. She stepped carefully across the gap between the new porch and the old house and returned a moment later with two more Pabsts.

"Did you happen to see the TV news this evening, Mrs. Wilson?" I said.

"Nah, I just got home a bit ago. You got the big check with you?" she asked, watching me expectantly and raising her beer can, poised for a toast. "You bring ol' Kay that big, beautiful hunert 'n' eighty grand from Crane?"

"No such luck," I said.

She shrugged and drank anyway. "I didn't s'pose you would. Crane said when the big day came he'd bring it out himself. Hell with it anyway. We ain't gonna get it."

"You seem resigned, Mrs. Wilson."

"Kay. Crane calls me Kay. Yeah, I know we're screwed. Hell with it anyway. Old Dot Fisher, she's not gonna give in. She's one tough old cookie, Dot is."

"She says you used to visit her sometimes."

"Yeah, I know Dot. We got no water pressure here sometimes, so I go down and draw from Dot's spring. She's real nice. I always liked talking to her. I damn near shit a brick—pardon my French, Bob—when I saw on the TV last year Dot was one of those women goes for her own. She never laid a hand on me, I'll say that much for her. Knew she hadn't better try, I s'pose, with Bill around. I ain't been down to her place for a time. Bill's mad at her, so why start trouble when you got enough already." She gulped from the Pabst can and fanned her face with the *Enquirer*.

"I guess," I said, "you don't know about what's been going on at Dot's place in the past twenty-four hours." I explained about the graffiti and the threats. She listened with big eyes and an open mouth.

"Now that stinks!" she said when I'd finished. "That just makes me want to puke. Now who on God's green earth would want to go ahead and pull a stunt like that?"

"That's what I'm trying to find out. I'm a private investigator."

"A cop?" She looked startled. "You said you worked for Crane."

"I do. I'm a private detective on assignment for . . . Crane. He asked me, as a matter of fact, to drop by here, Kay, and convey his warmest personal regards to both you and Mr. Wilson. And to ask you and your husband if you had any idea who might be harassing Dot and Mrs. Stout. Crane is disgusted by what happened, and he wants to put a stop to it." I nearly added, "He's paying me ten," but didn't.

"That Crane, he's quite a guy," she said, nodding and wistfully remembering. "Tell him we'll have him over again real soon, soon as ol' Kay gets herself organized. I'm on the two-shift at Annie Lee till Labor Day and when I get home I'm just too pooped to pop. But after Labor Day I can draw unemployment again, and then I'm gonna just lay back and take it easy for a time—shoot, I've earned it—and then Bill and I'll start having people in again."

"I'll pass the word. I take it, Kay, there's no one you know who might be mad enough at Dot Fisher to threaten her in any way to try to force her out of the neighborhood. Or is there?"

"Oh, boy," she said, making a face. "Oh, boy. Oh, boy." She nodded at her beer as she considered the possibilities. "Well," she said with a snort, "there's Wilson. Or he *was* mad, anyways. A month ago Bill was so P.O.ed with Dot Fisher I was afraid he was gonna march right down there and just slug her one. A couple of times, as a matter of fact, he'd had a few drinks and was really gonna go down there and do it. Just pop her one, show her who's boss. He'd've done it too—used to try the rough stuff on me thirty years ago until my brother Moose hadda set Wilson straight one night. Hasn't laid a finger on me since then, and knows he hadn't better try.

"Anyways, Wilson says he's gonna go down there and pop Dot, he says. Well, I just put a stop to that right then and there. I said, Bill, I'll call the cops on you, you dumb son of a bitch. And I meant it! Even if she deserved it, Dot's an old lady and it wouldn't've been right. Anyways, Bill got over it after a while—finally got it through his thick skull that the old lez wasn't gonna give in, and he just said the hell with it.

"Coulda used the dough, though. I mean, could we ever! But then Bill went off on some *other* tangent of his a week or so back. Some hotshot idea of his that's gonna make us rich, so he says. So then he forgot all about Dot and Millpond. Bob, I wish I had a nickel for every time Bill Wilson was gonna make me a rich woman."

"Where does Bill work?" I asked. "What does he do?"

"Presently," she said, popping the tab on the second Pabst she'd brought out, "Bill is employed at the Drexon plant. He's a forklift operator. Bill's the restless type, though, so who knows where he'll be next week. Wilson wants so awful much to get ahead. He asked Crane if Millpond had anything, and Crane said he'd keep an eye open for the right spot for Bill. Crane didn't mention anything about that to you, did he?"

"I'm sorry. He didn't."

She laughed, but not with amusement. "Sure. Well . . . Bill means well. He's got all that Wilson energy. If he could just learn to apply himself . . ." She looked away wistfully, then back at me. "Know what I mean, Bob?"

I nodded knowingly. She watched me, then grunted, knowing I knew that we both knew that Bill Wilson was not, at his age—mid-fifties, I now guessed his wife to be—going to get into the habit of "applying himself." Though I did wonder what Wilson had applied himself to lately that might make the Wilsons rich. And if Crane Trefusis had, in fact, found a "spot" for him that he hadn't mentioned to Kay.

I said, "Were you at home last night, Kay?"

"Sure. Why do you ask that?"

"I thought you or your husband might have heard some unusual traffic after midnight sometime. I don't suppose you get a lot of cars going back and forth on Moon Road. Was Bill here too?"

She cocked a moist yellow drawing of an eyebrow. "Course, Bill was here. Nah, we didn't hear nothin'. Hey—where'd you think Bill was? He's my husband, iznee? Think he was out foolin' around with some woman who's younger and better-lookin'?"

"I thought maybe he'd worked late."

"I'll bet you did, ha-ha." She gave me a significant look. "The fact is, Bob," she said in a confidential tone, "my husband don't play around no more. And neither do I. At least . . . not a whole lot." She eyed me appraisingly, the pink tip of her tongue protruding from between lightly clamped teeth. Her leg shifted, and the *National Enquirer* slid to the floor. She said, "Every wunst in a while, Bob, I *do* meet a man who finds me quite sexy for an older woman. Somethin' like that Joan Collins on *Dynasty*. And if that man is someone I myself consider to be attractive . . . we-l-l-l-l . . ."

I said, "I'm gay."

"Huh?"

"I'm a homophile."

"*What* kinda file?

"I go for men. Like Dot Fisher goes for women. I'm a homosexual. 'Gay,' we call it. Even if *The New York Times* won't. Kay, I'm a fruit."

After a confused couple of seconds, it hit her, and she threw her head back and whooped with laughter. "Oh,

shoot, ha! ha! Oh, that's a good one kid, ha! ha! Oh, fer—
that's the first time any man ever dropped *that* one on
me!"

She laughed and coughed uproariously for a good minute, then gradually settled down and gave me a sweet,
understanding look.

"You don't have to say a thing like that about yourself,
Bob. Truly. Shoot, I know I'm not as attractive as I used
to be." She tried to smile again.

"None of us is," I said, knowing that some people did
age beautifully—Timmy would, I could tell already—and
that others, like Kay Wilson, peaked in physical allure at
the age of thirty, or twenty, or fourteen.

We spent a not entirely relaxed couple of minutes ex-
changing clichés on aging, and then I took out from my
wallet a photo of Timmy and me, arms entwined, at the
1978 gay-pride parade in New York City. She studied it
with lips pursed and kept looking up at me to see if I was
really the man in the picture. Finally, satisfied that I was,
she relaxed suddenly, grinned, and said, "Ho-boy. You're
somethin', Bob. Hyo-boy. Wait'll the girls out at the
home hear about *this* one."

Kay brought us both some potato chips, and then I
asked her if she had other family members or friends who
might be mad enough at Dot Fisher to harass or threaten
her. Kay used the opportunity to describe her six grown
children, none of whom seemed to be likely suspects.

Two of the Wilson offspring were in Southern California, two lived in Queens, one was a career Army man in
Germany, and the youngest, Crystal-Marie, was in a
downstate mental hospital. None had visited Albany recently. As for friends, yes, all of them were sympathetic
and put out, Kay said, but she could think of none who'd
shown any sign of providing the Wilsons with an un-
requested assist in ridding the neighborhood of Dot
and Edith.

I thanked her and said I'd return the next day to speak with her husband.

"Sure thing, Bob. Just give us a call first and make sure we're on the premises and ain't stepped out. And you tell Mrs. Fisher I'm real sorry to hear about her trouble. Maybe I'll just traipse down there tomorrow and stick my nose in. And you be sure to say hi to Crane for me, you hear? That Crane, he's quite a guy, quite a guy. And you know, Bob, *you're* quite a guy, too. *Lordy.*"

I had a quick triple burger at Wendy's. While I ate, I thought a lot about two people: Joey Deem and Bill Wilson.

I headed back down Central through the fuming Friday evening traffic, pulled into Freezer Fresh, and ordered a chocolate cone with sprinkles.

"Joey Deem here tonight? I'd like to talk to him for just a minute."

"Joey? No, he called in sick," I was told by a young black man in a Freezer Fresh paper hat.

"He won't be in at all tonight then?"

"Not if he's sick," the kid said blandly, dipping my cone in a bowl of multicolored specks of dubious digestibility. "Health department wouldn't like it."

From a pay phone I called Dot's place to find out if Lew Morton had arrived. He had, Dot said, as well as a patrolman whom Ned Bowman had left at the house to look after things until Peter Greco got back at midnight. There had been no further threatening letters or phone calls.

I drove on into the city, the sun melting into a gaseous black blanket spread across the sky behind me. As I drove, I thought maybe this whole business was going to be a lot simpler than I had feared it would be. Or maybe, since Crane Trefusis had a hand in it, it wouldn't. On the one hand this, on the other hand that.

5.

Word had spread among Albany gays about the incident at Dot Fisher's, and nearly fifty of them who'd seen the six o'clock news showed up at the Gay Community Center to be harangued by Fenton Mc-Whirter. Two hours later, twelve had actually signed up for the gay national strike. Twelve *thousand* were needed to make an impact locally, but McWhirter took what he could get. Donations for the strike campaign added up to $37.63.

I phoned Dot's house from the center and was told by her that yet another threatening call had been received. "Death to the dykes on Moon Road!" was what the caller had said, then hung up. Dot and Edith were in the kitchen with Dot's friend Lew Morton seated by the back door and an APD patrolman just outside. Dot sounded shaky but controlled and said she'd be just fine until Peter arrived at midnight to look after things.

At the center, I also picked up a phone message from Timmy. His car had broken down and he'd meet me later, up the avenue, the message said. I thought, For sure.

I looked for Peter Greco, and at ten o'clock I joined him and McWhirter and six other leafleting volunteers as we piled into my car and McWhirter's and headed toward Central Avenue to further signal the revolt.

The sultry streets were alive with sweating crowds, and the bars even hotter and more chaotic, but revolt did not seem imminent. There was a blurry, enervated feeling to the night. I couldn't tell whether this resulted from the suffocating heat or from the simple fact that these were now the eighties, a decade in which, so far, most people, straight and gay, couldn't quite settle on what to do next and so didn't do much of anything at all. It was the fifties all over again, except with Reagan this time, and the New Right, the AIDS epidemic, and the Bomb multiplied ten thousandfold. It was the age of nervously milling around.

The music in the discos that night was no help: cold, sarcastic punk stuff that kept only the dance junkies sporadically on the floor. I'd heard the old funky, sensuous, friendly dance music of the seventies was still alive and well in Manhattan—preserved in West Village private clubs, like family genealogies in a Mormon vault—but on this night Albany didn't even seem to have the energy for nostalgia. The music did seem louder than usual, as if more were better, but the higher volume didn't help either. At Coco-nuts, the ersatz South Seas disco where the Lacoste crowd hung out, even the tropical fish in the aquarium seemed to be clapping little fish hands over their ears.

Nor did Fenton McWhirter's presence anywhere cause enthusiasm to break out. Most people received the flyers and leaflets cordially, then studied them, and you could see their eyebrows shoot up at the point where they got the drift of what the leaflets were asking them to commit themselves to. One person asked McWhirter if he'd lost his marbles, but the rest only thought it.

There was only one "incident." At the Watering Hole, McWhirter screwed up the pool shot of a golden-maned, mean-eyed, drugged-up "cowboy"—who could well have been a real one, in town after the drive from Abilene to Schenectady, as he smelled powerfully of the stockyards. Or, it could have been a new scent, Shitkicker, from the makers of Brut. The cowboy grabbed McWhirter by the scruff of the neck and instructed him to "get your faggot ass outta my way," but I rapidly separated the two, and Greco placated the cowboy with a rum and coke and gamely attempted to recruit *him*. The cowboy suddenly recognized McWhirter and Greco from the TV news, and Greco's pitch did seem to set some wheels spinning in his mind, but he said his parish priest wouldn't like it and he didn't sign up.

At the Green Room, McWhirter worked the back-room disco while Greco made his way into the smog of beer breath and smoke of the front-room piano bar. I tagged along with Greco into the crowd of alcoholic fifties queens up front, even though the room had always made me uncomfortable. The problem was, I always left with the nagging feeling that I belonged there. The yellow-haired cowboy from the Watering Hole came in just after Greco and I did. He peered around, seemed to decide that *he* didn't belong there at all, and fled back into the night.

At the piano bar, Greco unexpectedly ran into his old lover of ten years earlier, Tad something-or-other. It seemed to be a night for that. Timmy was still nowhere to be seen.

Greco and Tad were startled to see each other. Their brief conversation was awkward. I didn't listen in, but, trained and inclined to be nosy, I took in what I could by glancing their way from time to time. Tad, who'd been alone at the bar and sullenly preoccupied with a snifter of something warm and murky, grew quickly hostile, and Greco, looking injured and confused, soon retreated.

"An unhappy reunion?" I said.

Greco shrugged, trying to look philosophical, but his dark eyes were bright with hurt.

"You can't go home again," I said, and looked around to see if Timmy had come in the door. He hadn't. "When it's over, it's over. Never apologize, never explain. Never look back, or something might be gaining on you. What are some of the other ones?"

Greco didn't laugh. "Tad asked me for the money

back," he said, shaking his head in disbelief. My immediate assumption was that Tad, my age or older, had once "kept" Greco. "All he could talk about," Greco said glumly, "was his lousy three thousand dollars. Of our whole year together, that's the only thing he remembers. God."

"Tad's quite a bookkeeper," I said.

"He never called it a loan *then*. That's so unfair. It really is. 'Where am I going to get three thousand dollars?' I said. He just said, 'You get it! Before you leave Albany!' It's the only thing he'd talk about. And how his business folded last year and how broke he is these days. Well, jeez. I'm sorry things aren't going well for Tad, I really am. He deserves better. He was always extremely possessive, but he was also loving, and generous—"

Greco began suddenly to cough and gasp, and said the foul air was bothering him, so we walked out into the oppressive but smokeless night and stood alongside my car.

I said, "Tad took you in when you first came out?"

"Oh, no," Greco said, laughing lightly and breathing more easily now. "It was nothing like that. I'd been out since I was fourteen and on my own since I was eighteen. Tad was ten years ago. I was twenty-four then and I'd already had several lovers. Tad must have been the—I don't know—fifteenth or twentieth."

Persons of the New Age. When I was twenty-four I was getting my kicks trying to decipher whether or not Ishmael might actually be getting it on with Queequeg.

"I didn't really settle down," Greco went on blithely, "until the year after that when I met Fenton and realized what I wanted to do with my life and who I wanted to do it with. No, the thing with Tad was . . . he was in love with me, and he paid to have my first volume of poems printed. I was reluctant. I knew I wasn't as crazy about Tad as he was about me. But I was too excited about seeing my work in print to think straight, and I let him do it. I know it cost him a lot of money, but—God, how can somebody be that bitter after *ten years?*"

"Right. You'd think in all that time a person's feelings about someone would have gone through a lot of changes. Gotten milder, mellower." I watched for Timmy's yellow Chevette to pull in off Central.

"Oh, jeez, it's time," Greco said, glancing at his watch. "I've gotta get back to the house by midnight and stay with Dot and Edith so their friend can go home. Are you coming out for a while?"

I looked at him, wondering if the invitation was significant in a particular way. Being a not unattentive fellow—fifteen or twenty *lovers* by age twenty-four—he saw my interest.

"We could go out for a swim in the pond and lie down together under the stars," was what I first thought I heard him say, but what Greco actually said was "We could run off some more leaflets and wait for Fenton to get home. The mimeo machine's in the trunk of the car."

Ethics. Had I had them once? Could I again?

I said, "No, thanks. Timmy—my lover—is probably looking for me, so I guess I'll hang around here. I'll be at home later, so call if there's any problem out at Dot's. Otherwise, I'll be out there first thing in the morning."

"I'm glad you're helping us," he said, smiling. "Even if you're on the payroll of the Great Satan." His eyes shone with their sweet humor, and I wanted again badly to touch him.

"Better not let the Ayatollah Fenton hear you say that," I said. "He still has this crazy idea that just because I'm a minion of Moloch I'm somehow not to be trusted."

"Trust is something you have to earn with Fenton," Greco said. "But once you've got it, you've got it for keeps."

He grinned again, looking as though he were trying to

tell me something useful, and wondering if I'd caught on. Then he brushed my cheek with his hand again, the exasperating little shit, and we both went back inside the bar so that he could find McWhirter and get the car keys.

A few minutes later, I watched Greco head back out to the parking lot, and I rejoined McWhirter and the leafleters. They had signed up two men for the GNS at the Green Room, bringing the grand total for the bar tour to six.

By three-fifteen Timmy still had not shown up. By three-thirty I had befriended, in a narrow but specific way, a slender youngish man named Gordon whose black hair was as curly as Greco's, and whose eyes were as dark, though a good bit dimmer, as was the area behind them. At three-forty we pulled into the deserted parking lot of a Washington Avenue institution of higher learning. At three-fifty-one we pulled out again. He asked if I'd mind dropping him off at the Watering Hole, which wouldn't close for another nine minutes, and I did.

"Catch ya later, Ron," he said.

"For sure, Gordon, for sure."

Then I drove home.

The shower wasn't necessary except for purposes of general sanitation and cooling off. I wouldn't even have had to brush my teeth. Or wash both hands. But still I stayed under the cool—tepid—spray for a good, cleansing fifteen minutes.

I settled into an easy chair and lit an imaginary cigarette. I wanted a real one and thought about driving over to Price Chopper to pick up a pack; it had been more than four years since I'd been off the killer weed, but what the hell. No, I'd smoke a joint instead, just something to feel the soothing harshness on my throat.

I rummaged around in the freezer, but all the little foil-wrapped packages I opened contained chicken necks. Timmy, the world's only Irish anal-retentive, saving up for a chicken-neck party or some goddamn thing.

A car pulled into the parking lot down below. Zip, back to the easy chair. I opened *Swann's Way* and sat there frowning toward it, as if I had been absorbed in the book since the second Eisenhower administration, which, intermittently, I had.

His footfall in the corridor. His hair would be mussed, his shirttail out. Cum on his eyebrow. Anal hickeys.

His key in the lock.

"So, there you are, you elusive devil!" He laid his jacket on the couch and bent to kiss me. "I've been all up and down the avenue since ten-thirty. Everywhere I went I just missed you. You must have left the Green Room about a minute before I got there. Sorry about the screw-up, but my damn radiator sprung a leak. Seems half the cars in Albany overheated today, so I ended up with a rental car for the weekend. How'd it go tonight?"

He was busily climbing out of his Brooks Brothers work clothes, noticing with horror, of course, the jacket he'd just dropped on the couch, and carrying it to the closet, where he smoothed it out and hung it carefully on a wooden hanger.

"Oh, it didn't go too badly," I said, my finger poised with conspicuous impatience on the line in *Swann's Way* where I'd left off in the spring of 1977.

"I met McWhirter at the Green Room," he said airily, taking off his pants and clamping them authoritatively into a pants hanger. "*He* didn't think it had gone all that well. He seemed pretty depressed, in fact. In the bars, only five people signed up for his big national strike. No revolt of the masses on Central Avenue."

"Oh, really? You saw him? He told you that? When I

left the Green Room at three-thirty, there were already *six* signed up."

"Yeah," he said, neatly folding his dirty shirt before placing it in the laundry hamper. "But one guy changed his mind and came back and crossed his name off the list. McWhirter had a few choice words for the poor bastard too. It wasn't nice to see. I felt sorry for both of them."

I said, "Oh."

He slipped out of his briefs. His cock was limp, shrunken, exhausted.

"I'm going to take a quick shower," he said casually. What an act. "And then let's *fuck*."

I said, "Wait." My heart was thudding and snapping like my office air conditioner.

He turned in the bedroom doorway to face me. I said, "How did *your* evening go, anyway? With Boyd-boy. You neglected mentioning that."

"Oh, shit," he said, shaking his head and looking wearily amused by it all. "Boyd is such a flake. I'll tell you all about it in a minute. Just hold on. Boy, do I stink!"

No doubt. He sped into the bathroom to, I assumed, scrub down his eyebrow.

I read in *Swann's Way* the words "But, whereas" several times, then reinserted the yellowing bookmark. I waited. When I heard the water stop running, I opened the book and reread, "But, whereas."

"But, whereas."

"But, whereas."

"But, whereas."

Timmy came back, theatrically erect. Quite the athlete, Timmy.

"I love your ass, Donald Strachey," he said in a low voice, and dove at me with the concentrated enthusiasm he generally reserved for a misplaced article of clothing.

I said, "Did you and Boyd-boy do it? You know—'it'?

The famous and ever-popular but-still-controversial-in-some-circles 'it'?"

He halted in midair, hung there briefly, then descended to his dumb, ugly puce shag rug I'd never liked.

In a tight little voice, he said, "No. We did not. Boyd and I did not do . . . '*it*.'"

He stood there hot-eyed, waiting, his mind working, not so extravagantly prepossessing below the waist now, but staring hard at me, as if he had just been fucked—in the metaphorical sense this time. A well-rounded evening for Timmy.

I said, "Just thought I'd ask. When you came in you had some kind of goddamn dried white flaky stuff on your eyebrow."

"On my eyebrow. On my *eye*brow. Ooops," he said, looking mock-guilty and clamping a hand over one eye. Then the anger surged through him and he spat it at me: "Ooops! Ooops, ooops, *ooops*."

His face was an inch from mine. I turned away. He was sweating, breathing hard, eyes like blue and white saucers.

He said, "Look at me."

I said nothing.

He said, "One of us doesn't trust one of us."

I could feel myself flushing.

He said, "*You* are the one who doesn't trust one of us."

I knew what was coming.

He said, "You don't trust the one of us who picked up a SUNY student in Price Chopper in June and was seen doing it by Phil Hopkins." Hopkins, that insufferable busybody. "Which aisle was it, lover? I want to know. I want to find out which are the cruisy aisles at Price Chopper in case I ever start doing again what the mistrustful one of us does now. Which aisle is the hot one? Is it fresh produce? Oral dentifrices? Day-old baked goods?"

I looked into his face now. I opened my mouth to speak, then closed it. Then I opened it again and croaked out, "The meat department, naturally. In fact—poultry."

He tried not to laugh. I tried not to laugh. We laughed.

We lay together on the comfy puce shag rug and shared a joint. Ever the cautious bureaucrat, he'd hidden it in a pint of Häagen-Dazs boysenberry with a false bottom. We ate the Häagen-Dazs too.

"I apologize," I said.

"Mmm."

"It *was* me I didn't trust. I knew that. Sort of."

"Uh-huh. So, how many have there been? *Since* June?"

"I thought you never wanted to know the sordid details."

"A number is not sordid."

That's all he knew. "Since June? Oh . . . about three."

"Approximately three."

"More or less."

"Uh-huh. More or less."

I said, "Seven."

He sighed, very deeply. "Look, Don," he said. "I don't like it. You know I don't like it. Maybe I shouldn't care. But I care. I'm not a man of the brave new world. You know that. I'm just me, Timothy J. Callahan, an aging kid from St. Mary's parish, Poughkeepsie, and I care.

"But I also know that if you're going to do it, you're going to do it. And apparently you *are* going to do it. You told me that a long time ago. However," he said, leaning up and looking sadly into my face, "*if* you're going to do it—and I'm *not* giving you permission, because you're not a child and I'm not your parent, so I'm not in a position to either give or withhold permission, and as a free adult you're not in a position to ask for it. But, *if* you are going to do it once in a while, I want to ask two things of you, okay?"

"Ask away."

"One: Don't get herpes or AIDS."

"I promise."

He sighed again. "And, two"—he looked at me wistfully now, with just a lingering trace of bitter resentment—"don't assume, Don, that I'm doing it too."

I said nothing. I couldn't. I knew that it would be so much better for both of us if I changed. And that I wouldn't.

Finally I said, "Gotcha."

"So," he said, going through the motions of relaxing again. "Don't you want to hear about my drink with Boyd?"

"Sure. What was it like?"

"Glorious," he said, grinning. "We went up to his room at the Hilton and fucked the bejesus out of each other."

I slowly turned and studied his face with great care.

"Oh," he said, shrugging. "It didn't *mean* anything, Don. Hell, it was just for old times' sake. That was all. I mean, it had nothing to do with *us*."

He couldn't keep a straight face for long—he never could—and when he began to laugh I grabbed him. He'd been ribbing me, the mischievous rascal, I was 93 percent certain.

We were just getting going again, and then, too exhausted to do it, to fall asleep together instead—when the telephone rang.

I groped onto the end table and snatched down the receiver. "This is Strachey."

"Is Peter with you?"

"Peter? No. Is this . . . Fenton?"

"Peter's not here. He didn't come home. Where is he?"

"He left the Green Room before midnight, didn't he? In your car. I saw you give him the keys."

"But he's not *here!*" McWhirter whined, a clear note of fright in his voice. "The *car's* not here."

"Don't go anywhere. Don't leave Dot and Edith. I'll be there in twenty minutes."

We dressed. As we headed out Central Avenue in my car, I brought Timmy up to date on the day's events at Dot Fisher's. He didn't react much, but he didn't like the sound of any of it.

We pulled into the parking lot at the Green Room. The place was quiet, deserted. One car sat in the far corner of the tarmac lot, McWhirter's old green Fiat. We got out and examined it. The windows were rolled up and the car was empty and locked. The keys were not in the ignition.

As we sped on out Central, dawn broke in a cloudless sky.

---

6. When Ned Bowman arrived at nine-fifteen I was still on the phone. I had spent nearly an hour rudely awakening people I remembered seeing at the Green Room the night before, describing Greco and asking if anyone had seen him leave the place, in a car, on foot, alone, accompanied. No one had, though none of the twenty or so men I spoke with was entirely alert and in command of his full faculties at the hour I called.

Detective Lieutenant Ned Bowman, decked out in his

customary uniform of white socks, dark sport coat, and clip-on brown tie, greeted Dot formally, exchanged scowls with McWhirter, suffered through an introduction to Timmy—homosexuals not wearing pleated skirts always confused Bowman—then came over to where I stood by the wall phone and whispered, "Hi, faggot."

"Top o' the mornin', Lieutenant. A grand day, isn't it? Be right with you."

I finished up my last phone call—still no luck—and joined the surly assemblage at the kitchen table. Dot hadn't slept well and was red-eyed and shaky. McWhirter, Timmy, and I hadn't slept at all and were beginning to feel the effects of the heat, which was coming back fast. Bowman, who most likely had slept nicely in an air-conditioned lair in Delmar, did his characteristic best to stimulate the conversation.

"So, who's the alleged missing person? This Greco's the little guy I saw hanging around out here yesterday? He's your roommate, Mr. McWhirter?"

"Peter Greco is my lover," McWhirter said in a clenched voice. "Peter Greco has been my friend and lover for nine years. Yes."

"Oh, is that a fact? Uh-huh." Taking his time, Bowman carefully printed something out in his notebook. We sat watching him. Dot picked up her coffee cup, which rattled in its saucer.

"And what is the subject's home address?" Bowman asked next.

"Four-fifty-five Castro," McWhirter said evenly. "San Francisco, California."

Bowman's eyebrows went up, as if he were already onto something. I leaned over far enough to see him write down "455 Fidel Castro St.—Frisco."

"Now then," he said. "Before I drove out here I checked the police blotter and the hospitals and found no record of your roommate's having run afoul of the law or having met with an accident." In fact, I'd run the same checks and come up with the same result. "So, tell me," Bowman said. "What gives you the idea that your friend is 'missing'? What went on last night, Mr. McWhirter, that put this notion in your head?"

McWhirter shot a look at Dot, who sat rigid and grim-faced. Timmy, witnessing for the first time the storied Ned Bowman in action, was taking it all in with a look of slightly crazed fascination. I got up and exchanged my coffee for a glass of iced tea, which I briefly considered pouring over my head, or Bowman's.

As McWhirter described the events of the night before, Bowman took notes. He interrupted once to mention that he had seen McWhirter on the six o'clock news. "Good luck with your strike, Mr. McWhirter," he said blandly. "Me, I'm an old union man myself." He glanced over at me, poker-faced, so I could see what he was thinking: This fruit McWhirter's a real laugh and a half.

". . . and Peter *always* lets me know where he's going to be," McWhirter nervously concluded. "And he would never just leave the car like that. I'm really afraid something's happened to him," he said, shaking his head in frustration. "A lot of people don't like us—don't like me. I've been threatened hundreds of times . . . and people know . . . they know how much Peter means to me, how much I mean to him, and—." His voice broke and he turned away, blinking, unable to speak.

Bowman screwed up his face, unsettled by this display of emotion one man could show for another. He stayed quiet for a moment and looked thoughtful. Maybe he'd seen this before. Or maybe he himself had felt something akin to what McWhirter was feeling, once a very long time ago, and had strangled the sensation at birth. Whatever his possibly useful thoughts, he rid himself of them soon enough.

He said, "Mr. McWhirter, has your friend ever gone

off with another man? Just for a little fling? Know what I mean? Doesn't he do that every once in a while?"

I let my peripheral vision take in Timmy for a few seconds. His cheek twitched accusingly, but he didn't look my way. Dot harrumphed and did look my way. I shrugged. McWhirter slowly turned toward Bowman, and when I saw his murderous look I glanced around to make sure there was no lethal object within his reach.

Through clenched teeth, McWhirter said, "You *would* assume that, wouldn't you?"

"Well," Bowman said, unfazed by McWhirter's anger, which Bowman apparently took to be routinely defensive, "I think you have to admit that a lot of your people can't seem to help being . . . promiscuous." He glanced at Dot. "I hope you'll pardon my language, Mrs. Fisher."

I sneered at Bowman but avoided looking at Timmy.

"That's quite all right, Lieutenant," Dot said. "You may say 'promiscuous' in this house. If that's the word you consider to be appropriate."

She gave me a little half-wink, which meant "Just don't say 'rotgut.'"

McWhirter, not easily amused under the best of circumstances, was seething, just barely under control. When Timmy and I arrived at five-thirty, McWhirter had been frantic, unable to stop talking or to stand still, demanding that a posse be organized, the National Guard called up. Then, following a sudden violent outburst of anger at Greco for having let something happen to himself and "fucking up *everything*," McWhirter had plunged into a desperate sulk, which lasted for an hour or so, during which he simply sat and stared. Now the rage was back, but with a new target.

"You pathetic ignoramus!" he hissed. "You know *nothing* about Peter. You know nothing about *me*. Your bigoted head is so full of homophobic stereotypes and . . ."

McWhirter made a speech. The gist of it was that gay ways of living were as varied as straight ways of living. Except, he pointed out, those gay men and women who were "sexually active"—a group that no longer included himself and Greco, he emphasized—were more relaxed and open and "joyously fulfilled" about it than were straight people who lived the same way. This was hardly the whole truth, or even half of it. But it didn't much matter that McWhirter was fiddling the facts, because Bowman, tapping his pen on the table and whistling under his breath, wasn't listening anyway.

When McWhirter concluded with a rude suggestion as to what Bowman could do with his "outmoded, mind-slave, cop-think attitudes," Bowman glanced coolly at his watch and said, "I'm due at the first tee at Spruce Valley at noon, Mr. McWhirter. If you provide me with a photo of your roommate, I'll see that the subject is listed as a missing person first thing Monday morning."

McWhirter stood up abruptly and charged out of the room. Ignoring him, Bowman turned to Dot. "I'm glad to see that you're getting along nicely, Mrs. Fisher, and haven't been troubled by any more vandalism problems or threats. If you want a patrolman to come by periodically during the night to check out your property, just let us know. And believe me, we're going to utilize every resource at our disposal to make an arrest in this case. I'll have a man out here Monday morning to check out the neighbors, and if you don't feel safe in the meantime, it might be a good idea to stay over for a couple of days with a relative or friend. I wouldn't take the threats too seriously, though. It's most likely kids or harmless kooks, and you've gotta roll with it till either it stops or the department makes an arrest."

He closed his notebook, stood up, and playfully waggled a finger at me. "I'd say you're plenty safe with this guy on the job," he said, grinning. "Strachey's got clout now. I hear you're on Crane Trefusis's payroll these days, Strachey. I wouldn't mind a little piece of that action myself. How about putting in a good word for an old cop next time you run into Crane?"

"You wouldn't be comfortable at the new Millpond, Ned. Crane's turned into a gay libber. That's why he hired me."

"Is that a fact? Crane's tastes sure have changed all of a sudden. The word I hear is, Trefusis is spending a lot of time out at the Heritage Village apartment of that long-legged Miz Compton who parks herself outside his office door, while Mrs. Trefusis is up to Saratoga playing the ponies and taking the waters. But you never know, you never know."

Dot got her dog-fart face on, as if Trefusis himself were in the room. Timmy stared, open-mouthed. I walked with Bowman to his car.

"You're wrong, Ned," I said, once we were out the door. "These two guys don't mess around with other men. Something's happened to Peter Greco. You ought to look into it. Really, you should. I know Greco a little."

"They had a spat, didn't they?" Bowman said.

"No."

"Greco and this McWhirter mouthy asshole had a little tiff and the kid ran off. Used to be the story of my life, these domestic squabbles, back in the olden days when I was on a beat. You been around as long as I have, you'll know a lovers' quarrel when you see one, Strachey. When Greco gets tired and hungry he'll be back, and the love-birds will kiss, or whatever you people do, and make up. I'd give it till around suppertime tonight. When he shows up, give my office a call and leave a message, will you? Save me a shitload of paperwork Monday morning."

"You're wrong, Ned. As you so frequently are. Playing

the odds again instead of using your eyes and ears."

"Off my back, fruitcake." He climbed into his Dodge, slammed the door, and drove off.

I went back to the guest room where McWhirter was holed up. When I told him about Greco's chance meeting the night before with his old lover Tad—Purcell was Tad's last name, McWhirter said—McWhirter seemed surprised but unconcerned. He said yes, Peter might have wanted to talk more with Purcell, to come to terms in some way, but he would have informed McWhirter first, and anyway Peter was due back at Dot's at midnight and "Peter *always* does what he says he's going to do."

McWhirter was certain that some harm had come to his lover. He was convinced that the police would be no help in getting to the bottom of it, and then added, "Maybe the cops are even responsible. Yes. Oh, God. It's probably the cops!"

A sickening thought slid into my mind, but for the time being I kept quiet about it.

7.

I went back to the kitchen and dialed a number in the Pine Hills section of Albany.

A groggy male voice. "Yeah?"

"Don Strachey. I need a little assistance."

"Don't we all."

"Were you on duty last night?"

"Till three hours ago. I didn't go to bed when I got home though. I sat up in case you called."

"Don't give me a hard time, Lyle. I told you I probably wouldn't call. That I had a lover."

"Lucky you. Maybe I'll get one too. There's a hunk in the department I've got my eye on. He's gay, I know, and he knows I know. But he's shy. And has a wife and six kids."

"Better shop around some more."

"Uh-huh. Shop around."

"When are you going to make the move, Lyle? You're in the wrong town for your situation."

"Are there any right ones?"

"Probably not yet. Stockholm maybe. Or Copenhagen."

"Yeah. Too bad I don't speak Hindu. What do you want, if it's not what I wished it was?"

"Information. I was wondering if maybe the night squad goons were up to a bit of queer-bashing last night. Midnight or after, on Central, around the Green Room."

"I didn't hear about anything. But I probably wouldn't that soon. Unless it made the blotter, and even then I couldn't be sure. Some of the arrests that get made are the genuine article. You know, there are some *real* lawbreakers out there, Strachey. In case you haven't heard."

"I suppose those guys do stumble over an actual criminal once in a while. A matter of mathematical probability. But this one would be the other—the hate stuff. A phony rap on prostitution, solicitation, resisting arrest. Whatever they're dropping on people these days. A guy by the name of Peter Greco disappeared outside the Green Room at about a quarter to twelve. Slight, dark, curly-haired, cute. A bit boyish for your more mature tastes, Lyle, but ripe for picking by the bash-a-fag crew."

"I'll check around. But disappearances aren't those guys' specialty. You know about it, Strachey. They just grab people, drive 'em around, call 'em some names, maybe rough 'em up a little, then dump 'em. Some make it to the lockup, a few to the ER at Albany Med. A total disappearance would be something new."

"I know. It would."

A silence. "Uh-huh. Oh, yeah. Jesus. Well, it was only a matter of time, I guess. They're nuts—completely out of control. Maybe this time they've really done it."

"That's what I'm afraid of."

"Shit."

"Leave a message with my service if you pick up anything." I gave him the number. "I'll check now and again and get back to you. And one other thing. See if you can sniff out any recent coziness between guys in the department and Crane Trefusis. There might be a connection."

"The shopping mall wizard? That Trefusis?"

"The same."

"That one might be trickier. But as soon as I grab a cup of coffee I'll be out asking around. Sure as hell nobody here is gonna miss me. You know what I mean?"

"So long, Lyle. And thanks."

"'Thanks,' he says. Oh, sure."

Timmy agreed to stay at the farm and keep an eye on Dot and Edith. I put him to work phoning more Friday night revelers who might have been outside the Green Room around midnight and seen something unusual, or, if it involved the Albany PD, not entirely unusual.

Down at Dot's pond, Edith was seated on a flat stone with her feet in the moss green water, her skirt held demurely four inches above the water line.

"Good morning, Mr. Lovecraft. Going for a dip?"

"Hi, Mrs. Stout. I just want to cool off the old brain-pan for a minute. Maybe I'll get a chance to dunk the rest of me in later."

I leaned down and stuck my head in the water for twenty seconds, then stood up and shook off like a dog.

"Does your head swell in the heat?" Edith asked.

"Right. And then I can't get my hat on."

"That's what happens to my feet." She glanced back toward the house. "I guess I'd better watch my language. Dorothy can't *stand* the word 'feet.' Dorothy's rather eccentric, in case you haven't noticed. I'm terribly afraid she's going senile. But she's a grand girl and I don't know what I'd do without her. It's not easy for our kind, you know."

"I know about that. I'm one too."

She gazed at me for a long moment, thoughtful and a little puzzled. "Well," she said finally, "I suppose you know what you like, Mr. Lovecraft. But—two big hairy men? Hmmm. I hope you don't mind my saying so, but I can't imagine anything duller."

Chasms everywhere. Though this one we could laugh about. I said, "I can."

The old woman peered at me confusedly through her spectacles for a moment while the connections in her brain slowly got made. Then she said, "That's all *you* know, sonny."

Driving back toward Central, I slowed as I passed the Deem house but saw no sign of life. Neither car was in the driveway. I figured I'd catch up with Joey Deem later in the day. Meanwhile, Dot and Edith were being well looked after.

At the Wilsons', Kay was airing herself in the chaise alongside the new porch. A mammoth '71 Olds with rusted fenders and a gash along the side was parked under a maple tree. The car had a Howe Caverns sticker on the rear bumper and a sign in the back window that said MAFIA STAFF CAR. It was the kind of sad heap you see in front of K Mart, blithely or defiantly parked in the fire lanes.

I pulled in and shouted, "Crane sends his best, Kay.

He wished also for me to convey his warm greetings to your husband. Is Mr. Wilson in?"

"Oh. Hi there. It's you." She sat up looking wary. "Yeah, Bill's here." She heaved up her great chest and screeched, "*Willl-sonnn!*"

I got out and walked toward the house. The screen door flew open.

"What you hollerin' about now?" He spotted me. "Who's he?"

"Dunno. Says he's lookin' for you."

He was a good four inches taller than I was, broader, thicker, a jaw like an old boot, a flat cockeyed nose, and eyes full of simmering resentment. He wore dark green work clothes, and in a fist like a small hippo he was gripping a length of cast-iron drainpipe with a jagged end.

"Good morning, Mr. Wilson. I'm Donald Strachey, representing Crane Trefusis of Millpond Plaza Associates. May I have a moment of your time?"

His eyes narrowed. "Maybe. Maybe not. What's in it for me?"

"Crane Trefusis asked me to drop by and convey his fondest best wishes. And to ask for your assistance in looking into a problem that's cropped up."

He sneered. "Crane Trefusis is a lying, shit-eating, pig-fucking phony. I'll lend Crane Trefusis a hand the day he comes across with his big fat hunnert and eighty grand. Meantime, you tell Trefusis he can take his wishes and blow 'em out his ass. Now get outta here! I got a busted drain to fix."

"But, Bill! This man—"

"And you shut your trap!" Still watching me, he said, "You got them big bucks with you, mister?"

I shrugged.

"Then you climb back in that piece of Jap junk of yours and drive on out of here."

"It's German," I said. "And they make them in Pennsylvania now."

He looked as if his sense of humor was about to fail him. I said, "Y'all have a real good day now," and acted on Wilson's suggestion.

Heading on back into the city, I wondered again how Bill Wilson planned on making his wife rich any time soon. I could only be certain it wasn't going to be in the diplomatic service. But whatever Wilson's shortcomings— and I'd have to use other means for looking into them—I had to concede that he was an excellent judge of character.

Tad Purcell's address, as listed in the Albany phone book, was on Irving Street just off Swan. The block was a peninsula of gentrification jutting west from the South Mall renewal area. In another five years the orderly plague of marigolds in window boxes and white doors with brass knockers would likely spread as far as Lark Street, and where the dispossessed poor would go, no one knew. The local machine was preoccupied with obscure larger matters, and UNICEF was busy in Somalia.

"Hi, I'm Don Strachey, a friend of Peter Greco's. Could I talk to you for a few minutes?"

A quizzical look, not entirely friendly. "I've seen you somewhere recently," he said. "Where was it?" A cloud of Listerine breath hit me in the face like a visit to New Jersey.

"Last night at the Green Room," I said. "I was with Peter."

He tensed up, glanced over his shoulder, then looked back at me, undecided about something. He ran a well-manicured hand through his freshly blow-dried black waves that were touched with white.

"Oh. Sure. I guess that's where it must have been.

What was it you wanted to talk about?"

"Peter. He might be in trouble."

I watched him. His faintly creased oval face, on the brink between youth and whatever was coming next for him, was aglow with after-shave, and the pink now deepened. He pursed his lips, lowered his head as if to consult the alligator on his polo shirt, then looked at me again.

"Any friend of Peter's is a friend of mine," he finally said with a nervous laugh. "I have to go out in a couple of minutes, but I've got a second. Sure. Why not? C'mon in. You said your name was Rob?"

"Don. Don Strachey."

"Take a load off your feet, Don."

I followed him into a small living room decorated with menus from famously expensive local restaurants, and lowered myself into a canvas sling chair. To my left was a large console color television set with a framed photo of a young Peter Greco resting atop it. Purcell perched on the edge of the couch and lit a Kool. Somewhere above us water was running.

"Well, I must say, I'm not *completely* surprised to hear that Peter is in trouble," he said. His tone was sarcastic, but the apprehension came through. "Is he in trouble with the law?"

"Maybe. In a way. The thing is, Peter never showed up at the house where he was staying last night. Dot Fisher's farm, out on Moon Road. His friends are pretty worried about him."

He blew smoke at the ceiling and thought about this. "Is that right? Well. Where do his friends think he might have spent the night?"

"I thought you might know."

"Ho, really? Well. How about *that*. Now, where would anybody ever get such an idea?" He colored and bit the inside of his cheek, making it look as if he wanted to smile but was trying not to. Either he knew something and was acting coy, or he was simply enjoying the idea that I might think Greco had spent the night with him and was going to insist that both of us savor the fantasy, however briefly.

"Peter had been speaking with you just before the time he vanished," I said. "You asked him for three thousand dollars. Demanded it, he told me."

A jittery laugh. "Did he *say* that? God, Peter didn't take that *seriously*, did he? He must have known I was just bitter about . . . what happened between us." He went all pink again, bright as Dot's phlox, and rocked on his hams. "After ten years! God. You'd think he'd have remembered how I get after a drink or two. I mean, you know how it is."

I thought I was beginning to see how it was with Tad Purcell, but I wasn't sure yet. He dragged deeply on the cigarette, then flicked the ash several times, even when it was no longer there. "You know, Peter and I used to be lovers," Purcell suddenly announced with a proud, shaky half-smile. "Did Peter mention that?"

"He did," I said. "Peter spoke well of the time you two had together."

He relaxed a little and sat back, gazing at the photo on the TV set.

"Peter was a very, very important part of my life," Purcell said softly. "My memory of him is something I cherish deeply."

"I can see that."

"You see, the thing is, Peter was mostly on the streets before he met me," he said with a look of distaste. "Running around with hippies and flower children and so forth. But by the time we met, Peter was really fed up with street life. All that pointless rebellion and immaturity. We all have to grow up sometime, am I right?"

"Right."

Clearly grateful to have a new audience for this old story—his only one, I was afraid—Purcell warmed to the topic. "Well, I could tell immediately that first night I picked him up while he was crossing the park that Peter had just about had it up to here with his rather juvenile lifestyle. Peter was really disillusioned, ready for a change of course into something safe, and comfy, and sensible. He'd had a bad bout of hepatitis, and maybe that had something to do with it too. But I mean, not that the hepatitis was the most *important* thing."

"It would have been chastening."

"Anyway, we ran into each other and—can you believe it?—we just fell in love on the spot. Bingo! God, I was so head-over-heels nuts about that guy that I just went ahead and— Well, I did something, something reckless and foolish, I suppose you could say. Something that I hardly ever do. What I did was, I offered Peter the kind of life I could see he needed. I offered him my home to share with me. My home, and my love. I mean, every once in a while you just have to throw caution to the winds and take a chance in life, am I right?"

"Right. Once in a while."

"Well," he said with a nervous grin, "for once in my life, my kindheartedness—which is my biggest weakness—actually paid off. Peter agreed to stay with me. To accept my offer of stability, a home, someone to depend on to be there when you needed another human being. Except"—his face fell—"except it didn't work out. I mean, it *did* last eleven and a half fabulous months. But then, well, you see, the thing was, Peter had not *really* changed. No. Peter, as it turned out, was not *ready* to grow up. He was still too immature to accept my gift."

He sighed again and gazed at Greco's photo. "Oh, God, Peter was *so* sweet. So beautiful in so many ways.

But you know," he said, pursing his lips and leaning toward me confidingly, "I realize now that it wasn't just immaturity. There was something else Peter lacked. I can see that now. Do you know what I mean? Something missing in his upbringing, I suppose. A psychological type of problem that prevented Peter from learning to appreciate the true pleasures of hearth and home. Which is *such* a terrible shame. Poor Peter. I'm sure he's had his regrets. Missing out on such a golden opportunity. I know I have."

I nodded lamely. Purcell looked at me as if he were hoping for a more expansively sympathetic reaction, but I was unable to summon one up. Finally, I said, "You and Peter must have gotten to know each other pretty well, Tad. It seems odd that Peter would have misunderstood your statements last night about the three thousand dollars."

"Absolutely! That's what *I* think. How could he have taken me seriously about that silliness? Except . . . I guess it is true that I could handle my liquor a little better back when Peter knew me. Back then, I didn't used to get quite so . . . hyper. Not so sharp with people sometimes. I guess I got that way later, as a matter of fact, after Peter. And after a couple of other relationships that didn't work out. Relationships with people who were sort of like Peter. I'm sure you know the type I mean. People who can't appreciate what you have to offer. A lot of faggots are like that, I've noticed. Oh, well. What can you do? I suppose it's just my fate in life to be . . . unlucky in love."

The water upstairs was shut off with a clank. My mind attempted to construct a coherent thought, but again it failed. I said, "Sorry to hear about your run of bad luck, Tad. Good luck in the future. So. Tell me this. When did you last see Peter?"

"When? Last night. What do you mean?"

"I mean, what time? Did you speak with him again after your conversation at the bar, when I was with him? That was around eleven-forty."

He laughed dryly and tapped another nonexistent ash into a blue ceramic ashtray the size of a hubcap. "Well, I wasn't really keeping track of the time last night. Anyway, not until desperation hour rolled around. But, no. I didn't see Peter again after our . . . initial discussion."

Footsteps sounded above us.

Purcell said, "Would you excuse me for one minute. Back in a sec."

He bounded up the stairway behind the couch. There were muffled voices. I flipped through a copy of *Food Product Management*. I learned about the development of a square tomato to cut down on storage and shipping costs. Purcell bounded back, all pink again, like a winter tomato. What was making him blush?

I said, "Tell me this then, Tad. What time did you leave the Green Room last night?"

He lit another Kool. "Why do you ask that?"

"I thought you might have run into Peter later."

"Hah. If only. But no such luck. For what it would've been worth, of course. No, I hung around the Green Room till three-thirty, thinking Peter *might* come back and try to make me feel better. He always hated ending things on an unpleasant note. God, he was such a sweet person. But I guess he's changed. Gotten old and cynical like the rest of us, ha-ha. Anyway, about three-thirty I gave up on Peter and drove down to the Watering Hole. Last-chance gulch, right? Thought I might get lucky and fall in love again. It's been known to happen."

"I've heard. Peter said you told him you haven't been making out well lately. Had a bad year financially. I'm sorry to hear that."

He blinked, made a face, dragged on his Kool. "I lost

my food supply business last year. Reaganomics did me in. And I *voted* for that phony. But what I've got now isn't bad," he said with a tentative shrug. "I'm in food services at Albany Med. The money there's not too bad. Maybe I'll be out of debt by the time I'm eighty." He smiled sourly.

More footsteps above us. "It sounds as if you did get lucky last night," I said, glancing up. "Or do you not live alone?"

He shifted and looked embarrassed, with a touch of irritation. "Oh, you noticed. He heard your voice and he's waiting for you to leave. He says he doesn't want to be seen. He's cheating on his lover and doesn't want word to get back. I can't *stand* people who do that. I say either you're committed to another human being or you're not. There's no in between. Even though he says it's the first time he's done it in six months, I still hate it. The guy's really the dregs anyway. God, I must have been really plowed last night. My standards are not exactly what they used to be. Five till four at the Watering Hole. God. And I have this awful feeling the guy even has herpes."

I checked my watch. Eleven-fifteen. "Well, I hope your luck isn't quite that bad, Tad. You mentioned earlier that you weren't surprised to hear that Peter might be in some kind of trouble. Why?"

"Because," Purcell snapped, his face suddenly tightening, "Peter *uses* people. Sooner or later, treating people that way is going to get you into trouble. Your chickens come home to roost. You just don't get away with it forever. Squeezing what you can out of somebody and then dropping that person as if they have leprosy. Some people get mad. *Very* mad. Of course," he added with a tremulous sigh, "I got over that a long time ago."

I thought about telling him that Greco had been with Fenton McWhirter in an apparently mutually satisfying and entirely healthy relationship for nine years. But Purcell must have known that already and chosen not to accept what it signified. He was going to believe what he wanted to believe.

"Just do me a favor and call me if Peter shows up here or contacts you." I gave him my card and headed for the door. "Hope you don't come down with herpes, Tad. I hear it's murder."

He glanced up the stairwell and winced. "The pits," he said. "The absolute pits. Miss Sleaze of Eight-two. Ecchh."

I closed the door with the brass knocker behind me, thinking, Prepare. Prepare.

I walked up Irving to where my car was parked in front of a house with petunia-filled window boxes under every sill. From a little two-by-five patch of marigold-bordered lawn, a wrought-iron post rose up to hold a birdhouse, under whose single round opening was attached a miniature window box containing two tiny Johnny-jump-ups.

I unlocked my car and climbed in. The thing was ovenlike, hot enough to bake a quiche in. I rolled down the windows and sat there watching Purcell's house twenty yards down the street. The windshield was clouded from my breath and I turned on the defogger. Although Purcell's bitter stew of a biography had been just confused, self-deceptive, and sad enough to sound drearily plausible, I still wanted to witness who his overnight guest had been, or hadn't been.

Within two minutes Purcell's front door opened and Peter Greco emerged. I did not fully believe what I was seeing. The slight dark figure moved quickly down the wooden front steps tapping the wrought-iron curlicued hand rail as he went, and turned east toward Swan.

I was out and running.

"Peter! Peter!"

I caught up with him. He turned. He said, "Hey—Ron, was it? How's it shakin', good buddy?"

"Hi. Hi, there. Hi, Gordon."

It was the Greco lookalike I'd picked up in the Green Room and spent twenty-six minutes with the night before. For sure.

He said, "Let's you and me get together again sometime, whaddaya say, Ron? But I can't right now. Sorry. Gotta visit my grandmother in the hospital."

"Oh. Too bad. What's she in for, herpes?"

He glared, then began to look a little worried, as if I might be someone not to be trusted, the Irving Street Toucher or something. He turned and walked quickly away, glancing back once to see if I was coming after him.

I wasn't.

8.

The ransom note was discovered just after eleven.

Timmy had arranged for a tow truck to haul McWhirter's Fiat out to Dot's place until a locksmith could open it and the Fiat dealer could produce a new set of keys. The note, inside a plain white envelope, had been stuck under the Fiat's windshield wiper. The tow truck operator hadn't noticed it, but Timmy, always on the lookout for out-of-place objects, spotted it as the tow truck pulled in at Dot's. The envelope, which had *not* been on the Fiat at five in the morning when Timmy and I first discovered the empty and abandoned car, was addressed to Dorothy Fisher.

I heard about it from Timmy when I checked in at Dot's from the Price Chopper pay phone two blocks from

Tad Purcell's house. I bought a bag of ice and sucked on a cube while I drove straight out to Moon Road. The sun was brutal in a blinding white sky, and a puddle formed on the car floor where the ice bag leaked.

At Dot's I read and reread the note, which was handwritten in an inelegant, almost childish script that none of us had seen before. It definitely was not the same handwriting as in Friday's threatening letter to Dot.

The note said, "Pay one hundred thousand dollars if you want Pete to live, we will contact you Mrs. Fisher."

McWhirter was dazed. He paced back and forth across Dot's kitchen looking enervated, helpless, alone. As the rest of us moved about the room we had to bob and weave awkwardly to keep out of McWhirter's path.

I phoned the Spruce Valley Country Club and had Bowman paged from the locker room.

"Greco's been kidnapped. Dot Fisher received the ransom note. They want a hundred grand."

"You're making this up, Strachey. You'll go to jail for this."

"No. It's the truth."

"Kee-rist. On a Saturday. All right, all right, I'll be there in twenty minutes. This had just better be for real, Strachey, or you are up shit creek with me, you get that?"

"'Up shit creek with Ned if not for real.' Noted."

I reached Crane Trefusis at Marlene Compton's apartment at Heritage Village. "One of Dot Fisher's houseguests has been kidnapped," I said. "There's a ransom note. They're asking a hundred. Do you know anything about this, Crane?"

"Did you say kidnapped?"

"Uh-huh."

A silence. Then: "I know nothing about this, no, of course not. Have the police been notified?"

"They have."

"Who is the victim?"

"His name is Peter Greco. A friend of Dot's who happened to be staying with her for a few days. Maybe you'd like to put up the hundred, Crane, to get Peter back. Dot hasn't got a hundred grand. All she's got is a schoolteacher's pension and Social Security. Plus, of course, a house and eight acres."

A pause while the wheels turned again. Then, calmly, he said, "No. You are mistaken."

"Mistaken about what?"

"That Millpond has anything to do with this."

"Uh-huh."

"We have our limits, Strachey."

"Right. We are not a crook."

Another silence. Then: "I—I'll go so far as to put up a reward for the safe return of this young man. From my personal accounts."

"How much?"

"Five."

"This is a human life we're talking about, Crane."

"Of course. Seventy-five hundred."

"You're paying me ten to catch somebody who wrote on the side of a barn."

"Eight."

"Ten, at least."

"All right, ten." He sighed. "You're an extremely hard-nosed man, Strachey. You'll go far in this business, I'm sure." This business? "You know as well as I do that *you* are the man who's probably going to bring about an arrest and collect the reward. You play all the angles, don't you? My sources were correct in their assessment of your abilities. I'm impressed."

I'd been playing games with him over the reward money and hadn't, in fact, thought ahead to who might collect it. But the idea of an additional "ten" dropping my way for a particular purpose did not fill me with repugnance. It seemed, as I thought about it, that the ten could become useful, even necessary. The thing that scared me was the thought that the reward money would not be collected at all.

"I'll donate the money to charity if I'm the one to collect it," I lied. "Meanwhile, Crane, one question: Is Bill Wilson working for you in any capacity?"

"William Wilson of Moon Road?"

"Right. Kay's hubby."

"No."

"Kay told me you said you were keeping your eye out for the right spot for Bill."

"Yes, well. Regrettably the position of vice president for community relations at Millpond is occupied at the moment. But I'm certainly keeping Mr. Wilson in mind. Why do you ask about Wilson?"

"He was on your list of suspects, remember?"

"That was for the vandalism, not the kidnapping. Do you think the two are connected?"

"Could be. The motive for both appears to be forcing Dot Fisher to sell out to you, Crane."

He said nothing.

"Crane? Are you there?"

"I was just thinking."

"What did you think?"

"I was thinking, Strachey, that you and Mrs. Fisher and her friends might be—how shall I put it?—engaged in an unethical act? Is that possible? An act calculated to elicit public sympathy and bring pressure to bear on Millpond to increase its offer to Mrs. Fisher? Of course, it was just a thought."

"Think again, Crane. I work for you, don't I? I'm doing that because our interests have happened to overlap in a limited way, and of course I'm thrilled to be able to make off with your 'ten.' At the point where our interests diverge and I can't work for you anymore I'll let you know fast. Meanwhile, be assured that I will not plot against you. And I'm confident that your thinking vis-à-vis me is likewise. Am I right?"

"Of course," he said emphatically, hollowly. "What kind of man do you think I am?"

"Swell. I'll expect the ten-grand reward to be announced as soon as the news of the kidnapping is made public. For now, I think that the police, if they know what they're doing, will want to keep it quiet. But your offer, if I understand you, is in effect immediately. Agreed?"

"Agreed. And . . . meanwhile, you can inform Mrs. Fisher that Millpond is willing to raise its offer for her property by another ten percent."

"I'll pass along your timely point of information, Crane."

"Thank you."

A sweetheart.

I dialed the number on outer Delaware Avenue of a man whose family conducted games of chance in a well-organized way throughout the capital district. We'd enjoyed a couple of personal encounters seven years earlier, but broke it off over a conflict stemming from the disapproval each of us strongly felt over the other's way of looking at the human race. Vinnie and I still kept in touch from time to time, though, and exchanged confidences.

I asked Vinnie about Crane Trefusis's connections with the mob.

"Lotta dough. Crane makes it squeaky clean. Why do you wanna know this, Strachey?"

"I'm on his payroll for a couple of days. I like to know who I'm working for. But what I'm really interested in, Vinnie, is who Trefusis's muscle is. When he wants to make a point with somebody he considers dumb, who does he send out to make it?"

"I'd hafta check, but I think maybe it's one of his own. A guy in his security office. Dale somebody. Ex-cop. A boozer. You want me to find out for you for sure?"

"I do. Don't let anybody at Millpond know you're asking. But check."

"For you, I'll do it. Half an hour."

"I'll phone you back. Hey, Vinnie, who was that fair-haired boy I saw you with on North Pearl Street last month? Your pop know you're dating the Irish?"

"Heh-heh." He hung up.

Next I dialed a number in Latham belonging to a man I'd once helped out. Whitney Tarkington, fearful that his grandmother, a straitlaced Saratoga grand dame, would discover his homosexuality and disinherit him, had hired me five years earlier to take care of a blackmailer. I'd done the job, discreetly if a little messily, but Whitney's accounts were closely monitored by a committee of bankers and he hadn't been able to pay me an appropriate amount for my fee. Instead, he had promised me the assistance of his wealthy circle of gay friends if and when I thought they could be useful in a particular way.

"Hel-ooo-ooo."

"Hi, Whitney. It's Don Strachey. The day has come. I have a favor to ask of you beautiful upscale guys. I want to borrow a hundred grand."

"Good-bah-eye."

"Wait, don't hang up, Whitney! You'd have the money back within . . . three days. I guarantee it. And the trustees of your zillions, Whitney, will pin a medal on you. Because—now get this, Whitney—I'd be paying *ten percent interest*. Ten percent in *three days*."

"At the sound of the tone, you may repeat that last part. Beep."

"Ten percent in three days. That's what I said, Whitney baby. What a killing you'd be making! And if you haven't got a hundred grand in your wallet, you just ring up some of your railroad-and-real-estate-heir-type jerk-off buddies and collect, say, twenty grand each from five of 'em. And Tuesday noon, or thereabouts, I repay the hundred, *plus* an additional ten. In cash. Even a Pac-Man franchisee doesn't rake in *that* kind of money in three days."

"Donald, my dear, I must confess that you *have* piqued my interest. But really, Donald, haven't you *heard*? Wholesaling cocaine is against the *law* in the State of New York. We'd all be found out, and when word reached Saratoga, what would *mother* say? I have promised her, you know, that I would *never* embarrass her in public. And my getting dragged off to Attica in chains by some humpy state trooper in a Gucci chin strap *would* be a bit of a social blunder, don't you agree? And *grandmother*! Why, I'd be *finito* with Grams!"

"I can promise you that there is no dope involved, Whitney."

Except, possibly, me. My palms were sweating, my pulse interestingly elevated and erratic. I explained about the kidnapping, and he listened, uttering occasional little ooohs and ahs.

"Taking a bit of a gamble, aren't you, Donald?"

"Uh-huh. But don't mention the kidnapping to anybody, Whitney. Not yet. Just say it's a sure-fire investment opportunity that came up. Hog bellies from a freight train that derailed on Gram's croquet court or something."

"Well, my dear, this *is* simply dreadful. And even though, as you well know, I have precious little time for starry-eyed radicals, under the circumstances I suppose I have no choice except to—"

"Could you just hurry it up, Whitney? The banks in the shopping malls close early on Saturday. Now, here's where you can drop off the hundred. . ."

I went back to Timmy and Dot, who were attempting to calm McWhirter down with a cup of herb tea.

Timmy said, "Who was that?"

I said, "Manufacturers Hanover Trust. Saratoga branch."

"Oh, swell. They should be helpful. Did you open an account?"

"Nope. Just made a withdrawal."

---

9. Bowman sat scowling at the ransom note for a long tense couple of minutes, as if the mere passage of time might cause the letters on the sheet of paper to rearrange themselves into THIS IS ALL A CRAZY MISTAKE, LIEUTENANT. YOU CAN GO BACK TO THE GOLF COURSE NOW WHERE YOU BELONG. But it didn't. They didn't.

"This isn't the same handwriting as on the other note, is it?"

"No," I said. "It's different, messier. And the syntax and punctuation are even worse."

"Who here has handled this piece of paper?" he snapped. Four of us raised our hands. "I'll need prints from all four of you. You haven't made matters any easier for me, that's for damn certain. I suppose yours are already on record, Strachey, you being a famous certified pain in the ass and all."

"For sure, Ned."

Glowering, he went to the phone, called his bureau, and asked that two of his assistants be sent out to the Fisher farm.

"Now tell me again," he said, seating himself wearily, "what this Greco fellow was up to yesterday and last night. Take your time, and don't leave anything out. Where, when, who, and what for."

Very slowly, through clenched teeth, McWhirter said, "We have already *explained that*."

"Ah, so you have, so you have, Mr. McWhirter. And how would you like to run it by me once yet again? Just for old times' sake."

McWhirter was over the tabletop and at Bowman's throat before Timmy could finish shouting, "Holy mother!" Dot jumped up and yelled, "Now you two stop that right this instant!" as Timmy and I grabbed McWhirter from behind, pried his hands loose from the alarmingly empurpled Ned Bowman's neck, and dragged McWhirter thrashing and kicking out the back door.

"Down there!" I sputtered. "Fast!"

Edith was draped in a lawn chair under a pear tree squinting at the commotion, a frail hand raised to her throat, as we heaved McWhirter into the pond.

"I can't swim!" he gasped, flinging his arms and legs wetly about in a series of random and unproductive patterns.

"Oh, shit," Timmy said.

I said, "I don't think Price Chopper watches are waterproof. Anyhow, it's you who's into swimmers."

He was out of his clothes in a trice, or possibly thrice, and then, plunging, signed the vivid air with his bony ass.

McWhirter was dragged ashore coughing and gagging. He lay for a time on his stomach breathing hard. Then he pounded the earth very forcefully with his fist twice. He began to weep quietly.

I said, "I'm sorry, Fenton. Really. We didn't know you couldn't swim. It's just that strangling a police officer in Albany would cause eyebrows to be raised throughout the department. Among Ned Bowman's fellow officers the world would seem suddenly topsy-turvy, and in their confusion they would come and poke your right clavicle down into the region of your liver. We did you a favor, believe me. And now we're going to get Peter back for you."

McWhirter looked up at me balefully, and I could see his mind working. It was apparent that Ned Bowman's neck had not known the last of Fenton McWhirter's grasp. For the moment, though, McWhirter's rage had been sufficiently dampened. Timmy stayed with him while I made my way back into the house through the lacerating heat. The thermometer by Dot's back door read 99 degrees.

"When this business is finished," Bowman said, "Mr. Fenton McWhirter is going to pay a heavy, heavy price for this, Strachey. As will you yourself. I hold *you* responsible for what happened to me just now."

Dot was pressing a towel full of ice cubes against Bowman's neck. He looked wan but sounded livid.

I said, "That's an interesting piece of logic."

"For the moment, however, I am simply going to demand that you explain to me what the hell this mare's nest is all about. Is this alleged 'kidnapping' real, or is this some sicko stunt you and your fruit friends cooked up for me to waste my time on? Out with it!"

"Ned, one of the few things I've always admired about you is your Elizabethan felicity of expression. 'Out with it!' That's good. No vulgar street talk from your end of the detective division, and no glib and oily city hall locutions. A plain and forthright 'Out with it!' I like that."

He stood up abruptly and strode toward the door, the ice cubes clattering to Dot's polished oak floor.

"Better not do that, Ned," I said. "This whole ugly business is for real, I'm afraid. The feds will no doubt insist on poking their noses in sooner or later, and my guess is you'll want to have a head start and not end up getting outclassed by a bunch of guys wearing hats. Or were all those fedoras left on Hoover's grave when he died? Or in it?"

He returned to his seat, giving an ice cube a good kick

en route. He showed me a raging look that said, "You later." He barked, "Explain!"

I told him everything I knew, honestly and accurately—a novelty Bowman undoubtedly failed for the moment to appreciate—including the events as I had witnessed them or heard about them for the previous twenty-four hours. I described my relationship with Crane Trefusis, and Trefusis's to Dot Fisher, and how Trefusis stood to gain from Dot's sudden need to come up with one hundred thousand dollars in cash. Bowman allowed as how he had figured out that much for himself. I told him about my evening with McWhirter and Greco, about Greco's unhappy encounter with Tad Purcell, and my own underly fruitful visit with Purcell earlier that morning. Out of deference to Bowman's fragile sensibilities on sexual matters, I did leave out the parts about Gordon and his diseased grandmother.

I described the Deems and Wilsons and their interest in Dot's being forced to sell her property. I said it was possible, of course, that the kidnapping had no connection whatever with the Millpond situation, but that Greco himself had no known enemies in Albany—with the unlikely exception of the feckless Tad Purcell, who in any case was otherwise occupied Saturday night—and that anybody who disliked McWhirter enough to kidnap his lover must also have known him well enough to realize that his bank balance couldn't have been much above twelve dollars.

The Millpond–Dot Fisher state of affairs seemed to me to be the most promising avenue to explore, I said, and suggested that the Thursday night graffiti artist—Joey Deem? Bill Wilson?—ought to be quickly run down and looked at too, and either investigated further or eliminated as a suspect in the kidnapping. I did not voice my earlier suspicion about the night squad detectives, who struck me as much too crude a lot to pull off anything so sophisticated as a kidnapping.

Dot Fisher had sat quietly listening to all of this as Bowman grimaced and shifted about and made notes. When I'd finished, Dot calmly announced, "I'm going to sell the house."

I said, "No. No need."

Bowman watched us.

"Why, of course I will. What kind of person would I be if I didn't?" Her hands were trembling and she jammed them in the pockets of her shift. "From what you say, it's plain as day that I got Peter and Fenton into this dreadful mess, so I'll just have to get them out of it." She blinked repeatedly as she spoke, and her eyes were wet.

Bowman said, "You've decided to pay the ransom?"

"Why, my heavens, it never occurred to me not to! Peter's life is in danger. Just think how frightened he must be. It gives me the shivers. And I know he would do the same for me without giving it a thought."

"I'm sure he would, Dot. But really, it's not necessary."

"You shush! I phoned my attorney, Dave Myers, as soon as the ransom note arrived. I didn't explain the reason for my change of heart and he tried to talk me out of it, dear David, but I was adamant. He said he was going to wait until two o'clock before he called Crane Trefusis to accept Millpond's offer, and that I should think it over seriously in the meantime. I haven't *had* to think it over. What's to think about beyond getting Peter safely back here with us again?"

Bowman said, "It's five to two."

"Call Myers," I said. "Or I'll call him and tell him to forget it. I've got the money, the hundred. Or soon will have."

Bowman's eyebrows went up. "*You*? Where'd you

ever get a hundred grand, Strachey? You dealing coke?"

Talk big money these days and nobody ever thinks of U.S. Steel or General Motors anymore. A new America: computer chips, video games, and cocaine.

Dot said, "Oh, Don, that's extremely thoughtful of you, but I could never—"

"Not my money," I said. "Someone's lending it to us just in case it's needed. The kidnappers are not at all coming across as slick pros, and I'm reasonably certain that even if we have to hand over the hundred at all, we'll have it back in our grasp within minutes, or at most hours. It's just a precaution. A tool. Bait. The cash will be delivered here at three o'clock. Then we'll be ready for whatever comes next."

Dot opened her mouth to speak, then didn't.

Bowman, suppressing a grin, said, "I agree entirely, Mrs. Fisher. Mr. Strachey has thought the situation through very nicely. A tidy job of work he's done, I'd say. Oh, yes. Yes, if I were you, Mrs. Fisher, I would definitely take this man's money."

Dot hesitated again, then glanced at the kitchen clock. She rose quickly, came around, bent down and kissed me on the cheek, and moved for the phone.

I said to Bowman, "I'm counting on the Albany Police Department's full assistance in this delicate matter, Ned. I'm sure that under these rather special circumstances you won't let me down. Right?"

His eyes glazed over serenely and he looked deeply unconcerned. He shrugged. He attempted a yawn, but it caught on his uvula and he gave a little cough.

Trying hard to ignore the small mammals bouncing about in the pit of my stomach, I said, "I figure, Ned, that we have to buy time. When the kidnappers contact Dot, she stalls them. Agree?"

"Agree."

"I figure too that the amateurs we appear to be dealing with here might well be panicked by undue publicity, and that the whole business should be kept quiet for at least the next twenty-four hours. Agree?"

"Agree."

"Swell. Now, just so we both know where we stand with each other, Ned, you tell me what we *dis*agree on— beyond the obvious and enduring. Do us both a favor, lay it out now, and avoid a lot of hostile confusion later on."

"Oh, not much, I guess. I was just wondering whether or not you and your fag pals are perpetrating some kind of outrageous con job in order to make the Albany Police Department look bad. Tell me, Strachey. Is that a possibility? Is it now? The thought keeps nagging at me."

Maybe it was the heat, or my exhaustion, or both, but Bowman was starting to get to me. I said, "Gee, Ned. You mean some diabolical scheme to reveal to the voters that the criminal justice system in Albany County is essentially confused, inept, misguided, cynical, frightened, defensive, and riddled with ignorant hacks and cronies whose only interest beyond pushing faggots and black people around is in getting re-elected, reappointed, tenured, and properly positioned for a fair share of the grifts, graft, perks, and payoffs? Is *that* what you suspect, Ned? Nah. We wouldn't do that."

He glared. "I have my doubts."

"The machine's secret is safe with us, Ned. We'll never tell."

He was leaning close to me and about to let loose with some tiresome empty threat when the door opened and they all charged in at once: Timmy, McWhirter, Edith, two burly types in jackets who appeared to be the junior police detectives Bowman had phoned for earlier, and, in the midst of them, her great hips thundering out a five-plus on the nearest Richter scale, Kay Wilson. Kay held out a small package, which Dot Fisher, who had just completed the phone call to her lawyer, accepted.

"Why, thank you, Kay. Thank you so much."

"Somebody left this in our mailbox, Dot honey, but it's addressed to you, and I figured I better drag my old bones down here right away, 'cause you can see right there it says, 'Deliver immediately—life or death.'"

"Oh. Oh, my."

We all gawked at the small package. It was wrapped in a cut-up brown paper bag, and measured about eight inches by four inches by one inch.

Bowman gently pried up the lid and flipped it onto its back.

The handwriting was the same as that on the ransom note but again not the same as on Friday's threatening letter. "Immediately" was spelled "immeatetly."

Bowman asked for and was provided a pair of vegetable tongs and a paring knife. Without touching the package with his fingers, he slit through the cellophane tape holding the paper on and slid the wrapping aside. The cardboard box was fire truck red, the type a Christmas gift might arrive in, a wallet or fancy handkerchief. A sheet of notebook paper, folded in quarters, was taped to the top of the box.

Bowman asked Kay Wilson, Edith, Timmy, and me to step outside. They shuffled out. I stayed. Bowman went huff-huff, but he otherwise ignored my insubordination for the moment and went on with his duties.

The paper, unfolded, revealed these words: "Put $100,000 dollars in Mrs. Fishers mailbox tonight at 3 a.m. in the morning, or we will send Petes hart. If you follow the car Pete will die."

We stared at the box.

McWhirter, trembling, said, "Open it."

Bowman gently pried up the lid and flipped it onto its back.

McWhirter clutched the tabletop and groaned. Dot whispered, "My lord!" Bowman shook his head in disgust.

The object that lay damply, crazily, grayly atop a bed of soft white tissue paper was unmistakably a human finger.

10.

McWhirter, his voice breaking, barely audible, said, "We have to pay them."

Dot groaned. "Yes, of course, of course."

I said, "The money will arrive here at three. But we'll get it back, don't worry."

"Yeah," Bowman said grimly. "I guess we better have the cash ready. Just in case. Jesus, these people aren't fooling around." He sat gazing at the finger, tapping two of his own on the table. He looked up at McWhirter now and said, "Mr. McWhirter, I've heard of kidnappers who have . . . Well, let me just put the question to you directly. Are you certain that the finger in that box belongs to your friend Peter Greco?"

McWhirter blanched, looked away, and said quietly, "Yes. Oh, God, yes."

Bowman grimaced, in part no doubt at the thought that one man could know another's finger that intimately. Then he dispatched one of the junior detectives to retrieve some equipment from his car.

I said, "Obviously, we've got to get Greco away from these people fast. How do we set this up? We've got thirteen hours to do it in."

"Unless they're even dumber and sloppier than I think they are," Bowman said, "they'll arrive minus Greco in a stolen car, snatch the money, and off they'll go, thinking we won't dare follow so long as they've still got a hold of

Greco. I'll have to have this place totally covered, plus the other end of Moon Road, Central Avenue out to Colonie, and back as far as Everett Road. I'll order up a chopper too."

"At three in the morning?"

"No!" McWhirter croaked. "Just *give them the money*. Don't I have anything to say about this? You people are just going to get Peter *killed*, the way you're talking. Look at what these people are capable of. Just *look* at that." We looked. "Just . . . give them the money, and I'll . . . I'll pay it back."

"Mr. McWhirter," Bowman said, "I think I can understand how you feel—sort of." He shot me a warning look, apparently fearing that I might begin to think of him as human. "By that I mean," he sputtered on, "I can see, Mr. McWhirter, how you might be pretty scared and upset at this point. But believe me, the chances that we'll get your friend back in one piece—" We all looked down at the finger again. "I mean, by that I mean . . . the best way to make sure we get your friend back here alive is to not let these people slip away at the one time we can be sure we know where they are. You get what I'm saying? We let them run off with that hundred grand, and they might just get cocky and start thinking they can get away with *any*thing. If you follow my meaning."

McWhirter screwed up his face in agonized confusion. His mouth tried to make words, but he couldn't get them out.

I said, "Lieutenant Bowman has experience with these things, Fenton. He's right. You can be sure it'll be done with all the finesse the Albany Police Department is capable of."

Bowman looked my way, waiting for any qualifications I might be going to add, and when I offered none—nauseating flattery was called for here—he said, "You bet."

Dot Fisher's small fist suddenly hit the table. "Now, you people are just the absolute limit! Whom was that letter *addressed* to, may I ask? And the package. Whom was *that* sent to? Well?"

No one had yet called the finger a finger. It was just "it." Or "the package." I said to Dot, "The ransom note and the package were both sent to you."

"Exactly! So it seems to me that I should have some say in all this. And what I say is, you are all putting Peter in terrible, terrible danger. Well, I won't stand for it! The decision is mine to make, and I've decided. We will *pay* the kidnappers what they've asked for and let them go their way. And then, when Peter is safely back here with those who love him, *then* I will expect all of you to do everything within your power to retrieve that money and put those reprehensible savages in the penitentiary where they belong!"

Bowman said, "But—"

"And one other thing," Dot went on, waving Bowman into silence. "If the money is not returned to Mr. Strachey within seven days, I *will* sell my property and repay him promptly. No one can stop me, and that is that."

My options had now doubled in number. If the hundred grand somehow slipped away, I could then decide whether I wanted to be a monumental deadbeat or a mere son of a bitch.

Bowman had begun shaking his head and yammering on about how Dot would be making a big mistake by simply handing over the ransom, and it was out of her hands anyway, and it was well known among professionals that in seven out of ten cases it turned out that. . . .

Dot sat rigid, the lavender veins in her neck pulsing wildly.

I caught Bowman's eye. "She wants to do it her way,

Ned. It's Mrs. Fisher's decision to make. Not ours."

He glowered at me, and while Dot and McWhirter cringed and waited for him to pop off irrelevantly, I looked back at Bowman and lightly winked. He immediately got the point.

"Well," he said, throwing his hands up. "If that's the way you want it, Mrs. Fisher. If you insist, you go ahead and pay the ransom, and then we'll do all we can to track down these vicious perverts—sorry, no offense, Strachey —and then we'll get your money back. Or what's left of it."

McWhirter had been gazing fixedly at the finger, and now suddenly he reached toward it and touched it lightly. He moaned and flung himself out of his chair, across the kitchen, and down the hall. I guessed that the sound of a door slamming came from the downstairs bathroom.

The two junior detectives had entered the room during the discussion, and now one of them opened a plastic case full of foam pellets. He flipped the lid back onto the finger box and, using tongs, lifted the entire business, wrapping and all, into the case of pellets. The other detective opened a fingerprint kit and prepared to take the prints of those of us who had handled the ransom note and package. I was about to go outside and fetch Kay Wilson for the fingerprinting session when the telephone rang and Dot went to answer it.

Bowman came over to me and whispered, "I'll have fifty men out here tonight. We'll get 'em."

I said, "I have lied to my friends, Ned. That's not one of my usual bad habits. You guys hadn't better slip up."

"No sweat. And congratulations, pal. It's the first time I've known you to be all the way on the side of the law. I may shed a tear."

Dot slammed down the receiver. "Now this is just— beyond endurance!"

"Who was that?" Bowman snapped.

"It was . . . that *voice* again. 'You dykes better get out of there. You dykes leave or die.' If I ever get my hands on—"

The phone rang yet again.

"You got an extension?" Bowman asked.

"In our bedroom upstairs. The front, southwest corner."

Bowman said, "Pick up when I do," and trotted off down the hall. I placed my hand on the receiver. Midway in the fifth ring the phone fell silent and I lifted the receiver and passed it to Dot.

"Y-yes. Hello?"

We waited, watched her breath catch, then flow slowly out of her.

"It's for Timmy." She sighed. "It's not the voice. It's a man for Mr. Callahan. Oh me, oh my."

I said, "Did the first caller mention Peter?"

"Why no," Dot said. "He didn't. Or she. I'm still not certain whether it's a man or a woman."

Bowman came back. I said, "I think we've got two of them. Two separate people, or groups."

"Yeah. Or thirty-five. I've gotta get a tap and trace rig on this phone number, but fast."

Out in the yard, Kay Wilson had Timmy backed into a lilac bush and was singing the praises of Crane "Quite-a-Guy" Trefusis. Timmy's eyes were open, but I suspected he was nonetheless napping lightly. I'd seen him do it before at cocktail parties put on by insurance industry lobbyists. Edith was off by herself over by the peonies, gingerly emptying the Japanese beetle traps.

"Phone call," I said, ambling up to Timmy and Kay.

Kay turned. "For me? It must be Wilson, wants his lunch. Tell him I just left."

"No, it's for Mr. Callahan."

"Oh, your boyfriend, huh?"

"This is the man."

She snickered. "Hey, Bob. Tell me somethin', then. Which one of you's the boy and which one's the girl?"

Timmy quickly walked by me toward the house, his eyes raised heavenward.

I said, "Wouldn't you like to know. To tell you the truth, Kay, only our chiropractor knows for sure."

"Your *what*?"

I said, "What's your hubby up to today, Kay? Bill Wilson make you rich yet?"

"Hah! You pullin' my leg, kiddo? The day that bozo gives me more'n a lotta lip'll be the day Charles Bronson sends me a dozen roses and a case of Jack Daniel's. Say, don't you just love Dot's flower garden? Hey, what are you doin' over there, Mrs. Stout? Mealybugs chewin' up your tulips?"

"Eh? What's that, Mrs. Wilson?"

"I asked if you got chigs on your posies? Looks like you got 'em, all right. Up to your left tit. I got a can of Raid down to the house if you want to try a shot of that. That stuff'll fix 'em."

I said, "Kay, you're needed in the house for a few minutes. The police need a set of your fingerprints. So they can tell yours from those of whoever else handled that package you delivered."

Her eyes got big as we turned toward the house. "Hey, Bob, what the Sam Hill is goin' on around here, anyways? Police dicks crawling all over the place. This used to be a respectable neighborhood. What was in that package anyhow? Your lover boy wouldn't tell me what was goin' on. What's the big secret?"

I said, "One of Dot's houseguests is missing. The police are helping locate him. He'll turn up, though, don't worry."

"Maybe he was snatched," she said eagerly. "And they're sending him back here a piece at a time. I read in the paper how the Mafia does it like that. Is that what was in the package? Some poor clown's tongue, or left ear, or pecker? Hell, nobody's safe anyplace anymore. They're gonna getcha, they're gonna getcha."

I went queasy but didn't reply as we stepped into the house. Timmy was off the phone now and Bowman was on the line with, judging by his civil tone, a superior in the department. I presented Kay Wilson to the fingerprint man, and Timmy pulled me aside.

"Mel Glempt just called. You don't know him. At least I think you don't. One of the Green Room bartenders I phoned earlier ran into him a while ago and told him Peter was missing. Just missing, no more. That's all anybody knows so far. Glempt saw something last night, and the barkeep had him call me and tell me about it. Glempt saw some kind of fight or scuffle in the Green Room parking lot last night just before midnight. He'd just pulled in."

"And?"

"And . . . well, this must have been it. A young man—a 'kid,' Mel said, but it must have been Peter—this young man was shoved into a car. He seemed to be resisting, but a guy wrapped a bandage or something around his head so he couldn't see, and got him into the back seat of this car—some kind of big old dark green job—and then the car drove away fast. There were two men, the shover and the driver."

"And Glempt didn't *report* this to anybody? Shit." Timmy said nothing." Well, did he at least get a make and model on the car?"

"No."

"Did he recognize the people doing it?"

"No."

"Can he describe them?"

"One of them, he said. The one who was outside doing the grabbing, but not the driver."

"Which way did they go?"

"Out Central. West."

"We'd better clue Bowman in right away. Have his people talk to Glempt. I'll want to talk to him too."

I turned toward Bowman, who was still on the phone. Timmy said, "Wait."

He looked grim, his cornflower blue eyes taking on the November gray cast they had whenever he was apprehensive about something, or frightened.

Timmy said, "At least one of the two—the one outside the car, the one Mel got a quick look at—was a cop. A cop in a uniform. That's why Mel didn't call the police. He thought it *was* the police."

I looked over at Bowman, who, catching me watching him, turned his back to me as he spoke quietly into the telephone.

11.

I phoned Mel Glempt, who repeated to me what he had told Timmy. I asked him to tell his story to Bowman's people, and he eventually agreed, though, with considerable trepidation.

My service reported no messages. I reached Patrolman Lyle Barner at home and set up a meeting with him for three-thirty. He said, "You coming alone?"

I said no and asked him if he'd turned up anything in his check of the night detective squad. He said he hadn't. I told him he might need to check again.

Bowman's two assistants drove off, one of them to carry the finger and the two notes to the crime lab, the other to interview the Deems, Wilsons, and Tad Purcell.

I got Bowman off in a corner and described to him what Mel Glempt had seen outside the Green Room the night before.

Bowman said, "This is a con. You're setting me up. You're lying."

I shook my head. A setup was not out of the question, but I knew it wasn't mine.

He asked for the name of the witness. I told him and provided Glempt's address and phone number. I added, "He'll talk to you and your people, but he won't talk to the night squad guys and would rather they did not know his identity."

"How come? Why's that?"

"Because," I said, "certain elements of the Albany Police Department cannot be trusted to do what's right a good part of the time. Or even what's legal. Face it, Ned, that's the sad truth."

He threw his head back and snorted in disbelief, as if I had tried to convince him that the world was an ovoid slab supported by a three-pronged stick.

Bowman knew what I meant, though. He walked to the telephone and hesitated. Then, making sure his back was to me, he dialed a number.

Dot Fisher was fixing club sandwiches and Senegalese soup and setting out more iced tea. She moved about the kitchen muttering under her breath and forcing a wan smile whenever anyone addressed her.

McWhirter returned to the room and resumed his pacing. He had questions: "Has the FBI been called?" "Why don't you arrest this Trefusis mobster? *He* must be the one behind all this." "When could they have taken Peter? How?"

Watching McWhirter carefully, I told him what Mel Glempt had seen. He stood trembling for a moment, then slumped into a chair and buried his head in his hands.

Bowman completed his call and ambled back to the table. He was shaking his head, clear-eyed, his movements a tad jauntier than the occasion, as I saw it, required. He looked at me coolly and said simply, "Uhn-uhn." As if that was the end of that: Glempt had been mistaken about the cop he saw, or lying.

Timmy caught this and gave me a look. Here was an education for this sunny, optimistic fellow who had spent much of his adult life in the more wholesome and uncomplicated atmosphere of the back rooms of the state legislature.

Bowman did say he was sending two of his own men out to interview Glempt to get his "confused account of the abduction," and Bowman further announced that he now had half the detective bureau working on the case and needed more information on Greco's background and recent activities, as well as Dot's and Edith's. I convinced McWhirter that I would personally follow up on "the cop Mel Glempt saw"—this made Bowman writhe with indignant disgust—so for half an hour, over lunch, a tense, snappish interrogation went forward.

It yielded nothing. Greco's family had moved to San Diego eleven years earlier and he had no known remaining Albany connections other than Tad Purcell. Nor could Dot come up with names of any "enemies" of hers or Edith's—former students, colleagues, relatives, neighbors—beyond the ones we already knew about: the Wilsons, Deems, and Crane Trefusis.

Bowman said he had detectives out at that moment checking into the activities of Dot's Moon Road neighbors and would personally interview Crane Trefusis, which struck me as a wonderfully droll waste of time. Bowman allowed as how his bureau was also looking at some of the notorious local "hate groups," although he was clearly disinclined to investigate further the particular hate group which the only evidence we had pointed to.

"Lieutenant Bowman," Dot said. "You're not eating your Senegalese soup. Could I get you something else?"

"No, no, I'm fine. What's in this?"

"Tons of fresh vegetables straight from our garden. The herbs and spices are from Edith's little plot."

"Nnn. Looks good." He contemplated the greenish-yellow curried soup.

There was a light rap at the door and Dot heaved herself up.

"It's for you, Don. A man with a beautiful suitcase."

I went outside and watched Whitney Tarkington, in white ducks and a burgundy Calvin Klein polo shirt, place a Gucci bag on the terrace. He unsnapped it and held it open.

"It's all here, Donald. One hundred thousand—soon to become one hundred ten thousand—big ones."

"Dollars, you mean."

"Of course, dollars. What else?"

"In that bag it might have been lira."

"Ha-ha."

I peered into the bag and did a double take. "I see dollars, yes. I also see . . . *Checks?*"

"Twenty-eight thousand in cash, seventy-two thousand in checks. Best I could do on a Saturday, Donald. God, I had to bust my carefully toned buns just to come up with *this* on three hours' notice. I mean, a hundred grand in *cash?* You think I'm *Grams* or somebody?"

"*Checks*, Whitney? You think kidnappers are going to accept *checks* for a ransom payment?"

"They're good. Really they are."

"Crap. That's hardly the point. Crap."

"I mean, all of them *will* be good first thing Monday morning. They'll be covered, for sure. You can bet your life on it, Donald."

"Not my life, Whitney. Peter Greco's life. Thanks anyway."

"That's quite all right. I owed you one, didn't I? Now we're even. Or will be, when you hand me a hundred and ten thousand dollars—U.S. currency, please—seventy-two hours from this second."

He grinned dazzlingly and touched his perm.

"Of course," I said. "See you Tuesday, Whitney. Same time, same place. I might even return the bag."

"Just have it dry-cleaned if it's smudged," he said. "Toodle-ooo." He climbed back into his canary yellow sports car and drove off.

Timmy looked out. "Is that a Porsche nine-eleven? You don't see those around here too often."

"Looks like a Gloria Vanderbilt to me," I said, and went inside.

I phoned Crane Trefusis again. "I have to cash a number of checks. Seventy-two thousand dollars' worth. They're good. But the banks are closing, and Price Chopper revoked my We-Do-More-Club card last March over a minor incident involving a rib roast, a bunch of asparagus, and a smallish check the State Bank of Albany inexplicably declined to take seriously. You'll help me out, of course."

A pause. "Of course. Have you found the culprits yet?"

"Which ones?"

"Any of them."

"Not yet."

"You will."

"You bet, Crane. Have you come across any information that might help me in my labors?"

"I'm sorry, but I haven't. I don't actually spend a great deal of time with criminals in my business, Strachey."

"How much?"

"How much what?"

"How much time *do* you spend with criminals in your business? An hour a week? Three days? Forty-five minutes? What?"

"None that I'm aware of. Not that I'll ever convince a professional skeptic like you."

"Just keep your ear to the ground, Crane. That's all I ask. You never know."

"Of course."

We worked out details for the check cashing and I rang off.

Bowman had neglected his Senegalese soup but was finishing off a second sandwich.

I said, "Hey, Ned. What if the kidnappers are hiding out at the bottom of that soup bowl?"

He blew me a tiny kiss. Dot, a woman of apparently limitless reserves of charity, shook her head, embarrassed for Bowman, a man very hard to be embarrassed for, if not about.

McWhirter was pacing again.

"I've got the money," I said. "Part cash and part in checks that I'll cash and get back here in plenty of time."

McWhirter stared at the bag with fear in his eyes, as if it might contain eight pounds of severed appendages.

Dot said quietly, "Thank you."

Bowman said, "Wish I had friends like yours, Strachey. Good work. Looks like we're all set. I'll get a man out here to mark the bills and record serial numbers."

"What do we do now?" Timmy asked. "Just wait? I could use some sleep."

"Come on," I said, removing the checks from the valise and stuffing them into a bread bag I snatched from the kitchen counter. "You can sleep tomorrow. When this is all over. Right now we've got places to go, people to see."

"Where? Who?"

"You'll find out. We're both going to be busy. I've got a little list."

"Now don't you get in the way of my people," Bowman warned. "And if you hear anything I need to know, I want to know it goddamn *quick*. You got that, Strachey?"

I said, "Got it, Ned. You know me. For sure."

12.

Passing the Deems' house, I told Timmy, "I'll stop back here later. I don't think the Deems are the main problem in all of this. Maybe none at all. But there's something I want to check. You can help me out by looking into another nagging matter."

As we bumped past the Wilsons' I explained to Timmy what I wanted him to find out about Bill Wilson.

"I'll do what I can," he said, "but this whole thing is starting to scare the hell out of me. I'm not sure I'm cut out for this rough stuff. It started out as some homophobic vandalism, which was sickening enough. And now people are actually getting hurt. *Mutilated*."

"I don't like it either."

"Imagine having your lover's finger arrive in a box. Of course, it could have been worse."

"It wasn't his," I said.

We turned onto Central.

"It— What wasn't whose?"

"That finger wasn't Greco's."

"Come on. Really? How do you know? I thought Mc-Whirter told Bowman it was."

"Greco has thick black hair on the tops of his fingers. I know. He touched my face. It tickled a little. The finger in that box was slender like Greco's but practically hairless. And what little hair there was was lighter than Greco's."

"He *touched your face*? Kee-rist, Donald." He undulated awkwardly in his seat belt. "Do you want to describe the circumstances, lover, or should I just draw my own sensational conclusions and stick it all in your 'Seven Since June' file? Crimenee. You're just—incredible."

"He did it once standing in Dot's front yard and once standing in the parking lot outside the Green Room. It's a habit Greco has. Touching faces. He's a sweet, affectionate, uninhibited guy. It's no automatic High Homintern cocktail-party-kiss kind of thing. It's just something he can't help doing. Unconventional, but winning. Not that there's anything calculating in the gesture. You can't not like him."

"'Like.' Right."

I turned onto Colvin, south into the Pine Hills section of the city. I said, "Now who's not trusting whom?"

He threw his head around, sulked, threw his head around some more. Then he looked over at me in utter amazement. "But . . . McWhirter must have known!"

"Ah-ha."

"Presumably McWhirter is familiar with his lover's finger."

"A safe assumption."

"But then— Why did he lie? Dot told me McWhirter identified the finger as Greco's."

"Beats me. Before the day is over I'll ask him."

We swung left onto Lincoln.

"And *you* didn't say anything because . . . ?"

"I figured the news should be broken to the authorities by the loved one. The fact that it wasn't seemed to me a piece of information almost as fascinating as the fact of the finger itself. I *think* I know why McWhirter didn't speak up. But I'm not sure."

"I'm surprised Bowman didn't doubt his word. Press him on it. Maybe take him downtown for a lineup. 'Mr. McWhirter, is any of these eight fingers that of the man with whom you participate in an un-Godly relationship?'"

"Bowman will rely on the lab people," I said. "And they'll most likely come up with nothing, because I doubt that Greco has ever been fingerprinted. He hasn't been in the armed forces, and he's probably never been arrested. Even in demonstrations that turn messy Greco's not the type cops go after. Anyway, until I've discussed the matter with McWhirter, let's keep mum about it. If Ned knew, he might draw some hasty erroneous conclusions. To the effect, for instance, that this *is* some kind of scam McWhirter's cooked up."

"Or some hasty correct ones."

"There's that possibility. But I think it's something else."

"What?"

"Let me run it by McWhirter first. It's just a guess. It has to do with McWhirter's frequently justifiable glum outlook on the world."

Timmy sat sweating energetically and drumming his fingers on the dashboard as I turned onto Buchanan. "But if it wasn't Greco's finger," he said after a time, "then whose finger *was* it?"

"Good question."

Lyle Barner's living room, on the second floor of an old soot brown frame house, was full of dark oversized "Mediterranean-style" furniture with a plastic finish. Ischia via Dow Chemical. The gleaming leviathan of a bar was from the same discount house the couch and chairs had come from, as was the console TV set with an Atari hookup, around which the other furniture had been arranged. A carpet of dust covered everything except the center section of the couch and the midsection of the coffee table in front of it where Barner propped his legs. The only reading matter was the *Times Union* TV section. The room contained no decorative objects, artwork, or photographs. It was the room of a man with no past he wanted to remember and no future he could bring himself to believe in.

Ignoring Timmy, whom I'd just introduced, Lyle said, "You want a beer? Christ, I hate this fucking weather."

"Thanks, but we'd be blotto after half a can. We haven't slept."

"Uh-huh. Well, I'll have one."

Lyle Barner was a squat, well-muscled man with an incipient beer paunch and a lot of straw-colored hair on his shoulders. Both the mouth and eyes of his nicely arranged big-featured face slanted down at the corners with a kind of ferociously controlled tension, as if he were frozen in a pose for a Mathew Brady daguerreotype. Barner's curly hair was lush and full except for a half-dollar-sized bald spot on top, which I had once had the opportunity to observe for several minutes. He was clad, as he lumbered into the kitchen and then back to us again, in black nylon bikini briefs.

I was seated with Timmy on the couch. Dropping into an easy chair and slinging one leg over the armrest, Lyle looked over at me—only me—and said, "Been a while since I've seen you in the flesh, Strachey. Glad to see you're sexy as ever."

"What did you find out?" I said.

He swigged from the beer can. "You know, Strachey, I haven't had a whole lot of sleep either. Except I was out protecting the public last night. What were you doing? Out partying as usual, it looks like."

He glanced briefly, dismissively, at Timmy, as if to say, Where'd you pick this up? I'd had some half-formed cockeyed idea that it might be helpful for Lyle Barner to observe two healthy, relaxed gay men more or less at peace with themselves and each other, secure in their loving relationship and in the knowledge that its evident riches were a goal nearly all gay men could aspire to and achieve. But I was beginning to suspect I'd picked the wrong day for an object lesson of this particular sort, or the wrong couple to employ in it.

Timmy said sourly, "It's hot in here. I think I'll wait in the car. A pleasure meeting you, Lyle." He shot me a look.

Lyle nodded once and continued to watch me carefully while Timmy got up and walked out the door. We listened to his footfall on the staircase. The downstairs door slammed.

"Hey, that one's real cute," Lyle said. "But, tell me, Don. What *would* your lover think?"

"Your bitterness is unattractive, Lyle. You should work to get rid of it. You might become an attractive man."

He winced and looked away.

I said, "Are you going to help me out or not? A life may depend on it. What did you find out?"

He sat staring at the wall for a long moment, the emotion building in him. Then, still not looking at me, he said, "I'm bitter because . . . because nobody will love me." His face contorted and he shut his eyes. He said, "I want somebody to love me." He fought to regain control, then sat not moving, hardly breathing, his muscular left leg spasming crazily.

"Right now, you're not lovable, Lyle. Self-pity is off-putting. Nobody loves a whiner for long."

His voice breaking, he said, "You loved me once."

An old story. I knew it. I said, "We sucked each other's cocks. That's just friendliness. I don't sneer at it, far from it, but most of the time I'd rank it only a notch or two above helping a stranger change a tire. Well, maybe six or eight notches. And yes, I know, it's a whole lot more fun. Plus, you don't have to wash your hands with Fels-Naphtha afterwards. Though, of course, after changing a tire you don't have to brush your teeth. On the one hand this, on the other hand that."

He wasn't about to be humored. He said, "It's as close to love as I've ever come."

"But not as close as you'll ever get."

He snorted.

"You've got to get out of Albany, Lyle. You'll never do it here. Go . . . west, maybe. In San Francisco they're recruiting gay cops. Go there. You've got a good record. Go to some half-civilized place and quit hating yourself and taking it out on other people. Find out how fine a man you can be, and go be that person for a while. You'll like it. Other people will like it."

"I can't," he said, shaking his head miserably. "I've never been anywhere. I can't."

"I know someone in San Francisco who'll help you. I'll call him."

"No, don't. I'll never do it."

"Of course, it'd be hard. But you owe it to yourself. And to Clyde Boo, from Yank-your-Tank, Arkansas, or whoever, who's out there waiting for you. You'll find that life with Clyde won't be easy either. But it'll be a hell of a lot easier than this."

He stared at the empty wall.

"In the meantime," I said, "you've got to help me out."

He looked over at me now, his eyes wet. "Will you come and lay down with me first?"

"Well, gee, Lyle . . . gee. Actually, I think Miss Manners would advise against it. I mean, with my lover waiting down in the car and all. I think you have a good bit to learn about timing—about the social graces. I'm pretty sure we'd both feel very, very bad afterwards. Also, these days I'm a bit overextended in that department."

He looked sullenly at his commodious lap for a long moment—it hadn't escaped my notice either—and then back at me. He shrugged, smiled weakly. "Can't blame a guy for trying," he said. "Can you?"

I didn't know about Lyle. Whether he would make it or not. If he did, poor Clyde.

I said, "No, I know what you mean. Acting bashful gets you nowhere. It's just that your sense of occasion is a little off. But it'll improve with experience, I'm fairly certain. Now then. You were going to answer a couple of questions for me, right?"

"Oh. Yeah. Sure. If that's the way you want it." He fetched himself another beer.

Before I left Lyle's apartment, I phoned my friend Vinnie, who confirmed what he'd told me earlier and added additional details. It squared exactly with what Lyle had found out.

Timmy had the car seat tilted all the way back and was snoring lightly.

"Wake up. Lyle was helpful. We've got a lot to do and little time to do it in."

"Huh?"

I took the first right and headed south toward Western. "Lyle says he can find no evidence of any of the night squad guys—detectives or patrolmen—off on any private hoots last night. It's not out of the question that a day man might have been in uniform after dark for his own reasons, but Lyle put me in touch with someone I'd heard about a few hours earlier who looks like an even better bet. Lyle knows an *ex*-cop—a former night squad bozo who'd still have his old uniform and might have it in him to misrepresent himself. The man is known to lift a glass from time to time and prefers to do it in 'classy' surroundings. Lyle has set up a meeting in a suitably stimulating environment. And also—now get this—the guy now does private so-called security work. Guess who his current employer is?"

Timmy squinted and rubbed his eyes. He looked at his watch. "Who?" he said.

"Crane Trefusis."

"Jesus it's—it's almost five-thirty. You were in there for nearly *two hours*."

"Right. We've got just over nine hours left. While you're checking out Wilson, I'll see Trefusis—I've got to cash these checks—but first I'm meeting—"

"You knew him, didn't you?" he said, wide awake now. "I mean, really *knew* him. Lyle was one of them, wasn't he?"

"What? One of the famous 'Twelve Since June'?"

Twelve. What number had I told him?

He started to vibrate uncontrollably, as if his suspension system was about to go. Then suddenly he snapped, "Let me *out!*"

"What?"

"I said let me out of this fucking car! Stop this car and let me *out. Now!*"

"Look, Timmy, you're tired, exhausted—"

He opened the car door as I swung left onto Western, and if he hadn't been belted in he'd have hurtled onto the pavement.

I pulled to the curb. He unclicked the belt and was out of the car in a split second. "But, Timmy—"

I watched him stomp down the street for thirty yards. He halted, hesitated. He turned and stomped back.

He leaned down to the open window. His red, white,

and blue eyes fixed on me through two ugly little slits. He hissed, "I'll check on Wilson. I said I would do that. I'll phone you at Mrs. Fisher's with what I find out. Then I'm going to sleep. Then I'm getting up at two-thirty in the morning and I'm—going out. I don't want to be with you. I want to be with somebody else. *Any*body else. You make me sick. Literally *sick*."

He leaned down, stuck two fingers deep into his throat, and vomited copiously into the gutter.

Love is.

"Look," I said, "it's twelve or fifteen blocks to the apartment. We should talk. Get back in and I'll . . ."

He had wiped his mouth on a snow white lovingly ironed and folded handkerchief, which he had carefully removed from his back pocket with two fingers, and now he reached in and dropped the foul thing onto the seat beside me. Additional words evidently seeming to him redundant, he turned and staggered off down the avenue.

I slowly followed him for two blocks while the fuming traffic behind me honked and swerved around me.

Then, figuring first things first—Peter Greco's life now, more complicated matters later—I speeded up and took the first left toward Washington Avenue. As I passed Timmy, I watched him out of the corner of my eye watching me out of the corner of his eye. The inside of my car stank.

13.

The bar at the new downtown Albany Hilton was a million-dollar flying fortress of mirrors, Swedish ivy, chrome, rosewood, spider plants, bamboo, rubber trees, cut glass, and ferns, as if Hugh Carey's jet had crashed in the jungle.

Dale Overdorf was away on his second trip to the men's room, and I signaled the barman. "Another Coors for the gentleman and a double iced coffee for me."

I checked my watch. Seven-twelve. Overdorf hadn't shown up until after six, and in an hour I'd bought him six homophobic bottles of beer and found out next to nothing. During Overdorf's first men's room break I'd phoned Dot's house and learned that there had been no further contact with the kidnappers—and no message from Timmy. Bowman told me a tap and trace had been put on Dot's phone by the authorities, and if I stayed on the line another ninety seconds he could tell me where I was calling from. I said I was at the Hilton bar.

"You people taking that place over too?"

"Yep. The Fort Orange Club is next. The name'll be changed to Orangie's Pub."

Click.

Overdorf, bulllike and sweating, his gold chains ting-a-linging, wobbled back toward me. Negotiating the stairs up from the lobby, he seemed to be attempting to impersonate a third-rate comedian imitating a drunk.

"Sh-sure is hot in here. Goddamn, it's hot."

The temperature inside the Hilton had been set at a defiant 35 degrees.

"You were telling me, Dale, about the way Millpond security operates. The 'special projects' stuff. 'Outreach.'"

He slid onto his stool and partook of the pale liquid. "Who'd you say you worked for, Life-raft—or whatever your goddamn name is?"

"Lovecraft. H. P. Lovecraft professionally, but you can just call me Archie. I run Cover-U.S. Security Systems, Ink, in Elmira. Remember?"

"Oh, yeah. Yeah, Lyle said you were goddamn private. Like me now."

"Right."

"Uh-huh. So, how you like Albany, Archie? Some

dead town, huh? Not much action here. You want action, you gotta go over to goddamn Troy. That's where all the action is. Troy."

"I didn't know that."

"Oh, yeah. Action's in Troy."

"Just like Elmira. You want action, you gotta go over to Corning."

"Yeah. Know what yer sayin'."

"Same everywhere. You want action, gotta go some-place else."

"Dead town. Goddamn dead town."

I slapped a five on the bar. "Another Coors for the gentleman *s'il vous plaît*."

The barkeep gave me a look but produced the bottle. I told him to keep the change.

"You were telling me, Dale, about the kind of stuff you do in shopping mall security, which I've never han-dled but I might want to get into out my way. Shoplifters, dope peddlers in the bathrooms, all that. You said there was some special stuff that comes up once in a while. Kind of rough, you said. You mean like holdups, or hostage sit-uations, or what?"

"Heh-heh."

"I mean, I'm just trying to find out what I can look forward to. What are the dangers, the risks?"

He leaned close. "Lemme tell you, Life-raft. Just lemme goddamn tell you. It gets heavy sometimes. Heavy, heavy stuff. Crane Trefusis is a real hard-ass son of a bitch. I'm telling you, you do not wanna fuck with ol' Crane."

"Sounds like the kind of guy I wouldn't mind working for. Doesn't take any shit."

"Ho-ho. Take shit? Take *shit*? Ehn-ehn." He made his blurry eyes get big and ran a large finger across his throat.

"Jeez, Dale, what kind of shit would anybody try to

pull on a guy like that? People'd have to be nuts."

"You'd be surprised. Lotta dumb-ass people in this world. You'd be surprised."

"You ever take anybody out for Crane?"

He glanced around the bar, then leaned toward me again. He said beerily, "No. But I busted a guy's collarbone once."

"No shit. Recently?"

"'Bout a year ago. Goddamn asshole was tryin' to hold Millpond up for a quarter of a million for a zoning approval out around Syracuse. Crane has me play a tape of a certain conversation for this shit-ass. I give him five grand, and then I knock him around a little to remind him he isn't dealing with goddamn Fanny Farmer. He got the point. Oh, he got the point."

"I guess a class outfit has to do business that way sometimes if it's going to stay on top. Stay in the big time."

"You better believe it. Competition'll eat ya alive. Gotta goddamn *push.*"

Overdorf made a pushing motion with his thighlike forearm. The bartender glanced our way, but I shook my head.

"Any action like that lately, Dale? I hear Trefusis is getting a lot of grief from some old broad in west Albany who's holding up his new project. Some crazy old lez."

"Nah. The word is Crane's handling that one himself. The only rough stuff I've had lately was back in June when Crane had me do a favor for one of the Millpond owners, a building supply guy who found out some goddamn smartass who worked for him had his hand in the till. I persuaded the gentleman to start making rinston-too-shun. Reston-too-shun."

"Why didn't they just bring in the cops?"

"Dipped if I know. Doing the guy a favor, I s'pose. I

was nice about it though. But not *too* nice. Just nice enough. When I was done, it didn't show. Much. 'Nother collarbone job. Hey—hey, Life-raft, what time you got?"

"Ten to eight."

"Yeah. Early. Too soon to head over to goddamn Troy. Albany's a . . . dead town."

"You over there last night, Dale? Over to Troy for the action? Or were you stuck on a goddamn job last night?"

"Yeah, I was over. Not much action though. This one chick—I was in Bill Kerwin's place about twelve o'clock—and this one chick, built like Polly Parton, this one chick comes over and says, 'Hey—hey, you wanna bite a real cute chick's neck?' And I says, 'Yeah, sure, and that's not all.' And she says, 'Okay, here,' and she hands me this goddamn chicken neck. Shit. Fuck. Real cute. She was cute, all right. But she wasn't so goddamn cute afterwards. Uhn-uhn."

"This was just last night? Jeez, I was all alone in my room watching the Carson show, having no fun at all."

"Yeah, but tonight I'll score. I mean, goddamn Troy on a Saturday night? You better believe it, Life-raft. You can't find some action in Troy on Saturday night, you may's well go back to Cobleskill. That's where I grew up, out in Cobleskill. Now, *there* is a goddamn dead town. Hey, you wanna tag along over to Troy? I don't make promises, but— Hey, I'll bet you're a real cocksman, huh? Look like the type. Real pussy chaser. Get it comin' and goin'."

"H-yeah. Gotta admit it. Comin' and goin'. But I'll pass on tonight, Dale. I've made other arrangements."

"That so? Don't leave nothin' to goddamn chance, huh? Well, drop one for me, pal. Case there's no action in Troy."

"No action in Troy? Dale, I find that hard to believe."

"*Nyaah*. These towns around here are *all* the same.

Dead! Goddamn dead towns. They all suck."

"Even Schenectady?"

"*Especially* Schenectady."

"Guess I'm lucky I'm heading back to Elmira tomorrow."

"Someday I'm just gonna pick up and go where the action is. Get the goddamn fuck out of these . . . dead towns."

"Where would you go, Dale?"

"Rochester. You want *action*, you gotta go to *Rochester*. Listen, Life-raft, lemme tell you about goddamn *Rochester*. . . ."

I crossed State Street and loped down the hill toward Green. It was just past eight o'clock and the temperature sign on the bank at State and Pearl read 87 degrees. The high-intensity arc lamps clicked on in the blackening dusk. In the orange glare the street looked like the portals of hell, though less populated even on a Saturday night.

Dale Overdorf had been a washout, I figured, but I kept thinking there was something I'd missed or hadn't picked up on. I went back over the conversation in my mind. When Overdorf had gone into his "cocksman" characterization I'd thought about dropping the good news on him, but concluded I might need to come back to him, and so failed to contribute to his worldly education. But there was something else. I didn't yet know what.

The captain at La Briquet led me past the sweat-drenched pols, lobbyists, and high-tech entrepreneurs waiting for a table. We crossed the main dining room to an alcove in the back. One table was occupied by a bishop and two lesser spiritual operatives celebrating a secular ritual involving a Lafite-Rothschild '76 and a coq au vin. At a second rear table were three men in blue-black suits, horned-rimmed glasses, and five o'clock shadows. They were listening thoughtfully to a slim black-eyed woman with a briefcase on her lap who spoke at the speed of light: "You know goddamn well the senator is not going to go along with this shit, so why waste our time with a couple of raggedy-ass proposals our people have looked at ten times already, and want to puke every time we . . ." The juke box was playing Telemann.

The banquette in the rear alcove was occupied by Crane Trefusis and Marlene Compton, the blonde who sat outside his office. She was holding an unlighted cigarette, and the captain, deftly producing a silver lighter as a magician might from his sleeve, held out a small blue flame, which Marlene utilized with the bored indifference of a woman not unaccustomed to having small blue flames produced for her benefit.

I thought, Trefusis is going to suggest to Marlene that she go powder her nose. Trefusis said, "Marlene, why don't you go powder your nose?" She went. I flopped the bread bag full of checks onto the linen tablecloth alongside a slim vase containing a single yellow rose.

"Seventy-two," I said. "Local banks."

Trefusis stuffed the bag into a side pocket and from his breast pocket retrieved a fat brown envelope.

"Seventy-two, U.S. currency."

"Where'd you get it?" I said.

"Hard work."

I folded the envelope in half and jammed it into the back pocket of my khakis. It bulged.

I said, "Did Dale Overdorf kidnap Peter Greco?"

He didn't blink. "Not that I know of."

"I didn't think so."

"Overdorf is never sober after five P.M. Friday. He'd be incapable of it on a weekend. That would be his alibi, Strachey, and a damned good one in court. Where did you get Dale's name, if I may ask?"

"It came up."

"Dale is quite reliable during the week. He runs errands for our security chief, fills in, handles special assignments."

"Uh-huh."

"For a man with your reputation, Strachey, I'm amazed you would even consider such a possibility. Even though I know you'd love to discover that Millpond is involved in this idiotic kidnapping in some way. Or even the vandalism."

"You're right, I waste a lot of time. But occasionally it pays off. And it's always instructive. In a general sort of way."

"Yes. You must know a great deal about the manner in which life in our time and place is lived."

"I do."

"Perhaps you'll write a book someday: *Memoirs of a— Gay Gumshoe*. Are people in your profession still called gumshoes?"

"That went out with Sam Spade. Anyway, most of us don't get gum stuck on our shoes while we're pounding the streets. I'm sure I won't. In here."

"Then perhaps you're spending your time in the wrong types of environment in your search for criminals these days, Strachey. As I look around this room, I see none."

"I count six or eight, but never mind. Is the reward money all set?"

"It is on deposit with my personal attorney, Milton Hahn. A public announcement will be made when you and the police have authorized me to proceed with it. I spoke with the chief after you phoned me today, and he concurs that this is the proper approach."

"Glad to hear it. The chief and I have never agreed on much."

"He alluded to that."

"Here comes your food," I said. "And your recep-
tionist. She seems quite . . . receptionable."

"You notice such things? You're even more versatile
than I've been told, Strachey."

"It's an old habit I picked up in the seventh grade. But
it never amounted to much."

"You boys through with your man talk?" Marlene said.
"God, I could eat a *horse.*"

The waiter, standing by a serving trolley and causing
flames to break out all over a chunk of dead animal,
winced.

"See ya in church, Crane," I said.

He laughed.

I left.

I turned the corner from Green and headed back up
State. I picked up a Coke, a burger, and three large fries
at McDonald's and walked back to my car in a lot on
South Pearl. I ate and drank and went over the whole
thing in my mind. My eyes ached. I wanted to close
them, but I didn't. I knew I'd missed something already,
and I couldn't risk missing anything more.

I stuffed the bag of McDonald's debris under the car
seat and drove back toward Central through the reeking
heat. I wished I'd paid the extra eight hundred three
years earlier and gotten a car with air conditioning, and
the hell with Jimmy Carter, wherever he was. Though
Timmy, of course—Timmy the eco-freak-with-a-ven-
geance—would have disapproved.

Timmy. That bastard. Timmy.

14.

I tracked down Mel Glempt at his apartment on Ontario Street. He repeated to me what he had told me on the phone earlier in the day, that he had been leaving the Green Room just before midnight and saw a tall man in a policeman's uniform mug and deftly blindfold a smallish fellow, and then quickly shove him into the back seat of a large dark-colored car, which immediately sped away heading west. Glempt said that in the dimly lit parking lot he had not gotten a look at the cop's face, nor at the person in the driver's seat. Glempt came up with no additional details. He said he had told his story to two police detectives who had come by, and that they had been "polite."

On out Central, I pulled into Freezer Fresh and asked a pale, long-haired kid with bad skin if Joey Deem was on that night. The kid blinked, took a step sideways, and said, "I'm him."

"You kidnap anybody?"

This time he stepped back and looked at me as if I were batty. "What?"

"I didn't think so. But let's try another one. Did you paint rude slogans on Dot Fisher's barn?"

He took another step back and banged into the nozzle of the chocolate glop machine. His eyes darted about to see who might be overhearing our exchange. A line was forming behind me. The kid's mouth opened in an attempt to form words.

"How about the threatening phone calls and the 'you-will-die' letter? Those yours too?"

"I don't know what you mean," he blurted, his mind trying to get a message through to his lower body to settle down, quit spasming.

"You want a new transmission for the T-bird in your front yard. It'll take you two years of busting your ass at this place to save enough money to pay for one. Your dad told you he'd buy you one if Dot Fisher sold out to Millpond and he could sell his property too. Mrs. Fisher was uncooperative and you decided to urge her in your unmannerly way to cooperate. Have I got it right?"

Deem stood there white-faced and bug-eyed, dumb with fright. A round-headed man with beads of sweat on his brow hove into view. "What's the problem?"

"This kid says you don't have any guanabana," I said. "What kind of ice cream stand you running here, mister, you can't offer a customer who's sweaty and pooped an icy, refreshing nice big scoop of guanabana-flavored non-dairy food product?"

"What? What kind?"

"It's okay, José. No sweat, Chet. Albany isn't Mérida or San Juan, even though it sure as hell feels like it tonight. I know when I'm diddled, so forget the guanabana. You got any Bingo-bango-bongo-I'm-so-happy-in-the-Congo ice?"

"I'm sorry, sir, but I'm going to have to ask you to leave."

"Zat so? Well, it's not as if I'm being thrown out of the Savoy Grill, I suppose."

The queue behind me three-stepped neatly to the side as I turned and made my way back to the car.

"Say-hey, Crane! You owe me ten for locating the graffiti artist."

But now what?

Both Deem cars were gone, so I parked up the road and walked back to their house in the semi-darkness. I didn't find what I wanted in the garbage cans, so I grabbed a tire iron and pried open the trunk of the T-bird. There was the red spray paint. This was circumstantial, but Joey Deem seemed so shaky that he'd tell all once Ned Bowman dropped by, said boo, and asked for a sample of the kid's handwriting. Lacking a satchel of foam pellets, I tossed the can in the back of my car.

The tension at Dot Fisher's place had dissipated into a prickly listlessness. Bowman's unmarked car sat in the driveway by the barn, where the fresh white paint glistened stickily in the wet heat. The red graffiti still showed through; another coat of white was going to be needed. A young sergeant in a sweatshirt and baseball cap sat in the passenger seat listening to the staticky jabbering of the police radio, to which he occasionally jabbered back. Above the house, stars were popping out across a blackening sky.

Dot was at the sink furiously scouring a pot as I went inside. Bowman gave me thumbs up.

I said, "What's that for?"

"We're set," he said, and winked.

Dot suggested I help myself to the mint tea, which I did.

"Where's McWhirter?"

"Asleep. Assaulting a police officer can wear you out."

"Maybe I'll do the same. Sleep, I mean. First things first."

He sniffed, tried to look surly.

I said, "Your people visited Mel Glempt. I saw him too. He struck me as a reliable witness."

"So I'm told. Except the man he saw was no police officer. I've looked into that. We're exploring other possibilities."

"Uh-huh. Maybe it was a bus driver. Has Timmy called?"

"Timmy?"

"Timothy J. Callahan. My great and good friend."

"No. You think I'm running a dating service around here, Strachey? Doing social work among the perverts?"

'I just asked if he'd phoned, Ned. Anyway, I'd never accuse the Albany Police Department of social work. Or even, in a good many cases, police work."

"Yeah, well, if you and all your fruitcake pals would just—"

Dot slammed down her pot and wheeled toward Bowman. "Officer Bowman," she said, looking gaunt, overheated, deeply exasperated. "Officer Bowman, *please*. I realize you are helping us, and I do appreciate your being here and doing everything you can for us and for poor Peter. But, really! I must ask you not to make anti-homosexual remarks in my home. You have a right to your opinions. But sometimes you really can be such an extremely *rude* man!"

Bowman apparently had not in recent years been called "rude" by a grandmother scouring a pot. He stood there for a moment looking uncharacteristically helpless, his mouth frozen in a little O.

I said, "Actually, rudeness is one of Detective Bowman's finer points, Dot. Don't knock it entirely. He has a foul mouth, but he's no hypocrite. There's a genuineness to his malice that some of us find intermittently refreshing in a city government full of burnt-out phonies."

Bowman glowered but just shifted about nervously. He would have liked to issue me a couple of obscene threats but didn't want to be called rude again by an old lady bent over a kitchen sink.

"Sorry, ma'am," he muttered to Dot. "When I talk like that, I certainly don't mean you, or your . . . or Mrs. Stout."

"I don't care *who* you mean. That talk is discourteous and insensitive and unbecoming of a public servant. Also, I might add, it betrays a narrowmindedness that is certainly discouraging to behold in this day and age. So much of the time, Mr. Bowman, you just seem to be so . . . so . . . full of baloney!"

I would have phrased it a little differently, but probably to less good effect.

Bowman actually blushed. "Well, I have to admit, Mrs. Fisher, that I'm . . . still learning." He was crimson now, looking as if he feared Dot might have him write "No More Fag Jokes" five hundred times on the blackboard.

"We're *all* still learning," Dot said. "And I congratulate you on being big enough to admit it."

Bowman relaxed a little, no longer worried that he might get sent to the principal's office.

The phone rang. Bowman, relieved, lunged for it. "Let me get that!"

Dot glanced at me and rolled her eyes.

"For you, Strachey. It's your— It's Mr. Callahan." He handed me the sweat-drenched receiver.

"I found out about Wilson," Timmy said.

"This line is not private," I told him quickly. "I'll call you back in fifteen minutes. Where are you?"

"At the . . . you know. On Delaware."

"Fifteen minutes."

I hung up and asked Bowman to accompany me outside. We stood under a pear tree and I told him about Joey Deem.

"I figured that," he said. "One of my men stopped by the Deem place earlier, and the kid took off with a friend when my man arrived. Out the back door, zip-zip. The kid's mother was defensive when asked about her boy's state of mind and activities, but in due course she allowed as how her son might conceivably be capable of criminal matters on a limited scale. We'll pay the lad a visit tomorrow morning and squeeze him. He'll own up."

"I don't doubt it, Ned. Not with irresistible you conducting the interview. Or have you mellowed after getting roughed up in there by Mrs. Fisher? 'Rude.' That's the word, all right. Dot put her finger on it."

His little eyes narrowed like those of the Ned Bowman I'd known five minutes earlier. "Don't you push my face in it, Strachey, I'm warning you! I've got a list and you're at the head of it. Sure, I'll lay off the informal talk when I'm around Mrs. Fisher from now on. Hell, I've got nothing against two broads doing it, even a couple of old dames like those two. I'm broad-minded. I've never disapproved of that. In fact, the idea of it has always kind of turned me on. But two *men*? That is sicko stuff, Strachey, and you'll never convince me otherwise."

Bowman the Bunny Hutch philosophe.

"Glad to hear you talk that way again, Ned. You had me worried for a minute. I was afraid word of your newly benign outlook might get around and your career in Albany city government would be jeopardized."

"Thanks for the sentiment."

"Tell me, are all those bushes out there in the dark full of your guys?"

"They will be by midnight. The go team is gathering now in my office."

"I'll be behind a bush too. You might want to alert your people. Just how crowded is it going to get out there?"

"Crowded enough. If they drop off the Greco guy, twenty men will be on top of them in nothing flat. If they just snatch the ransom and take off, there'll be unmarked radio cars doing relays a block behind them till they get where they're going. Just to be on the safe side, we've got a homing transmitter sewn into the bottom of the money case. When they get to where they've got Greco, we'll move in fast. They'll never know what hit 'em."

"Sounds close to being foolproof. It'd better be. Here's the rest of the cash."

I tugged Trefusis's envelope out of my back pocket and shoved it toward Bowman. He grinned.

I drove over to Central and went into a Grandma's Pie Shop. Grandma wasn't there that night, but the cashier, a comely grandson whom I'd seen around, directed me to a pay phone. I dialed the apartment.

"Hello?" His voice was scratchy, distant.

"It's me. I love you."

"Don't be manipulative. I'm in no mood for it. This will be a non-personal conversation. I obtained the information you requested regarding William Wilson."

"I apologize. Really. It'll rarely happen again. Hardly ever. Not often at all."

"Do you want this information or don't you?"

"Once every three months, about. That'd be it. And only in other cities. Never in Albany or any contiguous municipality. Doesn't that sound reasonable? Short of storing my nuts in a jar of vinegar, which you would keep locked in your desk drawer, that's the best I can do. I think you'll have to agree that it's fair, given certain chemical imbalances in my frontal lobe. So. Are we friends again? Lovers, at least?"

Cutesy sniveling got me nowhere. He didn't even pause. "Here is what I have learned. Are you listening?"

"Sure. Yeah. I'm listening."

"I talked to Gary Moyes out at the Drexon Company. The word is, Bill Wilson runs the plant baseball pool. Except there's some scam going on and nobody ever seems to collect any winnings. They're all 'reinvested' in the following week's pool—which is not the way the players understood the pool would operate. There's a lot of grumbling, and Wilson's time may be running out.

"Moyes guesses that as soon as one of the more impatient employees comes up a winner, Wilson will either have to pay everybody off or suffer dire consequences. If he's getting rich in a small way, it looks as if he'll need every dime of it for a new set of teeth and maybe a neck brace. Wilson definitely is in bad trouble, or soon will be."

"Nnn. Yeah. That explains Wilson's bragging to his wife about soon making her a rich woman, I guess. But it also looks as if he's in need of even more cash and must be fairly desperate to come up with it. This might lead Wilson to behave irrationally, criminally. Unless he's got all the pool money stashed somewhere, which he might. He doesn't appear to be spending it on anything or anybody at home. Can you check his bank records and the plant credit union?"

"On a Saturday night? Neither of us has *those* kinds of contacts."

"Yeah. Crap. It looks as if we're back to square one with Wilson. Not that I'm all that much interested in him anymore. Maybe Bowman will come up with something on him. His guys are checking too."

"I have now fulfilled my obligation to you. Goodbye."

"Hey wait. I want to talk to you! We've really got to sort things out. You know and I know that we've got too much going for us to let—"

"I just want to say one last thing to you, Don. Listen to this. Listen carefully. I was thumbing through your Proust a while ago and came upon a line that jumped right out at me. It seemed so apt, so perfect. It was Swann talking to Odette, but it could as easily have been me to you. He says to her, Swann says, 'You are a formless water that will trickle down any slope that offers itself.' How about that? 'A *formless water* that will trickle down *any slope that offers itself.*'"

He waited.

I said, "Yeah. How about that? Quite a phrasemaker, Proust. The man was a genius, no doubt about it."

"He summed you up in fourteen words. Goodbye."

"Actually, it's probably less harsh in the original French, and— Hello? Timmy? Hello?"

With a phone company click he was gone.

"A formless water." I'd done it.

I ate a slice of pie, got change for a dollar from grandson, went back and piled some dimes by the phone. I dialed the apartment. No answer. I dialed my service. No messages.

Later. For sure.

Back in my booth I went over the Trefusis-Greco-McWhirter-Deem-Wilson-Fisher situation in my mind yet again. I had my coffee cup refilled twice. My head buzzed with heat, fatigue, and caffeine, and I swiped at flies that weren't there. One dropped into my coffee cup.

I couldn't figure any of it out. I still was nagged by the idea that I had not picked up on something crucial, but I didn't know what. I had been preoccupied, and that had been my fault, mostly.

I remembered my meeting with Lyle Barner. I got out my address book, went back to the phone, and made a credit card call to San Francisco. It was nine-thirty-five in Albany, three hours earlier in California. He'd probably be home.

"Yyyyeh-lo."

"Hi, Buel. Don Strachey. You sound chipper enough."

"Don, you old faggot piss-ant! Son of a bee! You in town, I hope?"

"Albany. Grandma's Pie Shop on Central. We shared a Bavarian cream here once."

"Ah, so we did. And if my rapidly deteriorating memory serves me, the pie that night was the least of it."

"If Grandma had known."

"Well, shithouse mouse! If this doesn't beat all! An old trick calls me up from three thousand miles away six years later, when last Tuesday's passes me on the street today and looks right through me. Son *of* a bee."

"You sound as if you're in good shape, Buel. Still out there organizing the masses for the socialist judgment day?"

"Oh, yeah. In a manner of speaking, I am. To tell you the truth, Don, I am now actually gainfully employed. Can you believe *that*? I work at an S and L."

"You into that too? When I knew you, your sexual tastes were more or less conventional."

"That's a savings and loan. Hercules S and L. It's all gay. No more rude tellers and huffy loan officers for the brothers and sisters. It's a new day, Don. I love it. And we're growing like crazy. B of A's gonna have to either come out of the closet or move to Kansas."

"B of A, what's that? Belle of Amherst? Basket of apples? What?"

"Bank of America. Owns half the city, and the suburbs all the way to Denver. But not for long. Hercules is flexing its mighty muscle."

"I can't wait to see your logo."

"So, how you doing back there in Depressoville? How's Timmy?"

"Oh, Timmy's fine, fine. The reason I called was I know a gay cop here who needs to make a move. Is San Francisco still recruiting among the brethren?"

"In a small, halfhearted way, yes. You want a name? I'll get you one if you want to hang on."

I said I did. He came back on the line a minute later with a name and phone number. I wrote them down.

"Thanks, Buel. This might help. As you can guess, the

revolution has not yet reached the Albany Police Department. Speaking of which, one of your city's most notorious troublemakers is with us in Albany this weekend. Do you know Fenton McWhirter?"

"Oh, sure. Everybody knows Fenton. We worked together on the first Harvey Milk campaign. Fenton rubs a lot of people the wrong way, but I always thought he was okay. There's nobody more dedicated to the movement, that's for sure. And, I suppose, nobody more ruthless. Fenton can be counted on to make some noise at least, one way or another."

"Ruthless? How so?"

"Oh, let's see. Let me count the ways. Do you remember the story that went around about how Harvey had a brick thrown through his own window to get more press attention and public support? I happen to know that Harvey didn't do it at all. He might have known about it, but it was Fenton's idea, and Fenton tossed the brick. And it worked."

"Is that so?"

"Another time ol' Fenton got pissed off at some cop who'd roughed him up a little at a street demonstration but didn't leave any marks to speak of. Fenton went out and found some deranged hustler over on Turk Street and paid him ten bucks to break Fenton's nose with a pipe. Then he tried to pin it on the cop. Naturally it didn't stick though. You can hardly get them on the real stuff. Say, is Fenton back there recruiting for his famous gay national strike?"

"He's trying. But he's having his troubles."

"The last I heard, he and his lover—what's-his-name—were thinking of calling the whole campaign off. Fenton's so wacky that none of the fat cats will bankroll the drive, and he's practically flat out, I hear. No dough for rallies, nothing. It's too bad, in a way. Fenton has all of

Harvey's cosmic idealism, but none of his personality or political savvy. We're still making headway, Don, but it's just not the same anymore, without the heroes."

"Yeah. That's true. You know, Buel, this is some fascinating information you've given me."

"Fascinating? How so?"

"Well, I've run into Fenton a number of times in the last thirty-six hours. And now I have this whole new perspective on the man. It's . . . fascinating. Depressing too. Look, Buel, I have to run. Gotta see a man about a finger."

"Yeah, I'll bet. Take care now, Don. See you at Christmastime, maybe, if I get back there to visit the folks."

"Sure thing. And thanks again, Buel."

"Good talkin' to you."

I went back to my booth, shoved the plates and cups aside, and laid my head on the table. I slept soundly for five minutes and had very bad dreams. One of them woke me up, and I ordered a fifth cup of coffee.

Oh, Fenton, I thought. Say it isn't so, Fenton.

---

15. Bowman was seated in the driver's seat of his car, which was backed around to the rear of the barn. The young plainclothesman sat at his side. I walked up to the open window and barked, "Gotcha!"

He gave me his city hall gargoyle look. "What the fuck you talkin' about, Strachey? Geddada here!"

"Where's McWhirter? He still holding up?"

"Still asleep, far as I know. Mrs. Fisher and her lady friend are upstairs with the air conditioner running. My men won't get into place until after midnight, so as to not disturb the ladies. I've got a man inside the house who'll be there all night to reassure the gals—they still don't know about this army I've got deployed—and to keep McWhirter under control. My only concern is, who's going to keep *you* under control, Strachey? I do not want you gumming up this operation. You understand that? You screw this up, and you are *kaput* in the state of New York. Capeesh?"

"Check, Ned. Capeesh, *kaput*. Where's the ransom money?"

"Already out there in the mailbox. A man's in the woods across the road keeping an eye on it."

"I hope he's one of your best."

He chortled. The underling alongside him chortled too. I walked on into the house.

The kitchen light was on. A uniformed cop sat at the kitchen table gravely considering the *Times Union* sports section. He looked up. "Who are you?"

"Inspector Maigret," I said, and walked on down the hall.

I opened the door to the guest room where McWhirter was staying and went in. I snapped on a table lamp and shut the door. McWhirter did not awaken. He lay atop the flowered sheets, stretched out on his back in a pair of jockey briefs with a frayed waistband. The shorts barely contained a healthy erection. I averted my eyes somewhat.

I rummaged through a canvas traveling bag that lay open on the floor. It contained a pair of Army surplus fatigues, jeans, T-shirts, a reeking sweatshirt, socks, toilet articles. Underneath these was a recent copy of *Gay Community News* and assorted letters and postcards. I read McWhirter's mail, all of it communications from various contacts around the country, gay organizations or individuals he planned on visiting, or had visited, during the gay national strike campaign. I found no mention in any of this of an untoward or criminal plot.

I opened a beat-up old L. L. Bean backpack that contained more clothing, of a smaller size. Greco's.

McWhirter stirred. His right arm flopped twice against the sheet. His erection throbbed. I got one too. I looked away and pretended to myself that I was Buffalo Bob Smith. After a moment, McWhirter's breathing evened out again, as did mine. Above me I could hear the snapping and fretting of TV voices and the distant whirr of an air conditioner.

Under the crumpled clothing in Greco's pack I found a bound volume, *Moonbites: Poems by Peter Greco*. I read two, and they were Greco: simple-hearted, avid, appealing. Yet the craft and originality just weren't there. It was, as Richard Wilbur had cruelly put it, "the young passing notes to one another." Greco was less young than he used to be, and maybe there was other recent more accomplished work. I hoped so. I wished that Greco were a fine poet, the kind that gives you the shakes, turns you upside down in your chair. I feared that he wasn't. I wondered if he knew it. I guessed he would. I wanted to find him— actually kidnapped, and not involved in some idiotic scam with McWhirter—and spend some time with him again.

I thought of Timmy. I figured he'd probably end up in some dumb orgy somewhere that night, and the next day enter the priesthood, a dry-cleaning order, no doubt. And I would find Greco, set him free, and run off with him. To Morocco, maybe, where I could do consulting work with Interpol while Peter reclined on a veranda by the sea and wrote—mediocre poetry. That's what I'd do.

I laid my head against the side of the bed where McWhirter slept and realized how utterly bone-weary I was. I yawned, then made myself think startlingly wakeful thoughts. It wasn't hard.

I replaced the poetry book in the backpack and came up with another volume, a hardbound book whose final pages were blank, but which otherwise had been filled in with handwritten dated short paragraphs. It was Greco's journal. A private matter ordinarily, but under the special circumstances I began to read the recent entries.

July 30—Staying at Mike Calabria's in Providence. Air heavy, hot, suffocating. Mike big, noisy, generous, funny. Fenton heartsick at reception in Rhode Island. Newspaper refers to him as "Frisco Minority Activist." What that? Eleven men sign on; $12 raised.

Aug. 2—New Haven hot, Yalies cool. No students, but two cafeteria workers sign pledge. Stayed with Tom Bittner, here for a year researching colonial anti-gay laws. Great seeing Tom. Cicely still with him; I slept on porch.

Aug. 5—The Big Apple. Gay men everywhere—and nowhere. Temperature inversion over city produces vomit-green cloud. Could barely breathe. Fenton went unannounced to office of New York Times editor, but . . .

McWhirter groaned, raised his head, blinked at me. I let the journal fall back into the knapsack.

I said, "Just the man I want to talk to."

"*What?* What the fuck are *you* doing in here? Where's—? Oh, God."

"That wasn't Peter's finger in the package. You would have seen that. You said nothing. Why?"

He did a double take, then bridled. "What the fuck is going on? What time is it?" He grabbed at a wristwatch on the bedside table, glared at it, then wrapped it around the circle of white flesh on his wrist. "Christ, it's not even eleven yet."

"You ignored my question."

He lay back against the headboard and examined me

sullenly. Suddenly he snapped, "Of course I knew it wasn't Peter's finger! Of course I would know that!"

"You didn't mention it to anybody. That strikes me as odd. It gets me to thinking."

He blinked, looked alarmed. "Jesus! Do the cops know?"

"Know what, Fenton?"

"The finger—that it wasn't—"

"Where did you get it? I've been wondering. Men's fingers are hard to come by. Not as rare as . . . hens' teeth. But rare."

"Where did *I* get it?"

"Or whoever."

He sat up with a jerk and flung his legs over the edge of the bed. His feet stank. I backed away and eased onto a desk chair.

McWhirter's face had reddened. He sputtered, "I know what you think."

"What do I think?"

"That I set this up."

"Why would I think that?"

"Because I—You must have found out that I play the game by rules I didn't make. Rules that I don't like but that somebody else made, and for now they *are* the rules."

"Your nose is a little cockeyed. I hadn't noticed it before, but now I do. How come?"

In his confusion, he couldn't help grinning daffily. "You heard that story? Great. Well, so what? It's true. Other people had been bloodied by the cops that night, the fucking savages. But *those* cops had taped over their badge numbers. The one who hit me hadn't. And I had his number. Simple justice."

"Simpleminded justice. You became one of them."

"Ho, Jesus!" He shook his head, looked at me as if I were a bivalve. "The same old liberal bullshit. You should be a judge, Strachey, or write newspaper editorials."

I said, "You're digging your own grave."

"*What?*"

"This so-called kidnapping is right in character for you. You stage the abduction, stir up lots of attention and sympathy for the strike campaign—and collect a hundred grand to finance the rest of the drive. I'll bet Dot Fisher doesn't know about it though, does she? Dot's unconventional, but still a bit old-fashioned in certain inconvenient respects, right?"

He stared at me open-mouthed. "You think *that*? You think I'd do that to *Dot*?"

"So, where did the finger come from? Explain."

"Look . . . I . . ." He was sweating, fidgeting, balling up little wads of chest hair between his fingers. "Look, it *is* true that I knew it wasn't Peter's finger in that box. *Of course* I knew. But the reason I kept my mouth shut about it was not the reason you think. I just thought—I figured that the kidnappers—cops probably—were using the finger to scare us. To scare Dot especially, and impress on all of us just how vicious they could be.

"And since we were already having a hard enough time getting that Bowman asshole to believe us, to take Peter's disappearance seriously, it seemed better if I just . . . kept my mouth shut. And also—Well, shit, I was afraid somebody like you would have heard about—about my reputation. And that you'd think Peter and I set the whole thing up. Just like you do now. God, that's the truth!"

"Uh-huh. That's what I thought too, Fenton. At first. When I saw that the finger wasn't Peter's, and knew that you must have known it wasn't, I guessed that you were keeping mum in order to feed Bowman's sense of urgency. But I didn't know so much about you then. Now I do. And I have become skeptical. Highly so."

"How did *you* know it wasn't Peter's finger?"

"Dunno. Guess I'm just one of those people who once he's seen a finger never forgets it."

"Do the cops know this? What you think?"

"Not yet."

"Don't tell them. *Please*. It's not true! You'll just put Peter in more danger!"

I said, "Fenton, you're a self-avowed ruthlessly devious liar and con man. All for the larger cause. Wicked means to a just end. Pulling a stunt like this would be right in character for you. It fits the pattern."

"That is *not true*. You're talking like Bowman now. Use *friends* like that? Brothers and sisters? Never!"

"It's not your friends you're using. It's me. Strachey, the Millpond flack. *I'm* the one who came up with the hundred grand."

"Yes, but—I wouldn't have known it would work out that way, would I? When the ransom note came—and the finger—it was sent to *Dot*. Obviously by someone who knew that *she* would be able to get hold of a lot of money from Millpond if she absolutely had to. Somebody so rotten he didn't care at all if Dot lost her home. Do you think *I* would do that?"

"Nnn. I don't know."

"Or *Peter*? You've seen what kind of person Peter is. Would *he* do a thing like that to Dot? Or to anybody?"

"No. I expect not. Unless . . . unless he didn't *know*. You could have gotten rid of Peter for a few days on some pretext while you pulled off this elaborate heist to raise money to finance the rest of your bankrupt campaign. Sent him off to do advance work in the next town or something. And arrange for some other cohorts, up from the city or wherever, to stage the abduction at the Green Room last night."

He peered at me with disgust. "Oh, yes. I have this troupe of actors—McWhirter's Old Vic—constantly at my disposal. Sheee-it. And when *Peter* finds out how I've all of a sudden gotten hold of a hundred thousand dollars? Then what?"

"Nnn. Yeah. Peter would probably give it back."

He continued to stare at me with the nauseated condescension that was his most natural attitude. What did Greco see in this creep? Was demented single-mindedness Greco's idea of toughness, substantiality, strength of character? My estimation of Greco had begun to fall. I thought of Timmy. Where was he? Why weren't we together?

On the other hand, what McWhirter had just told me made sense. He was ruthless, but I'd heard no evidence that he had ever betrayed his friends. He was devious and cunning, but Greco, whatever his weaknesses, was not. On the one hand this, on the other hand that.

I said, "All right, Fenton. I'm more or less convinced. Pretty much. For now."

"And you won't mention any of this crap you were thinking to Bowman?"

"Not now. No."

He collapsed against the headboard. "Thank you. Now, just get Peter away from . . . those people. That's *all* I care about. And then you can say anything about me that you want. Just get Peter back."

"Right. That's what we're all trying to do."

"Is the money in the mailbox?"

"Yes."

"I'll pay it back. Wherever it came from, I'll pay it back."

Watching him carefully, I said, "Dot and Edith don't know this, but when the pickup is made tonight, the kidnappers' car will be followed. Very, very discreetly. No arrest will be made until Peter is free. But we're all reasonably certain that whoever has done this will be in the lockup by dawn."

He flinched and sat up again, breathing heavily. "You

told me you weren't going to do anything like that. You and the cops. You agreed it was too dangerous."

"We lied. We all concluded from experience that Peter's chances are better this way."

He stared at me with hard, bitter eyes. "Lying for the higher cause, huh? Wicked means to a just end."

"Something like that. Yes. To save a life. Nothing terribly abstract or arguable about that."

"But it's still just your opinion."

"An informed opinion."

He started to speak, then just laughed once, harshly. At both of us, I thought charitably.

I said, "The phone here has been tapped by the police. If you call anyone, you'll be overheard. Did you know that?"

"No. But why should I care?" He turned away from me onto his side, and lay still except for his breathing, which came and went in deep sighs.

I left him there in the sticky heat and shut the door as I walked out. I passed the cop in the kitchen and went outside again. I sat on the veranda under the stars and tried very hard to rethink the whole bloody mess. I was sure I had been conned by a master. But I couldn't decide who he was.

16.

I walked down Moon Road toward Central in the hazy starlight. A quarter-moon hung above the western horizon with three stars inside its crook, like an astrological sign. It was Saturday night on Central Avenue.

"Hi, bet you're a Taurus, aren't you, big guy?"

"No, but you're close. I'm a Presbyterian—born under the sign of a golf ball on a tee. I'm surprised you couldn't tell from the alignment of the divots on my skull."

"Well, *you're* certainly a weird one. Huh! Guess I'll just go dance some more. Last call's in ten minutes, but *I* could just dance *forever.*"

"For sure."

The air was still, wet, black. I passed the Deems' house. The living room was lighted behind closed drapes in the picture window. The screen door was open and I could hear raised voices.

"I don't care! I don't care! I don't care!"

"Get back here, I'm not finished with you!"

More distant: "Jerry, not so loud!"

"No one in this family has *ever* broken the law! Joseph, if your grandfather—"

"I don't care! I'm sick of you! I'm sick of this place! I'm sick of all of you!"

"Go to your room!"

"Jerry!"

"I'm going! I'm going!"

"Jerry, don't hit him!"

"You selfish miser! I know you! I know you!"

The wooden door was eased shut. The voices became muffled. I stood in the shadows and waited. The wooden door flew open again, then the screen door. Joey Deem burst out into the night, charged across the lawn, flung open the driver's door of the T-bird, then banged it shut. The lock clicked.

Sandra Deem stepped out in a bathrobe and hair curlers and stood for a moment on the low stoop. She pressed her fingers across her cheek several times. Then she turned and went inside, closing both doors behind her.

I walked on down the road.

A light burned in the Wilson living room, and I crept up to a window in the darkness. Wilson was seated in an easy chair, a row of Pabst empties lined up on the table beside him. His gaze was fixed on a noisy spot across the room. "And as we move into the top half of the eleventh inning, it's still *all tied up*, Yankees six, Brewers six." I could see Kay's immense bare legs hanging over the end of the couch.

I backtracked onto Moon Road and walked the remaining fifty yards down to Central. The Saturday night revelers traffic was heavy, but in the car dealer's lot across the avenue I could make out two figures seated in the front of a blue Dodge. It was the only Chrysler product in three acres of Hondas. I shot them a two armed Nixonesque victory sign, then turned and walked back toward Dot's.

Just after one-thirty I chose my spot. I brought an old Army blanket from the back of my car and placed it under the curtaining arch of a group of forsythia bushes, the kind of cool, secret bushy cave where I'd hidden from the world when I was eight. I stuffed one end of the blanket up into the thicket of branches to form a lumpy, scratchy backrest. The mammoth clump of bushes grew atop a slight rise halfway between a rear corner of the barn and the pear orchard, and I had an unobstructed view of the house, the mailbox, and, off in the other direction to my right, the farm pond.

I settled back and listened to the peepers, and the muted roar of traffic back on Central and from the interstate beyond the woods on the other side of Dot's house. A couple of times I heard rustling in the bushes down at the other end of the barn, and once I watched four men in flak jackets emerge from the barn and stumble into the foliage across Moon Road.

I smeared myself with insect repellant, which had little effect, though my constant scratching and slapping at the gnats and mosquitoes kept me from dozing off. The air was as heavy and tepid as a night in Panama. The fields smelled sweet.

At five to two the back door of the house creaked open. The outside spotlights had been shut off, but in the starlight I could make out McWhirter and the patrolman who'd been in the kitchen moving quickly across the lawn. They climbed into the back seat of Bowman's darkened car and carefully pulled the door shut, click-click. Then it was quiet again. I felt more alone than I wanted to.

At two-ten I was startled to see the back door of the farmhouse ease open yet again. Two figures emerged. One wore a long frilly bathrobe, peach-colored it seemed in the white starlight, and she poked the wobbly beam of a flashlight a few feet ahead of her.

Edith was followed across the veranda and onto the lawn by Dot, who carried towels and was clad in a red terry cloth beach robe, which hung loosely on her slight frame. The two women spoke in low voices and made their way across the damp grass toward the pond.

At the water's edge Dot set the towels on a wooden bench and let her robe fall away. Edith removed her robe and folded it carefully before placing it and the flashlight on the bench. Dot was naked, but Edith had been wearing a calf-length nightgown under her robe, and now Dot helped her hitch it up over her head and place it neatly alongside the folded robe.

Dot stepped into the water first and bent to splash her face and breasts.

"Oh, my! Oh, it's just grand, Edie!"

Edith moved her head about, up, down, right, left, trying to focus on the surface of the black water before stepping down to it. Dot reached out and guided her. The two women stood waist-deep facing each other for a moment before Dot squeezed Edith's hand, let go of it, and let herself fall backwards into the water. She backstroked languidly to the far side of the pond while Edith watched, then turned and sidestroked back again.

Lowering herself into the water with a little cry of astonishment, Edith lay on her back and let her feet bob whitely to the surface. Dot also fell back now, and the two floated in lazy circles, exclaiming softly from time to time, as the moon rose higher above them.

When the women rose dripping from the water after a time, they gently wrapped towels around each other. After a moment Dot let her towel fall away and wrapped Edith's around the both of them as they embraced. They stood holding each other for a long time before they lay down together atop Edith's towel on the moon-whitened grass.

I lay back and looked up at the stars through the leafy branches of my cave, and I thought about my life. I said, "Timmy."

17.

I tried to focus on the luminous dial of my watch, but it kept blurring out. I rubbed my eyes furiously, squinted, brought the watch up to within six inches of my better eye, backed it out to ten inches, and saw it. I squeezed my eyes shut, opened them, looked again, and said, "Christ."

It was ten to five.

I poked my head out of the bushes and saw Bowman standing with two cops on the veranda of the farmhouse.

The sky was gray above, pink in the east. I crawled out, shook and stretched as I moved, and crossed the lawn.

"You look like shit, Strachey."

"Where is he?"

"Where Izzy? Dunno. Where Heimie?"

"Greco. Is he inside?"

"Hey, Strachey, did I ever tell you the one about the rabbi and the monsignor who were up in a plane that flew through a storm? This plane is bangin' and bumpin' all over the sky, see, and the monsignor starts crossing himself, and—"

"They got away, didn't they?"

"—and then the rabbi, *he* starts crossing himself too, and the monsignor, he looks over at the rabbi and he says—"

"Spit it out, Ned. Who fucked up?"

He yawned lightly. "Your money's safe, pal. Not to worry. It's in the kitchen."

"Good. So what happened? I fell asleep."

That brought him to life. "Is that a fact? Fell *asleep*. Well, I'll be mothered! Hey, you guys hear that? 'Travis McGee takes a Nap.' 'The Deep Blue Snooze.' Hope you didn't flake out too early to miss the late show up by the pond last night, huh, Strachey? You didn't let that get by you, did you? Huh?"

He chuckled lewdly, and the two cops with him picked up the cue and joined in. They looked like shit too.

I said, "What happened? With Greco. Where is he?"

"Beats me. As a matter of fact, not a goddamned thing happened. It was no show. No pickup, no drop-off. The department paid out a lot of overtime, though. Boys don't mind that at all."

"*Nothing* happened? No car, no phone call, no nothing?"

"Zilch."

"Yeah. Well. I guess that could mean a lot of things. So, what's your next step, Ned?"

"Wait. Get some sleep and wait. We'll talk to the Deems again, and this Wilson character. And, I suppose I'm obliged to pay a call on your employer Mr. Trefusis, for the sake of neatness. But you'll see, Strachey, this is outside the neighborhood, only indirectly connected to this Millpond business. It's some tetched boyo who read the papers and got an idea in his head. Even dressed up like a police officer to make the snatch. He's a psychopath, but he wants that hundred grand, and he'll be in touch. The department is checking out all the weirdos we know of who might think up a stunt like this, and we might just land him fast. If not, my guess is he just got nervous last night, and he'll be back. We'll be here when he gets here."

"What about Greco in the meantime? These people are nuts. They might saw off another appendage."

"Well, it's not that I'm not concerned about that. Believe me, I am. But what choice have we got at this point in time?"

He still wasn't onto the finger scam. Nor was he aware of my suspicions about McWhirter. I thought, Should I tell him? I said, "Where's McWhirter? How's he reacting?"

"He was real twitchy a while ago. But he bounced back pretty good. He just jumped in Mrs. Fisher's car and went over to Central to pick up some doughnuts. The guy is tougher than I figured somebody like that would be."

One of the other two cops jerked his head around and said, "Hey, that's the radio!" He trotted over to Bowman's car, now parked out in the driveway. "Lieutenant, you better take this."

We all jogged puffing over to the car. Bowman spoke with an officer at Division Two Headquarters who told him that a phone call had been placed to Dot Fisher's house six minutes earlier and that the dispatcher had been trying to reach Bowman since then.

"Well, who was it, goddamn it? *What* was it?"

"I'll play you the tape."

"So play it, play it!"

"Here it is."

McWhirter's voice: *Hello?*

Male voice; harsh, tense: *You want your lover back?*

McWhirter (pause): *Y-yes.*

Voice: *In three minutes, call this number I'm gonna give you. Call from another phone. Call 555-8107. And bring the fuckin' money!*

McWhirter: *Let me write it down—*

Click. Click, dial tone.

Bowman snapped, "You get a trace?"

"Sorry, Lieutenant. Not enough time."

"What's 555-8107? You get that?"

"It's a pay phone on Broadway in Menands."

"Did you send some men out there, I hope?"

"As soon as the call came in. We tried to raise you, too, but—"

"Well, what have you *heard* from that car? What's the report?"

"We're . . . uh, we're trying to raise him now. Hang on."

Bowman's face was all purple again and I could see his pulse pounding on his left temple. I said, "The caller. On the tape. I've heard that voice somewhere."

"Whose is it?"

"I don't know," I said. "I can't place it. I can't remember."

The money was gone. No one could recall McWhirter's carrying anything when he drove off. Bowman said they would have noticed that and checked it out. One of the other cops said McWhirter had been wearing fatigues with oversized pockets and a jacket. Whitney Tarkington's hundred grand had slipped away. *My* hundred grand.

Three minutes later Bowman's radio squawked to life again. "We've still got two cars out at the pay phone on Broadway, Lieutenant. So far, no show."

"Weeping Jesus, we missed them! Crimenee! Damn it! Damn it to hell!"

I squatted on the dewy grass and tried to think. The air was heating up again. I waited for Bowman to ventilate. He took out his frustration on his underlings. They shifted from foot to foot and appeared to be thinking unclean thoughts. I was having a few myself.

When the junior dicks had slunk away, I stood up and said to Bowman, "There are a couple of things I should tell you about Fenton McWhirter."

The eyes in his potato face grew beadier than usual. He said nothing.

"This might or might not have anything to do with the last half hour's developments, but . . . McWhirter is not entirely trustworthy."

Now his eyes opened wide and he began to take on his purplish hue again.

"What! You held something *back* from me, Strachey? What was it? What?"

I described McWhirter's history of well-meaning duplicity. As I laid it out, Bowman's face registered all the colors the *Times* fashion supplement said would be big in the fall: burgundy, plum, mauve, fuchsia, and finally, disconcertingly, olive.

Through clenched teeth, he hissed, "I *was* set up."

"Maybe," I said. "Could be. *Es posible.*"

"You—you—you will pay for this!"

I squatted again, looked up at him, and said, "I already have."

That seemed to please him.

Driving back into the city, I caught the WGY six o'clock news, which had it already. Bowman had been swift.

"Capital area police," the newscaster said, "are mounting an all-out search for Fenton McWhirter and Peter Greco, two gay activists from San Francisco, who are wanted in connection with an extortion scheme involving a phony kidnapping.

"A hundred thousand dollars belonging to Albany private investigator Donald M. Strachey was taken in the scam. Strachey was unavailable for comment, but Albany police described the theft as a sophisticated operation in which the two alleged perpetrators tricked Strachey out of the cash, which was paid as ransom after a staged abduction of Greco. The two men planned on using the money for radical political purposes.

"According to police," the report went on, "McWhirter and Greco may be armed and are to be considered dangerous." A description was given of the car they were thought to be driving—Dot's little red Ford—and listeners were urged to phone Albany police if the car was spotted.

The weather forecast was for a hot and humid Sunday, followed by a hot and humid Sunday night, and then a hot and humid Monday. I switched over to WMHT, which had on a Schubert octet.

"Armed and considered dangerous." Bowman was having a lovely time.

And yet, something was not right. Before I'd left the Fisher farm I wakened Dot and told her what had happened. She said simply but firmly, "I do not believe it. It isn't true. Fenton would not cheat you or me. Perhaps his judgment has been bad, but his principles are unbending. If he ever stole, it would be from the people he considered to be his enemies. And *Peter steal*? Oh, my stars, what silliness! No. What you're telling me is all stuff and nonsense, and you should know it!"

Should I? Or was Dot Fisher so sweetly naive that her schoolmarm's imagination was incapable of absorbing an act so cynical as the one Fenton McWhirter now stood— thanks to me—accused of. Dot had met bitterness in her life, and stupidity and small-mindedness, but not, so far as I knew, desperate cunning. If she had never seen it, how could she recognize it?

On the other hand, Dot had spent most of her life among children, who can be as sophisticated in their treachery as the Bulgarian secret police. Maybe she *did* know cunning when she saw it, and she had not seen it in McWhirter.

And, there was yet another troubling matter: If McWhirter had staged the kidnapping, then who *was* this *third* party in the affair, the man who had written the notes, mailed the finger, and then called McWhirter from the pay phone in Menands? The ransom notes had been in neither McWhirter's nor Greco's handwriting; I'd checked that when I went through their belongings. And the voice on the tape had not been Greco's. I knew that because it was another voice I was certain I had once heard. Somewhere. Sometime. Briefly. I tried again, but I couldn't bring it back.

A *local* co-conspirator? Or were Dot's instincts sound, and I was missing something again, ignoring the obvious for the seemingly obvious. Crane Trefusis? Maybe. But Dale Overdorf, his thug-about-town, had not been . . .

My mind shut down. I'd had enough for a few hours. More than enough. I wanted only to sleep.

I stopped at my office, phoned Bowman, and said I'd

had second thoughts. I summarized them. I said I was nearly certain that McWhirter and Greco were *not* conning us all, gave my reasons, and said that *both* of them were probably in trouble now. I urged him to do something about it. He said he would consider my ideas after he napped for a couple of hours. I understood.

I drove over to Delaware. At the apartment, Timmy's car was not in his space. Nor was it in anyone else's, nor in Visitor Parking. I looked for the rental car he'd had but couldn't spot it either.

The apartment was airless, silent, dead. I wrenched open a window. I put some Bud Powell on the turntable but never got around to switching on the amplifier.

The bed hadn't been slept in. Or had it? He might have changed the sheets. I checked the hamper for dirty sheets. Two were in there—folded, naturally, probably in triangles, like the flag in repose. They could have been in there for days, though. I didn't know. Laundry was his job, not mine. Whenever the subject of household chores came up—had come up—I'd say, "You wash and clean, and I'll keep the windmill oiled and the hogs fed." A cushy deal I had. Had had.

His clothes were in their assigned places in closets and drawers, his luggage stacked beside the vacuum cleaner in the "pantry-ette." I searched for a note, a message on a mirror, a letter(-bomb), and found none.

In the bathroom the towels and washcloths were fresh and symmetrically arrayed, as at the Ritz-Carlton. His four varieties of shampoos and conditioners were lined up along the end of the bathtub: Maxine, Patti, LaVerne and—Zeppo.

Only his toothbrush and Aim were missing. Mister Sweetmouth. Mister Oral Hygiene. Clean Callahan, the Germ-Free Child.

I went back to the bed, fell onto my side of it, lay

staring at the ceiling for thirty seconds, or half an hour.
And then slept.

The ringing sound went on and on for days, weeks,
months, and when I realized that it was not in my dream I
reached out, snatched up the receiver from the bedside
phone, and placed it in the vicinity of my head. A mighty
act of will enabled me to focus on the alarm clock, which
read two thirty-five. I knew it had to be P.M., because
fierce sunlight fell across my legs, roasting them inside
the khakis I still wore.

The caller was not Timmy. It was Dot Fisher, speaking in a trembling, tearful, frightened voice. She told me
that Peter Greco was dead.

18.

I met Bowman at his Second Division
Headquarters office in the South End. The place looked
and smelled like the old school textbook warehouse in the
New Jersey town where I grew up, but instead of moldy
books about Charlemagne's horse it was full of shiny new
gunmetal gray desks, chairs and shelving, no doubt pur-
chased at a 300 percent markup from one of the mayor's
cronies. Albany was still back in the 1870s in that respect,
as in others.

"This thing is starting to get me down, Strachey.
Christ."

He'd slept on a cot in his office. A half-eaten Danish
lay on a pile of papers on his desk, and he sipped at some
oily black stuff in a foam cup.

"When did they find him?"

"About noon. A family out in their Chris-Craft spotted

him floating by a piling under the Dunn Bridge. The police boat brought him in."

"Cause of death?"

"Dunno yet. The coroner's office has him now. Preliminary says asphyxiation, but that's unofficial, not to be repeated. Anyway, that can mean a lot of things. Guy falls into a baloney machine and half the time the coroner will point to his remains wrapped in little plastic packages on the luncheon meat shelf at Price Chopper and say, 'That man there died from asphyxiation.' Once in a while an autopsy comes in on the money. Depends on who's doing it."

"When will you get a report?"

"Six o'clock, seven."

"Are you sure it's Greco? Who identified him?"

"Mrs. Fisher."

"Well, Jesus. I would have done it."

"She knew him best."

"What about McWhirter? Has there been any sign of him?"

"Just the car he'd been driving. Mrs. Fisher's. We found it about an hour ago in the V.A. hospital parking lot. I've got two men going over it."

I examined the dirty swirl of rainbow in his coffee cup. "This stinks. It is rotten. Loathsome."

"Uh-huh."

"It is also baffling. I don't understand it. At all."

"That it is, Strachey. You said it. And now I am going to tell you why I asked you to come down here."

Now it was coming. I leaned back.

"The Albany Police Department has officially requested your assistance, Donald M. Strachey, because," he said, trying to look pompous, "I have reason to believe that you are withholding information regarding a criminal matter. You held out on me once, Strachey, but you will do it again only at the risk of revocation of your New York State private investigator's license. Now. What else do you know about this goddamn rat's nest?"

I tried hard not to think about Peter Greco lying cold on the medical examiner's table, his bright eyes blank, and for the next half hour I described yet again my involvement in the case from the very beginning. My mind kept drifting back to Greco—had my distracted ineptitude helped cause his death?—but I concentrated hard, and I told Bowman everything I had seen and learned, how I had learned it, and the tentative or not tentative erroneous conclusions I had drawn at various points along the way. I left out only a little: all my contacts with Lyle Barner; my causing an ex-cop to become inebriated in the Hilton bar; the name of my San Francisco contact.

"I detect selected omissions," Bowman said when I'd finished.

"Oh? And what do you detect them to be?"

"Like, where you got that hundred grand."

Back to that again. What was he sniffing after? "I borrowed it from an acquaintance who owed me a favor. What difference does it make?"

"Uh-huh." He gave me his pal-sy 'I-know-you-you-sly-devil' look, which invariably meant that he was about to say something stupid.

I said, "Now what? Go ahead. Speak the words."

"You know what I'm thinking," he said sagely.

"I do not."

"Hah."

I waited. He leaned back in his swivel chair and peered at me across his cauliflower nose. "You're in on it," he said. "Aren't you?"

"'It'?"

"This big production. Scam, grift, fraud. Six-count felony."

I studied his face for signs of insincerity, which was not one of his eighteen character flaws. He looked as if he had meant what he said.

I said, "And Peter Greco's death was part of the plan? The big production?"

"That was an accident. Poor bastard Greco slipped up somehow. Ten to one the coroner will find accidental death, drowned in the bathtub, lemon-scented bubble bath in the kid's lungs. But instead of calling the whole thing off, you all decided it would work out even better this way with Greco dead. Oppressed minorities, all that garbage. Fruits'll come out of the woodwork all over the place now to sign up for this protest crap of McWhirter's. The hundred grand is just a prop in the drama, and when it's over the dough just goes back to your fag pals, and nobody loses so much as a dime. Am I right? Do I make sense, Strachey? You like my scenario?"

I stood up and walked out of the room. I could hear him yammering after me. "So maybe *you* weren't in on it, but you know goddamn well, you told me *yourself* . . ."

As I moved down the stairway and out the front door, no one tried to stop me. That was lucky for all of us.

The heat hit me like a tire iron. I rolled down all the car windows and drove over to the I-787 on-ramp. I headed north along the river, then west on I-90, then north again and got off by the Northway Mall. Inside Cines One thru Six the temperature was about sixty. My seat in a rear corner was comfortable. I don't remember what movie was playing. I think it was about some California kids and a short greenish guy from Mongo, or Chicago, or someplace.

From the theater lobby I phoned my apartment. No answer there, and my service had no messages. I called Dot and told her I'd be there soon. She said there had been no word yet from or about McWhirter, and no further contacts by the kidnappers. That scared me; during the movie I had concluded beyond all lingering doubt that I had been fooled, diddled, flummoxed—mainly by my own self—and that the kidnapping had all been for real right from the beginning. Now I was scared to death about McWhirter.

I stood by the phone thinking about calling Crane Trefusis, but not knowing what I'd say to him, what questions to ask. I considered breaking into his office and going through his files, but the place had seemed well protected and it wouldn't have helped just then to be caught with my finger in my employer's back pocket. Marlene Compton was a possibility; she'd have keys, though I figured unless I could convince her I was really King Hussein or Lee Iacocca, her interest in me would not be sufficient to overcome her numerous and varied loyalties to Crane "Quite-a-Guy" Trefusis.

In any case, the more I thought about it the less likely it seemed Trefusis's files would yield up anything usefully informative. Persons of his special station in life rarely wrote down anything incriminating. And unlike, say, Richard Nixon, the personally secure and unkinky Trefusis would not likely have bugged his own office in order to admire his own excretions at some later date. Because I didn't know how to approach him, I put Trefusis on the back burner yet again.

I phoned Lyle Barner and told him that Peter Greco was dead.

"I know," he said. "That sucks. The news hit me hard. I'm gonna ask around some more, see what I can pick up."

"Do that."

"And . . . I want to apologize."

"Don't bother. I understand the shape you're in."

"No, really. The way I came on to you yesterday. My timing was terrible, Strachey. I felt like a real shit after."

"Good. But let's let it go. I've got a name for you in San Francisco. A gay liaison with the cops out there. You should give him a call."

A silence. "Yeah. Well. Guess I should. I'll get the name from you next time I see you. Are you . . . doing anything later tonight?"

I wondered if I was hearing what I thought I was hearing. I said, "I'm busy for a few days, and so are you. But I'll check with you later to find out what you've turned up. Leave a message with my service, wherever you are."

"Right. Sure thing. I'm not on duty tonight, but I'm going to be out and around. I'm gonna take off right away, soon as I grab something to eat. I'll be in touch, Don. I'll give you a call."

"Thanks, Lyle. Dredge up what you can. On renegade cops, ex-cops, Millpond, Trefusis, professional thugs, loonies, whatever. This thing is no bad joke anymore. And it can only get worse."

"Yeah. I guess it can."

I rang off and tried the apartment again. There was no answer after twenty rings.

As I turned off Central and headed down Moon Road, Kay Wilson was standing by the roadside peering at something in her hand. She looked up, saw me, and began energetically waving what looked like an envelope. I pulled over.

"You missed 'em again! Those crazy queers stuck another letter in our box, and just like the last time the cops are all off in the doughnut shops somewhere instead of out here apprehending perper-trators. Those bastards keep using our mailbox, people are gonna get the idea Wilson and me are mixed up in this crap. We got enough trouble already, and I want somebody to put a stop—"

I said, "What 'crazy queers,' Kay? What have you got there?"

She thrust the envelope through the window at me. It was addressed, as before, to Dorothy Fisher, and said, "Open imeatedly—Life or Death matters."

"I saw 'em, this time!" Kay bleated excitedly. "I was out by the back stoop chuckin' horse chestnuts, tryin' to knock down a wasps' nest up under the eaves, when I heard a car stop, and I peeked around the corner and saw 'em just when they backed into the yard and then took off back out to Central. This time, I'll tell you, I got a good look, a *real* good look."

"That's terrific, Kay. That's great. Did you get the license number?"

She jammed a finger into the flesh at the corner of her mouth and looked like a cartoon character looking thoughtful. "Well, no. Didn't get a good look at that. But I saw the car."

"What kind was it?"

"Big."

"Big like a—what?"

"Like an Olds, or Ford. Or Chevy maybe."

"What color was it?"

"Sort of brownish, like Wilson's. Or blue maybe. Coulda been green, I guess."

"How about the people in it? There were more than one?"

"Two."

"Both men?"

"Yup."

"What do you remember about them?"

"They were . . . white."

Or green. "Take them one at a time. What about the one driving?"

She thought some more. "Matter of fact, I didn't get a

real good look at him. Shoot. It's hard to remember. I was way out back, ya know."

"What was he wearing? The driver. Sports shirt? T-shirt? What?"

"Nothin'. He wasn't wearing nothin'. I mean, no shirt, ha-ha. Probably had pants on, though you never know these days. One time out at the home I was on my break, and I walked into the canteen, and this one nutty aide we used to have by the name of Neut Pryzby, he was standing by the soda machine with—"

"The man driving the car, Kay. He wore no shirt? The car window was open?"

"His arm was hangin' out," she said. "Yeah, that's right. Drivin' with the other arm. Nice arm, the one I saw. Thick and muscle-y, like Wilson's used to be. Nice big round shoulders. I like that in a man." She gave me a look.

I said, "You must have seen the side of his face. Did he have a beard?"

"Nuh—don't think so. Nope. No whiskers."

"Big nose? Little nose? Pointy? Flat?"

"Yeah. Nose. Guess he had one. Average, I'd say."

"Right. What about the other guy?"

"Hoo. Jeez. Guess I didn't really get a good look at that one."

"He was in the front seat, too?"

"Yup."

"How do you know it was a man?"

She snorted. "Huh! You think I can't tell the difference? I ain't *that* old yet."

"You mentioned 'crazy queers.' What made you think they were—queer?"

"Because it was on the radio. Cripes, it looks like I know more about all this crazy shit flyin' around here than *you* do."

"There was nothing about the two men you saw, though, to make you think that they were gay? Or their car?"

"No wrists flappin' in the breeze, if that's what you mean. Say, we could use a little breeze, huh? Anyways, Bob, you told me before that *you* was one of them. Bet that was just a line, though, wasn't it? Huh? You ready to own up to ol' Kay?"

She gazed at me forlornly. Happily, I was able to say, "I'm queer as a three-dollar bill, Kay. You want a good reference, check with officer Bowman. Not that I've ever passionately nibbled the man's lobotomy scar. Nonetheless, he will vouch for me in a forthright manner. Check it out."

She hooted. "G'wan! Next think you'll tell me Rock Hudson's one!"

"Yeah. Or Liberace."

Her laughter thundered out into the neighborhood and she slapped her great thigh with delight. The clap was like a sonic boom rippling across Georgia.

I said, "Listen, Kay, the cops will undoubtedly want to ask you some more questions about the car you saw. Meanwhile, I'll see that Mrs. Fisher receives this envelope."

"Glad to help out. Hey, is that Greco guy really dead? Lord, I about peed my pants when I heard that. Radio said he drowned. I mean, was he really kidnapped, or did he steal your money, or what the hell's goin' on around here?"

I said truthfully, "I don't know, Kay. I wish I did."

"When Wilson gets back here he's gonna kick up a real storm when I tell him the cops'll be back. Bill don't take to cops. He was kind of a juvenile delinquent when he was a youngster and had some pretty rough times with the law. When I tell him, I hate to think."

"Where is your hubby, Kay? He doesn't work Sundays, does he?"

"Hadda meet some people. Somethin' about the ball games. Business." She looked at her feet, then up at me again, not happily. "I won't tell him it was you that was here, Bob. Wilson's the jealous type. If I told Bill not to get his dandruff up, that you was just a homo, he'd call me a liar and a lot of other names. Wilson cares a lot about my reputation, I gotta say that. He puts me on a pedestal." She smiled feebly, and I smiled feebly back.

I told Kay I'd be in touch, then drove on down the road. I pulled over in front of the Deem house—both cars gone, no sign of life—and opened the envelope.

The note, in the by-now-familiar handwriting, read: "If you don't want Fenton to die like Peter pay $100,000 dollars again Mrs. Fisher. We will contact you. And this time no cops."

19.

Dot was on the phone with Peter Greco's mother in San Diego. "Oh, no, Mrs. Greco. No, Peter did nothing to bring this on himself, you can be dead certain of that." She winced, and went on. "Peter was one of the sweetest, most considerate people I've ever known, and this thing is just the most unfair— Yes, I'm afraid it's not a mistake. I saw your son's body myself and— Is there someone there with you, Mrs. Greco?"

She stood slumped against the wall, her eyes half shut in a face collapsed with age and grief. As I passed her, our eyes met and she shook her head in spent resignation.

I went over to the cop seated at the kitchen table, apparently on guard against sugar bowl thieves.

You guys screwed up," I said. "This was tossed into the Wilsons' mailbox fifteen minutes ago." I dropped the envelope on the table. "How come their place wasn't covered?"

His jaw dropped and he snatched up the letter. His mouth clamped shut as he opened the envelope, and when he read the note his jaw dropped again. Getting up, he said, "I better notify the lieutenant."

"Right. This puts a new light on things. Or an old one."

The cop trotted out to his radio car as Dot went on speaking with someone who seemed to be a neighbor or friend of the senior Grecos'. After a moment, she placed the receiver on the hook but didn't move. There was a long silence. She glanced at me, then looked away. I could see what she was thinking.

I said, "It's no one's fault. Except the people who did it. They are the only ones to blame. When I find them, I'll tell them how we feel about what they have done."

"I offered them the money," Dot said in a broken voice. "What more could I have done?"

"Nothing."

"But if I had sold the house three months ago—"

"Yes, and if armadillos drove mopeds, fish could fly kites."

She gave me a funny look. "Why, that makes no sense at all."

I shrugged. "The point is, you've done the right things all the way down the line. Anyhow, you've got to stay strong and think about the present, Dot. And the future. Another problem's come up. Fenton is in trouble."

"I know."

"You do?"

"Of course. Fenton's been kidnapped. He took the money to the kidnappers this morning, hoping to buy Peter's release, and now with Peter dead the kidnappers are holding Fenton. Any fool could see that. I suspected as much when Fenton left this morning with the money and didn't come back. Peter's death confirmed it. Has there been another ransom note?" I nodded. "They'll kill Fenton, of course. Because he's seen them now and he'll be able to identify them. Do you think that's why they killed Peter? I think so."

The effort expended in getting all that out was too much for her, and, her face gone white, she clutched at the countertop. I helped her into a chair.

"Where's Edie?" she said.

"I don't know, Dot. I haven't seen her. Is she upstairs maybe?"

"Oh, yes. Yes, she's up there with the air conditioner running. Good God, it's hot! Is it me, or is today even more of a scorcher than yesterday? I used to think that when I was a child the summers were hotter and the winters colder. But now I'm not so sure. I suppose it's me. I guess it's just this dilapidated old sack of flesh and bones I drag around in. I think I'll go up and lie down for a bit. Edie's got the right idea. Cool off by the air conditioner. Yes, that's the ticket."

Dot insisted she needed no help climbing the stairs. She said that if I was hungry I should fix myself a sandwich and some salad. Which I did. The sun was low above the pear orchard. It was after six o'clock.

Bowman arrived within twenty minutes. He examined the new ransom note.

"Oy vey."

"You think McWhirter sent it?" I asked. "That it's part of the plot, the big production?"

"Maybe not. I guess not." He scratched his head.

"Did you get prints off the first note?"

'Yeah. Yours, Mrs. Fisher's, and Kay Wilson's. These people are dumb, but they're not that dumb. There were traces of latex on the note. Bastards wore rubber gloves. But I'll have this one checked anyway, just in case."

"What about the finger?"

"Nah, no prints on that. Just its own."

"Whose was it?"

"No record. The lab guys did come up with one thing though. The finger had been washed up with Albany tap water—you can't miss that stuff—but there were still traces of formaldehyde in it too."

"Is that a fact? So. That suggests a hospital or lab."

"We managed to deduce that on our own, Strachey. We're asking around."

"And nobody's reported a stolen finger?"

"Of course not. You think I wouldn't have heard about *that*?"

"Maybe it's Rockefeller's. Middle, upraised. Have you checked the state museum?"

He blanched at the sacrilege.

"And Greco's both hands were intact when he was found?"

He grunted.

"What did the coroner have to say? Is his report in yet?"

He rolled his eyes. "Asphyxiation," he said disgustedly. "So far, that's it."

"From drowning, or what?"

"I said, that is *it*. No. Greco did not drown. No water in the lungs. And no signs of strangulation. He'd been bound at his wrists and ankles, and it looked like he'd tried hard to get loose. There were cuts and rope burns where he'd been tied. And he'd been gagged, but not so tightly that he couldn't have breathed. His nose hadn't been covered, and he hadn't swallowed his tongue. The coroner hasn't figured it out yet. He's working on it, narrowing it down."

"Drugs?"

"No sign of any. They're still checking. He could've been locked in an airtight enclosure. Car trunk or something. Don't know yet."

"How long had he been dead?"

"Twelve, fourteen hours. That'd put it between ten and midnight last night."

I said, "I don't get it."

"Me neither."

"He died from three to five hours *before* the ransom was to have been picked up. Why would they kill him then? Even if they'd decided Greco would have to die to prevent his identifying them, why risk doing it before the cash was in hand?"

"So, they got cocky, overconfident. We know they're stupid."

"No, we don't know that, Ned. We only know they're poorly educated, can't spell."

"Jesus. You liberals."

"Or they want us to *think* that they never got past sixth grade. I want to hear the tape again. The call from the pay phone to McWhirter."

He shrugged. "Suit yourself."

"I'd like to hear the original. Is it in your office?"

"Nnn. I'll set it up. I'm hanging in out here in case they call again. Some of my crew will be joining me. Are you putting up the hundred grand again this time, or what?"

A shiver went up my back, then down again. I said, "Stuff a box with Monopoly money. It looks as if it hardly matters at this point. Christ, these people are vicious beyond belief."

"Maybe Mrs. Fisher wants to cough up the dough this

time. She really is kind of a nice batty old broad. I like her. Wouldn't mind having her on my side if I ever got in a tight spot."

"She doesn't know yet what the tab is this time. When she finds out, don't let her call her lawyer. Ask her to talk to me first."

"Well, now. I'd say that'd be up to her."

Watching him, I said, "Have you spoken with Crane Trefusis today, Ned?"

"We chatted," he said nonchalantly. "He's clean."

"Sure. No one in Albany with an income of more than a hundred grand a year has ever committed a crime. That's a given."

"I didn't say that."

I studied him again. I was nearly certain that he was just acting cute to irritate me, but not entirely certain. I waited, but he had nothing to add on the subject.

In the gathering dusk, I drove back into the city. My car still stank in the heat, as did I.

A police technician in Bowman's office played the tape for me five times.

"Hello?"

"You want your lover back?"

"Y-yes."

"In three minutes, call this number I'm gonna give you. Call from another phone. Call 555-8107. And bring the fuckin' money!"

"Let me write it down—"

Click.

I had heard the voice. Where? In another case I'd been involved in? In a public place? A bar, restaurant, airport, bus station, shopping mall? Why did I think it had to have been a public place? Because it was not someone I'd known well enough to meet, or even just overhear, in a private place? Or was it because of—noise. *That was it.*

I associated the sound of that voice—harsh, sullen, unappealing—with *background noise*. The sounds of people talking at a large gathering in a public place. But which one? When?

I couldn't remember.

On the way out of Division Two Headquarters I passed Sandra and Joey Deem seated morosely on a wooden bench near the front door. Sandra's eyes were bloodshot, the only color in her entire being. Her son wore a jacket and tie and looked frightened. Sandra explained that Joey had just been booked on the vandalism charge and would appear in juvenile court in late September.

"It's his first time," I said. "The judge will go easy. Just don't show up there a second time." This wasn't quite true. It was only about the fifty-seventh offense of this type that could get you into real trouble.

"There won't be a second time," Mrs. Deem said wanly. "Will there, Joey?"

He shook his head once and stared at the floor. I didn't envy him his necktie in the heat.

"Joey's father is pretty upset with him," Mrs. Deem said with a cracked smile. "But if Joey stays out of trouble for a year, his dad is going to buy him that transmission. He told him that this morning. Didn't he, Joey? That's what Dad promised."

The boy nodded, didn't look up.

I offered what encouragement I could, then left them there in the Arch Street gloom.

The apartment was empty, undisturbed, unvisited.

I stood in the bedroom and screamed, "Timmy, you asshole! You finicky mama's boy! You tight-assed Papist! You creep!"

There was no response.

* * *

My service had no messages. I dialed Lyle Barner's number and got no answer. I reached Bowman at Dot Fisher's. He said the kidnappers had made no further contact and that the coroner had not yet established the exact cause of Peter Greco's death.

I thought of Greco alive. I felt his fingers brushing my face. I went into the bathroom and threw up. Go-Buick week on the Hudson.

I showered and changed clothes for the first time in two and a half days. The improvement was noticeable. I phoned Tad Purcell's number but got no answer. I checked my watch. It was seven-forty. I drove out to the Green Room and found Purcell at the piano bar. Artur Rubinstein in white bucks was pounding out a medley from *Finian's Rainbow*.

I slid onto the stool beside Purcell and said, "Did you hear about Peter, Tad?"

Weakly: "Yes." He looked it. His face was as white as Pat Boone's shoes. His eyes were pinholes. His hair was slick with sweat and spraynet.

The philosopher king said, "Everything stinks sometimes. Some of it can't be explained."

Barely audible: "I know."

"But in this case there is an explanation," I told him. "I intend to find it."

He peered over at me glumly. He said, "Good luck." He lifted a glass of something festively colored and consumed a third of it.

"Where were you last night, Tad? Were you here till closing?"

With a nervous giggle, he said, "Where else?" This was so easy to check on that anybody with half a mind wouldn't have said it if it hadn't been true. I'd check anyway.

I said, "You work for Albany Med. Who would I talk to over there if I wanted very discreetly to find out if any body parts were missing? From a lab, or morgue, or whatever."

With a look of mock disgust, he said, "God, you are *weird.*"

"Like a finger, for instance. I've got to find out where a certain finger came from."

"Why? J'catch something from it?" His remark amused him hugely and he glanced around to see if anyone nearby had been fortunate enough to overhear it. Artur segued into the theme from *A Letter to Three Wives.*

"It's possible the finger came from somewhere else," I said. "A lab or college or one of the other area hospitals. But Albany Med is the biggest local repository I can think of for odds and ends of human body parts, so that's where I'm starting. Who would know about such things?"

"Newell Bankhead's in charge of the pathology lab," Purcell said with a shrug. "He'd be the one to talk to about blood and gore, I guess."

"Would he be on tonight? Or will I have to track him down at home or somewhere?"

Purcell giggled again. "Newell works weekdays. But he's not at home, I can tell you that for a certainty."

"How can you be so sure?"

"Because," Purcell said with a drunk's sly I've-seen-it-all-and-nothing-surprises-me-anymore grin, "Newell's right over there. He's the pianist."

I looked off to my right and saw Artur's right hand swoop through the air at the completion of a crashing arpeggio. He caught my eye and winked.

Newell Bankhead, a tall, gaunt, bright-eyed man of a certain age (mine), said he thought we would find fewer distractions if we chatted at his apartment around the corner

on Partridge Street. Newell managed to provide a somewhat unnerving distraction of his own, but when I walked
out of his apartment an hour and a half later I had what I
wanted, so what the hell.

The list I carried had on it a hundred and six names.
Most were employees of Albany Medical Center, though
Newell had made a few phone calls and was able to add
names from Memorial, St. Peter's, and three other area
hospitals.

It would be very difficult, Newell had told me, to account for every detached finger that came and went at
Albany Med or any other large hospital. None had been
reported missing, that he knew of. Often, he said, in cases
of severe mutilation, as occurred in certain unusually brutal car accident fatalities, the assorted remains of the de-
ceased were promptly hauled off to a funeral director for
whatever cosmetic reconstruction was possible, or were
sent in plastic bags for a closed casket service. Occasional
odds and ends of body parts, however, were sometimes
kept in the pathology lab for study. Or they were simply
disposed of: wrapped, sealed, and incinerated.

The names on Newell's list were of men and women
who would have had easy access to these body parts at
one time or another. There were pathology department
workers in various capacities, and a large number of
emergency-room doctors, nurses, and aides who carried
out a variety of functions. At the end of the list was the
maintenance worker at Albany Med who ran the incinera-
tor.

Newell pointed out that the list was not at all complete, so he starred the names of gay friends and acquain-
tances of his who, if I needed them, could provide
additional names for the list. When I counted the stars—
there were 27 out of 106—it looked as though Fenton
McWhirter was right. During a gay national strike, it

would not be wise to have an accident or become ill in the United States of America.

Bankhead also told me he had heard from a co-worker friend on weekend duty that two police detectives had visited the hospital that afternoon seeking the same kind of information. My opinion of Bowman's professional abilities went up, though I was afraid it would take Bowman's bureau three days to interview and, where necessary, investigate everyone on the list. I doubted we had that much time if we were going to save Fenton McWhirter.

I knew what I had to do. It was going to take five or six hours of drudgery, but there was no other way. I was going to make 106 phone calls, and I was going to listen for a hard, tense, distinctive voice that I would recognize.

I drove down Central to my office. I wrenched open the window above the burnt-out air conditioner, reached around and removed a loose brick from the face of the building, and used it to prop the window open. Then I sat at my desk, spread out Newell's list, opened the phone book, and began to dial.

"Good evening, I'm Biff McGuirk, calling from his honor the mayor's office. Are you Mr. Lawrence Banff?"

"Yes, speaking."

"Mr. Banff, the mayor is surveying the Albany citizenry to learn if there are ways city government can improve its services to the beautiful people of this extremely interesting town we all cohabit. May I ask if . . ."

After a grueling half-hour of this, I'd had enough. Too much. I had completed only three calls and had listened to a large number of moderately affecting stories having to do with potholes, water rates, potholes, property taxes, potholes, mad dogs, and the humidity on Ten Broeck Street. I had not heard the voice of the kidnapper.

I stared at the phone. It all seemed futile, a very chancy long shot at best. The kind of approach you took when you had the time to pick up the thousand loose ends you invariably came away with. I couldn't even be certain that the owner of the voice of the kidnapper I'd heard was even on my list. Or on *any* hypothetical list of hospital employees. Maybe it was the *accomplice* who'd stolen the finger from some lab or emergency room, the accomplice whose voice I had never heard and would not recognize at all.

I thought about it some more and came up with one semi-bright idea. Bowman, I figured, could get quick voice prints of all the area ER and pathology lab personnel—this could be accomplished within twenty-four hours—and then match them against a print of the voice on the tape. I calculated the odds at about fifty-fifty that our man *was* a hospital employee, and if so, this would be a way of zeroing in on him fast.

I phoned Bowman's office, was told that he was still out at the Fisher farm, and was patched through to his radio car.

The man himself came on the line thirty seconds later. "Better get your ass out here, Strachey, if you don't want to miss the excitement. Your mysterious voice called up. Mrs. Fisher is going to deliver the cash."

"*Dot* is?"

"That's who they asked for. She says she's gonna do it."

"Crap. Oh, crap."

20.

The call from the kidnappers had come at nine-twenty-two. Bowman had a copy of the tape and played it for me.

DOT FISHER: *Yes, hello.*

VOICE: *You want the other one to live?*

DOT: *Yes. Yes—*

VOICE: *Then you listen to what I say—*

DOT: *All right. Believe me, whoever you are—*

VOICE: *Now, listen, missus. Get it straight. Put the hundred thousand in a small picnic basket with a handle on top. At twelve o'clock midnight take the basket to the pay phone at the Westway Diner on Western Avenue near route one-fifty-five. You understand?*

DOT: *Yes, I do.*

VOICE: *Wait by that phone. And no Alice Blue this time, missus!*

Click.

The voice again. I knew it. I'd heard it. Somewhere. And now I knew something else. "Alice Blue." A nickname for cops used only, so far as I knew, by a distinctive subgroup of a certain larger social group. The kidnapper himself was gay.

Bowman had not failed to research the terminology. "One of my boys tells me he's heard this 'Alice Blue' shit, Strachey. Sounds like this creep is one of your people. So sorry to hear it. My condolences."

"Thank you. Where did the call originate?"

"Another pay phone. Colonie Center this time. He was gone by the time we got a car out there. And nobody around there had seen whoever'd used the phone. A royal pain."

"So, what's your plan?"

"She's going. Mrs. Fisher's one tough cookie, she is. We'll follow, discreetly."

"She knows you'll be along?"

"Yes. She wants these punks as much as I do. And she knows what savages they are."

"Is she taking the money?"

He nodded, a little guiltily.

In the heat, I felt cold. I said, "Where did she get it?"

"It's not here yet," he said, looking around for something to distract him. "The cash'll be here any minute now."

"Uh-huh. And who's bringing it?"

"Your employer," he said, not looking at me. "Mr. Crane Trefusis."

"No. She didn't."

"She did. Well, she did in a manner of speaking. What I mean is, it's an option on the property cancelable by the seller up to twenty-four hours after signing. After that it's binding, no matter what. Mrs. Fisher's lawyer got on the horn with Trefusis and okayed the language."

"Twenty-four hours. Crap. That may not be enough time."

"It's more than enough if these nuts show up for the drop."

"Yeah, if. But they're unpredictable, aren't they, Ned? They often seem to have the audacity not to follow to the letter the plan tucked away inside your head."

He snorted. "So, what do you suggest, bright boy? What have you come up with that's worked out any better? Unless you've got a niftier idea, maybe you'd just better keep your fat yap shut for a while, huh?"

I kept my fat yap shut for a while.

Dot had been upstairs with Edith, and now she appeared in grass-stained old jeans, sneakers, and a sweatshirt with words across the front that read: "My grandmother visited Hawaii and all she sent me was this dumb sweatshirt."

A cop came in and called Bowman to the radio car, and he went out puffing into the night.

I said to Dot, "I understand why you did it, but we could have come up with the cash some other way. It's an awful risk you're taking, Dot."

"Oh, it doesn't matter all that much. I'm just worn to a frazzle. Enough is enough. And Edith does hate the winters here so awfully much. Do you think I'm too old to take up surfing?"

"Probably not in Laguna Beach."

"I'll bet there's an Old Biddies' Down-the-Tubes Association out there, wouldn't you think?"

"I would. But you haven't lost it yet, Dot. Not at all. There's time."

"Yes. I hope so. Though, really, I'm not at all optimistic about getting Fenton back here safely. Are you? Not after what they did to Peter. But we have to try, don't we?"

"Yes."

A wicker picnic basket lay atop the kitchen table. Dot went over to it. "This basket was a present from Edith on my fiftieth birthday. It was full of cheeses from all over the world, and a card that said, 'You're the big cheese in my life.' Wasn't that a dumb, funny, lovely thing?" She perched on the edge of a chair and gazed out the window at the orchard and the moonlit pond.

The door opened and Bowman came in, followed by Crane Trefusis, who saw me first and came toward me with a glad hand out.

"That was a superb piece of detection, Strachey, the way you zeroed right in on that Deem boy. Congratulations."

"Congratulations? That's all?"

"The check is in the mail," Trefusis said brightly. "Oh—Mrs. Fisher, it's nice to see you again."

"I'm sure it is," Dot said, not smiling.

"I want to tell you how sorry I am—"

"Yes, yes, thank you, Mr. Trefusis, but let's just get this over with."

Trefusis looked a little hurt and peeved that his condolence speech had been cut short, though if the alternative was doing business, his nimble mind was prepared to accept that. He produced from his jacket pocket a sheaf of documents and a gold-plated pen.

"I'll just be a moment," Dot said, accepting the papers but not the pen. At the kitchen table she shoved a pair of reading glasses onto her nose and laid out the documents to compare them to the agreement her lawyer had dictated over the telephone.

Trefusis said to Bowman, "Lieutenant, I wish you all the luck in the world in getting hold of the maniacs responsible for this malicious crime. What are the odds that you'll make an arrest in the near future?"

"Excellent," Bowman said.

Trefusis ceased breathing for a second or two, but his expression didn't change. "Glad to hear it," he said with too much enthusiasm. I didn't doubt that he wanted the matter tidied up, though if it happened twenty-five hours from then, that would have been preferable.

Dot came back with the binding option agreement signed. In essence, it stated that unless the $100,000 was returned to Millpond Plaza Associates within twenty-four hours, Dot was obligated to sell her house and acreage to Millpond for $350,000 within a week's time.

"I need a witness to my signature, Don. Would you mind?"

I minded, but I signed. Then Trefusis signed and Bowman signed as his witness. The ritual was repeated over a second copy of the agreement, which Dot kept.

Handing over a canvas sack full of money, Trefusis said, "Included is a list of the bills' serial numbers as per Lieutenant Bowman's request. You know, Mrs. Fisher, I'm so sorry this had to happen under these sad circumstances, but in a sense you are actually quite fortunate that Millpond was available to—"

"Take your papers and go, Mr. Trefusis. Please. Before I . . . give you a piece of my mind!" Her color was rising, and Trefusis swiftly backed off and fled out into the night, the option agreement clutched in his fist.

I said, "Sweet guy."

"We all have our loyalties," Bowman piped up.

"Ned, that's the fifteenth or sixteenth most fatuous statement I've ever heard you make."

"I was only just saying, goddamn it, that—"

"Don't squabble," Dot snapped, opening an aspirin bottle. "Please. Not now."

Bowman and I stood there, heads bowed contritely.

To break the silence, I asked Bowman, "Who was on your radio just now. Anything new?"

"Not much. Just that the coroner now thinks the Greco kid had some kind of allergy or something. The asphyxiation was caused by an internal chemical reaction. But they don't know yet what set it off."

I said, "Dot, was Peter allergic to anything that you know of?"

She looked perplexed. "Why, I don't think so. He never mentioned anything like that. Goodness knows, people with hay fever have a devil of a time this season of year. But Peter never seemed bothered by it. Fenton would be the person to ask."

We all looked at each other.

Bowman said, "Hopefully we'll have an opportunity to ask him in an hour or so."

"Yes," Dot said. "One hopes."

Bowman didn't pick up the lesson in English usage, but he had more pressing matters to think about. As did I.

While Bowman and Dot stacked the hundred grand in bills in the picnic basket and Dot was fitted with a hidden microphone and radio transmitter, I went into the guest room and dug out Greco's journal.

I flipped through it and after a minute found the entry I remembered.

> Aug. 2—*New Haven hot, Yalies cool. No students, but two cafeteria workers sign pledge. Stayed with Tom Bittner, here for a year researching colonial anti-gay laws. Great seeing Tom Cicely still with him; I slept on porch.*

I checked other pages at random and came up with two More examples of what I was looking for. The June 26 entry for Portland, Maine, included the remark "Supposed to stay with Harry Smight but had to clear out after 20 minutes. The usual."

On July 2, in Boston, Greco wrote, "Great to see Carlos again but couldn't stay at his apt. and ended up at his sister's. At C's, bloody beasts were everywhere!"

Back in the kitchen, Dot and Bowman had gone outside to his car. I phoned New Haven information and was given the number for a Thomas Bittner on Orange Street. I dialed the number and explained to the sleepy male voice that answered who I was and, briefly, what had happened to Peter Greco.

"Oh, God. Oh, no."

"Listen, Tom, you can help us find the people who did this. Peter died of asphyxiation, and the medical people think an allergy may have caused it. Was Peter, by chance, allergic to cats?"

"Oh, Jesus, yes, he was. Deathly. I mean— Oh, God—"

"Thanks, Tom. You've helped. Regards to Cicely."

I rang off and dialed Newell Bankhead's apartment.

"Don Strachey, Newell. I have a small favor to ask. Actually, it's quite a big favor, but it might help save a life. I need a list of everybody who works in pathology or an ER in area hospitals who's gay. The partial list you gave me isn't enough. I need 'em all. Real fast. Can you do it?"

He laughed. "That'd only take me about six weeks. And twelve reams of paper."

"Look, you just get on the phone and call three people, then they get on the phone and call three people, and like that. It shouldn't take more than a couple of hours. In the end, everybody gay in Albany knows everybody gay in Albany. Eventually you always end up in the bed you started out in. I mean, this is the Hudson Valley, Newell, not West Hollywood. You can do it."

"I've been watching the Channel Twelve news. Does all this have to do with that horrible kidnapping business?" he asked. "That sweet young man who died?"

"It does."

"Oh. Oh, Lord. All right then. Yes. I'll do what I can. But it's after eleven, you know. A lot of people will be in bed getting their beauty sleep. People who go on duty at seven in the morning."

"Wake them up. Tell them how important it is. And one other thing, Newell. This complicates matters slightly, but you can handle it. I want to know not only which men in pathology and the ERs are gay, but who among them own cats. Or have lovers or roommates who own cats."

"Cats? Which ones have cats?"

"Right. Cats."

A silence.

"It's crucial," I said. "Life or death."

"Well. Hmm. I'll . . . do what I can." He sounded doubtful.

"Thanks, Newell. By the way, I forgot to mention how much I enjoyed your rendition tonight of the theme from *Ruby Gentry*. I've always been a big Jeannie Crain fan myself."

"Why, thank you so much. But it was Jennifer Jones in *Ruby Gentry*. Don't you know *anything* about music?"

"Oh. I guess I was thinking of *The Unfaithful*."

"That was Ann Sheridan."

"Of course. Sorry, but during the fabulous forties my parents only took me to see *Song of the South*. Do you ever play 'Zippity-doo-da'?"

"Occasionally, around three-thirty in the morning," he said dryly. "If someone requests it."

"Well, I'm going to do that some night. So, be ready. Meanwhile, I've got work to do. And so do you."

"I'll say."

"I'll get back to you in a couple of hours, Newell. Thanks."

"Nnn. Surely."

I went outside, where Dot had just climbed into her car, the picnic basket full of money on the seat beside her. Edith was in a bathrobe standing by the open car window and leaned down to kiss Dot goodbye.

"Now, you be careful, Dorothy, and don't try to give those people an argument. Just hand them the money, and then you come right on home."

"Don't worry, love."

"Well, I *am* going to worry, and you know I am."

Bowman called out from his car, "Time to go, Mrs. Fisher. We'd better get rolling."

Edith backed away clutching her robe. A patrolman stayed behind to keep watch over her. I bent down and kissed Dot good luck, then yelled to Bowman that I'd follow in my car. He yelled back that he wanted me where he could keep an eye on me and commanded me to get into the back seat of his car, which is what I'd had in mind.

As we bounced up Moon Road toward Central, Dot half a block ahead of us, I explained to Bowman about Greco's allergy to cats and how this might have led to his dying, probably accidentally. Which would have explained a lot of things.

"Jesus," Bowman said, choosing for the moment to miss the point. "Couldn't stand cats? What kind of a faggot *was* this guy?"

Then the ride became very quiet.

---

21. The Westway Diner was lit up like a small city in the black night. A glass-sided outer lobby contained a cigarette machine and a pay telephone. From across the avenue we watched Dot step out of her car at eleven-fifty-nine and climb the few steps into the lobby, where she stood by the phone. From a special radio speaker mounted on Bowman's dashboard we could hear Dot's breathing and accelerated heartbeat. The picnic basket hung on her arm.

At midnight, the telephone beside Dot rang.

"Hello?"

The diner pay phone had been tapped, and from the regular police radio speaker we could hear both Dot and the caller.

"Drive down to Price Chopper." The now-familiar voice again. Where had I heard it? "Wait by the pay phone out front."

"Which Price Chopper?" Dot quickly asked. "The one at the Twenty Mall, or the one down Western Avenue toward Albany?"

"Down Western. We'll call in two minutes."

Click.

Bowman sputtered, "Jesus, Mother, and Mary! We'll never get into that line in two minutes! Can we?"

A metallic voice from Second Division Headquarters, seven miles away, said, "We'll try, Lieutenant. We're workin' on it."

Dot was back in her car and turning east onto Western Avenue. Traffic was light and she swung out into the four-lane thoroughfare with no difficulty.

"You hear that, Conway?" Bowmaan barked into his microphone. "Boyce? Salazar? It's Price Chopper, back down Western."

"Got it, Lieutenant."

"We heard."

"On the way."

The parking lot of the all-night supermarket was practically deserted. Dot had pulled directly up to the pay phone near the brightly lighted entrance. Again she climbed out and stood by the telephone with her picnic basket. The phone rang.

"Yes, hello?"

Now we could hear only Dot's voice, the tap not yet completed.

"Yes, yes, I understand."

Bowman muttered, "Repeat it for us, lady. *Repeat* it."

"Yes," Dot said. "I'll do that right away."

Dot hung up and entered the supermarket, the basket dangling from her arm. Her voice came out of the radio speaker again.

"He told me—I hope you can hear me, Lieutenant Bowman. The man told me to go inside the store and to . . . to buy a chuck steak. That's what he said. And then to go back outside and wait by the telephone."

Bowman writhed in his seat. "A chuck steak. Shit. He *couldn't* have said a chuck steak. Strachey, is the old doll hard of hearing, or what?"

"Not that I know of. I'd say no, she isn't."

"Oh, my land!" Dot's voice again. "My word, I didn't bring a cent with me. All I have is the money in the basket! Well, that will just have to do. Let's hope they can't count."

Bowman squirmed some more, shook his head. "I don't believe this is happening."

"I've got the steak," Dot said after a minute. "It's a bit fatty, but fine for stew. The roasts look nice, but the man said steak, so steak it is."

From our position across the highway we watched a dark blue Dodge identical to Bowman's pull into the Price Chopper lot, come to a stop at the edge of the woods on the western side of the lot, and douse its lights.

A young, tired female voice said, "That's four sixty-seven."

There was a pause, during which Dot's heartbeat quickened.

"Don't you have anything smaller than a hundred?" the cashier asked wearily.

"No, I'm sorry— Oh! Aren't those nice little TV sets! Just what I need for the den. I believe I'll just take one of those along. How much are they?"

"Eighty-nine ninety-five. There'd be sales tax on that too."

"Oh. Yes. And how much would that make it?"

A silence. Then: "Ninety-five thirty-four for the TV. And four sixty-seven for the meat."

"Fine," Dot said. "That's just fine."

Click, click, ring.

"That'll be one hundred dollars and one cent."

The heartbeat again. I thought I detected a slight mitral valve prolapse.

"Oh, heavenly days, I seem to have only another—"

"Forget the penny," the young woman said.

"Oh, thank you. Thank you so much."

"Have a nice night."

"Yes. You too."

She came into view again, the picnic basket over her right arm, a grocery bag clutched in her right fist. Her left hand grasped the handle of a small portable television set.

Dot quickly placed the TV set in the back seat of her car, then went and stood by the phone again. She said, "Do any of you have a hundred dollars? What if they count it?"

Bowman froze, but Dot made no move away from the phone.

A minute went by.

"Where the hell are they?" Bowman rasped. "What kind of crazy goddamn treasure-hunt-of-a-stunt are they pulling this time?"

The phone rang, startling all of us.

"Hello?"

Then another voice on the police radio: "Phone company's got it, Lieutenant. We're patching."

"Do it."

"—and go home. And take all those fuckin' cops with you!"

"But there are no policemen with me. As you can see— Can you see me? I'm alone. I wouldn't let them come."

"You just do like I said, missus!"

"Is Fenton nearby? Are you releasing him now?"

"Just do what I *said*."

"All right. I'm doing it now." Dot hugged the receiver between her neck and shoulder so that both hands were free. She bent down, took the package of meat out of the grocery bag and seemed to unwrap it. "I'm placing the meat in the basket," she said. "And now I'm putting the basket down on the pavement by the phone."

Bowman and I both said it at once—"A dog!"—as the form shot out of the woods on the eastern edge of the parking lot, snatched up the basket handle between its teeth, and hurtled back across the tarmac and into the deep woods.

"Oh, my stars!" we heard Dot shout. "Get back here with that! Get back here, you damnable mutt!"

She was exclaiming only to herself and to us. The phone line had gone dead.

"Salazar, around the block! Boyce, you follow me! There's a street on the other side of those woods!"

We sped down Western a third of a mile, then hooked sharply left onto a side residential street that paralleled the woods the dog had run into. The street dead-ended after a block, and the woods spread out to the left and right. We couldn't see the end of them in any direction.

We leaped from the car and stood listening. We heard peepers.

While Bowman and the eight or ten other patrol cars that suddenly materialized rushed pell-mell up and down the streets and back roads of Guilderland, I jogged back to the Price Chopper parking lot. Dot was seated in the driver's seat of her car, the radio on, tuned to WAMC. The midnight jazz show was on, with Art Tatum playing "Sweet Lorraine."

I climbed into the car and we sat and listened for a few minutes. Neither of us spoke. When the song ended, we exchanged seats and I drove us back to Dot's house. Edith was waiting in the kitchen, and we all had a sandwich and a beer.

No one said much. Dot and Edith were exhausted, defeated. I was watching the clock, and waiting.

22.

At one-twenty the patrolman guarding the Fisher farmhouse received a call from Bowman inquiring whether Dot had gotten home safely. He was informed that she had. Bowman reported that no trace of the kidnappers, the dog, or the basketful of meat and money had been found, but that the woods and streets in a six-square-mile area were being combed. As the patrolman passed this information on to me, I heard a helicopter roar overhead.

At 1:25 A.M., with the temperature at 80 degrees, Dot and Edith went out for a dip in the pond. They wore bathing suits this time.

At exactly one-thirty I dialed Newell Bankhead's number. The line was busy. I got hold of the operator and informed her that Mr. Bankhead's grandmother had been killed when the bus she'd been riding in plunged over a cliff on the outskirts of Katmandu, and would the operator please interrupt Bankhead's conversation? She grilled me according to phone company protocol, duly noted my lies, was gone for a few seconds, and then put Bankhead on the line.

"Newell, I'm sorry to be the one to break the news to you, but your grandmother Ruby Gentry was killed when the bus she'd been riding in plunged over a cliff on the outskirts of Katmandu."

He chuckled. "My, my. Sorry to hear it."

"I thought you'd want to know. So, what did you find out?"

"Six people hung up on me, and several others hung up on some friends of mine who called around. But I've got a list that's pretty complete, I think. There are fifty-eight names. Do you want to write them down?"

"I'm set. All these people work in pathology or in ER, and they're all gay?"

"These are the ones we're sure of. I've got another list of eighteen deep closet cases we can't be certain about but would be willing to bet money on."

"I'll take them all, cat owners first."

"We came up with sixteen of those. There are sure to be more, but these are the ones we know about."

"Shoot."

Bankhead dictated the list and I copied it down in my notebook, filling five pages. Several of the names I recognized from the earlier list he'd given me at his apartment.

When he'd finished, I said, "I know I didn't ask you this before, Newell, but on the off chance you can help me out, what about dogs?"

He chortled lewdly. "Eight or ten of them are *absolute* dogs, honey, but I thought you wanted this list for a kidnapping case."

"Ha, ha. Dog *owners*, Newell. As with the cats."

"I really don't know a lot of these people, but hold on a sec." He hummed the theme from *A Summer Place* while he perused his list.

"Here's one," he said. "Martin Fiori has dogs *and* cats. I've been out to his place, and it's an absolute menagerie."

"Oh, really? What kind of dogs? Are they trained?"

"Yes, I happen to know that they do do tricks. There are two poodles who can jump through a hoop, and a Pekinese who faints on command. Martin'll say, 'Have the vapors, Patsy,' and the little pooch will roll right over and faint dead away. I'll tell you, it's an absolute scream."

"Martin doesn't sound promising. Who else have you got?"

"Let's see. Oh, here's one. Buddy Strunk has a dog. Some kind of mongrel, I remember. Real friendly. The sniffy type. Visitors to Buddy's apartment sit all evening with their legs locked together. But I don't think Buddy has a cat. No, no cat at Buddy's."

"Keep going."

"Dr. Vincent has a dog. And a cat."

"Who's he?"

"Dr. Charles Vincent. He's on the ER staff at Albany Med. He has a big bash once a year out at his place in Latham that I've gone to."

"What kind of dog? Do you remember his dog? A German shepherd maybe, or something else in the smart, mean department?"

"Gosh, I don't think so. I'd remember a big, ugly beast like that. I think Charles's dog is reddish. An Irish setter probably."

"Yeah, okay. I'll check that one. Who else?"

"Unn. I think that's about it, I'm afraid. There are probably lots of others. But you didn't ask about dogs. Just cats. So I didn't inquire."

"Crap. Okay. Well, this is something anyway."

"Oh, here's one more who doesn't have a dog or a cat that I know of, though he might. But his brother does. His brother trains dogs."

"Who's that? Tell me all about him."

"He's Duane Andrus, an aide in the Albany Med ER. His dad was a vet and used to run the Andrus Kennels out on Karner Road in Guilderland. The old man drank himself to death years ago, and then the brother—Glen, I think his name is—he's a security guard at Albany Med—"

"A security guard who wears a uniform?"

"Yes, he would."

"Go on. Tell me more."

"Well, Glen kept the kennels open for boarding after the old man died, until the place was shut down after the SPCA complained about bad treatment of the animals. The place was a real hellhole, from what I read. Filth, starvation, beatings. That was just last month, I think. Or late June maybe. It was in the papers. The only animal that came out of that place healthy was Glen's dog, the one he trains. Duane helped out out there, I know. Which doesn't surprise me. He's the type."

"The type for what?"

"Meanness, carelessness, flakiness. A real asshole."

'What else do you know about Duane?"

"That man is a criminal if there ever was one. Hustles his ass, and has a monumental coke habit, or so I hear. He's been in jail for assault, that I know for sure. Duane always seems to have money. He's got some sugar daddy in town, I'm told. He hangs around the pool table at the Watering Hole. He's mean, dumb, and ugly, but not nearly as ugly as he is mean and dumb, ha-ha. Hunky though, in his vulgar way. If that's the type you go for."

I let the tape play in my head again. I heard the voice, and the background noise. Friday night at the Watering Hole. The mean-looking cowboy whose pool shot Mc-Whirter ruined. The one who smelled like the stockyards. Or a kennel.

I said, "You're a sweetheart, Newell. That's my man, I'm all but sure of it. Listen, is it possible that Duane Andrus would have been one of the people your friends called tonight? *You* didn't call him, did you?"

"Duane is really not my cup of tea, honey. I go for the strong silent type. Deep. Like Richard Gere. And no, I don't think anyone else would have called him either.

Duane is not exactly what you'd call approachable. Unless you've got a hundred-dollar bill in your hand."

"Newell, thank you. You've done something important tonight. If there's any justice, you'll get a shot at the Troy Savings Bank Music Hall for this."

"Why, thank *you*, darlin'. I'll pack the place for sure if it's two-for-one on a Wednesday night."

I rang off and asked the patrolman guarding the farmhouse how I could get in touch with Bowman.

"The lieutenant said he was going up in the chopper. I hadn't better bother him now."

"Bother him," I said. "On this one, he'll have your ass if you don't."

I told the cop where I'd be and what I'd be doing and to relay the message to Bowman as rapidly as the department's bureaucracy could manage it.

I wanted a gun with me but couldn't take the time to drive all the way back to my office to pick up my Smith & Wesson. I dialed Lyle Barner's number. After ten rings I was about to hang up when he answered.

"Yeah? Who's this?"

"Don Strachey, Lyle. I need help. Now."

"Don— Oh. What's the problem, Don?" He sounded nicely relaxed and distracted. Too relaxed. I regretted doing this to him.

"I want you to meet me in fifteen minutes—ten, if you can—outside the Star Market at Western and Karner Road. Come armed."

"Hey, man, hey. I've got— There's someone with me."

"Get rid of him. I know who the kidnappers are and where they are. I'll need help. Bowman will turn up eventually. But I need a strong man who has experience with unruly types and can handle a gun, and I need him now."

"Oh, right, Don. Ten minutes. Star Market, Karner and Western."

The cop was in his car trying to raise someone on the radio when I pulled out of Dot's driveway and went pounding up Moon Road.

The lights were out at the Deem and Wilson households. I supposed they were all asleep, dreaming of untold wealth. The wealth that they would be within hours of collecting, were it not for my rushing out to Karner Road to take it away from them.

23.

Lyle's Trans Am roared into the Star Market lot five minutes after I did. I was standing beside my car when he pulled up beside me.

"Listen, Don, let me explain something. It wasn't my idea—"

The passenger door on the other side of Lyle's car opened. A man stepped out and looked at me across the car roof. His face rang a bell.

"Hi, sport," I said. "Long time no see."

He gazed at me coolly.

"He insisted on coming," Lyle burbled on. "I mean, jeez, if I'd thought he was going to— I mean—"

My impulse was to flatten them both. Drag Lyle from the seat of his pretentious hotdogger's shitwagon and knock him the hundred yards over to Dunkin' Donuts and shove him into the artificial-vanilla-flavored cream machine. Then come back and kick the other one's ass down Western Avenue the six miles back to the apartment.

Instead, I strolled into Star Market, bought a gallon jug of spring water, brought it out, uncapped it, took a swig, then poured the rest of it over my head. Ga-lug, ga-lug, ga-lug. The stuff wasn't particularly cooling, but it was wet and cooler than my body temperature, and it had its effect.

Lyle stared at me with his mouth hanging open. Timmy looked away, trying with everything he had not to laugh. Not that his newly hardened heart wasn't thudding inside his tank-topped chest.

Wiping my dripping face on my shirtfront, I said, "We'll go in my car. I'll explain on the way. Get in. Now."

They obeyed.

I drove past the kennels, a long, low white clapboard building with a pink and black CLOSED sign stuck in the window of the main door. I parked a quarter mile down Karner Road, and the three of us hiked back toward the kennels. Twenty yards south of the building we entered the scrub pine woods and moved closer.

The front section of the building was in darkness, but from the woods we could see a light burning in a rear wing that had small slitlike windows running high up along its length.

With only one gun among us, we stayed together. We crept up to the side of an old dark green Pontiac parked in the rear yard, and then on to the wing, where we flattened ourselves against the wall.

Lyle and Timmy bent down and formed a two-sectioned platform with their backs, which I climbed up on and peered through the window. I saw no people, just a security guard's uniform hanging from a hook—that of the "cop" Mel Glempt had seen grabbing Peter—and a long row of metal cages lined against the wall opposite me.

The window I looked through was covered with rabbit wire but the glass was broken and half fallen away. The foulest stench I had smelled since south Asia hit me like an airborne sewage pit.

I climbed down.

Timmy whispered, "Catshit."

"Yeah. Catshit. And, even worse for Peter, cat fur."

Standing there, I had a picture burned into my mind of the filth-ridden cages I had just seen. I knew then how Peter Greco had died.

I doubled over and began to heave silently, but Timmy whispered, "Later! Later!" and I kept it down. It was a subject Timmy was such an expert on.

We moved to the rear corner of the wing and saw that thirty yards away a second one-story wing extended back from the main front building, and it too was lighted on the inside. We slowly crept toward it, and as we approached, the sound of voices came from one of the high windows. Lyle drew his revolver.

Again, I was raised up to peer inside, and I saw them. McWhirter, inside a stiff-wire dog cage, was bound with rope at his wrists and ankles, a gag in his mouth. Two men were just below me. I could see the bare right arm of one and heard the voice of the other, whose body was not within my visual range.

"Tell him they jewed us out of a hundred bucks," said the man with the arm. "Fuckin' dyke skimmed off a hundred. We oughtta go back there and bust her lip."

"Shut up, Glen. That don't matter!" said the voice of Duane Andrus. "Listen, baby, I want that fifty back within a week, or you are *finished*. You got that? I mean *finished*."

A long silence. Andrus apparently was speaking not to his brother but to someone on the telephone.

"Listen, I told you that was an *accident*, and I'm not gonna keep listening to you yap about that. The Greco guy was blindfolded and never would have recognized us, but this asshole's different—he's seen us—and what the fuck difference does it make? We're in it up to our tits now anyways, so you just shut your fuckin' pansy mouth!

Some big fuckin' help you've been anyways, so you just piss off! And you get me that fifty back, or your ass is fuckin' *hamburger*."

The receiver went down with a bang.

"He's such a worthless piece of shit, I don't know why I ever—"

"Shhhh!"

The low growl was no more than ten feet behind us.

"That's Brute," came a voice from inside the building.

None of us moved. None of them moved. The only sound was of the breathy, wet snarl, a pent-up animal rage gathering itself to explode. I turned my head slowly and saw it in the hazy moonlight. I knew they were usually trained to go for the neck, wrist, or groin, and I tried to decide which of those on me was expendable. I voted for wrist.

Focusing all my attention on the dog, I hadn't heard the movement inside the building, but suddenly a man I took to be Glen Andrus appeared around the back corner of the wing.

"Brute, *kill!*" he shouted, which was less original than "Have the vapors, Patsy," but more useful for the owner's purposes under the circumstances.

The beast hurtled toward our idiotic pyramid, and Lyle's gun thundered a bright charge into the night, its impact sending the dog cartwheeling through the air away from us. Our pyramid collapsed at the same moment, and Glen Andrus charged around the back of the other wing toward the Pontiac. Lyle took off after him. Timmy and I rushed around the corner of the wing where McWhirter was tied up inside.

I collided with Duane Andrus as he exploded out the door, and the two of us bounced off the door frame and found ourselves rolling together across the soft, warm, shit-littered earth. I wrestled him onto his back and was about to throttle him—not necessarily fatally, though it

could have happened—when his head came up and he
clamped my left ear between his teeth. I worked my
thumbs in hard against his esophagus. A continuous siren
sounded inside my head and I heard a couple of sharp
cracks that I thought might have been gunshots.

Andrus flailed at my lower back with his fists and bit
harder with his teeth. Later, I could not remember feeling pain; there was just the sound, the shrieking of a siren
a few inches outside my head, or a few inches inside it.

Timmy's hand hove into view. I knew that lovely a-
little-too-well-manicured graceful thing with its soft blue
veins as well as I knew my own. The hand was wrapped
around a brick, which landed hard against Andrus's sku!!
He gagged, fell away from me, spit something bloody i
my face, then lay moaning.

I stood up, felt sick, then squatted and lowered
head as Lyle came bounding around the corner of the
building.

"You guys okay? I shot the other one in the ass. He's
not going anywhere. Better call an ambulance."

McWhirter, whom Timmy had set free while I was
tussling with Duane Andrus, staggered up to us, stooped
and bent from having been tied up for eighteen hours.

He stammered, "They're not even cops! They're—
they're *worse*."

"It can happen," Lyle said.

Timmy turned toward the kennels. "I'll call Bowman
and the ambulance."

"You won't need to call anybody," I said, as the police
helicopter roared into view above the woods off to the
east. "But see if you can scare up a flashlight in there. I
think I'm missing something."

Timmy was waiting when I was wheeled into my room at
Albany Med. I was drugged up and didn't remember the
conversation, but later he told me we had this exchange:

"I'll never leave you again," he said.

"I know, not for a minute. I was afraid of that."

"The doctor says you're going to be okay. He says it's back on. It'll look a little funny—not his words—but what the hell."

"Right. It'd be no fun for you trying to nibble at a hole in the side of my head."

"I told him that if the ear was too far gone, I knew where he could get hold of another spare appendage to sew onto your head in its place. When I said it, he didn't hoot with merriment."

"Plastic surgeons are not famous for their whimsicality. If they were, we'd all have faces like Valentino's. And cocks like Lyle's."

He laughed nervously and said, "In your left ear.'

I said, "Yeah. Thank God."

"You'll be out of here in two days, the doctor told me. The bandage will come off in a week."

"Two days? No way. That might be too late."

"Too late for what?"

Most of all, I wanted my strength back then. So I didn't reply. I just shut my eyes, and slept.

Through the night, I dreamed over and over again about a conversation I'd had two nights earlier in the bar at the Albany Hilton.

---

24. I opened the bedside drawer and took out my watch, which a nurse or aide had thoughtfully left for me along with my wallet and keys. It was ten-fifteen. It had to be morning, because the sun was blazing in at me yet again.

Tossing aside the thin sheet that covered me, I swung

my legs over the side of the bed and let my feet touch the metal stool below as I pushed myself upright.

My head throbbed. I touched the bandage wrapped around my skull and the bulge of packing on the left side. I stood up, felt light-headed, blinked, and made the faintness go away. Holding on to the tubular sides of the other unoccupied bed in the room, I made my way to a narrow door. It was not the clothes closet, but I made use of the appliance therein nonetheless and then splashed tepid water on my face.

The clothes closet was behind the door next to the lavatory, but my clothes were not in it and I knew I was going nowhere in my hospital nightie with its little bow holding it together.

I removed the sheets from both beds and fashioned one into an East Indian dhoti, a kind of bulky loincloth, in the manner Timmy had once shown me. Whoever said nothing much tangible had ever come out of the Peace Corps was mistaken. Another sheet I wrapped around my waist skirt-fashion, and a third around my torso with a long flap hanging over my shoulder. I ripped the sewn-up end off a pillow case and made a crude skull cap to cover my bandages.

Snatching a long-stemmed plastic rose from the vase on the windowsill, I shuffled out into the corridor and down to the nurses' station.

"Hare Krishna," I said happily, and offered the rose.

"You people are not supposed to be up here! You're supposed to stay downstairs in the lobby, and you know it!"

I was ushered swiftly to the elevator.

Timmy, ever-dutiful peon to the tattered gentry in the legislature, was not in the apartment and evidently had gone to work. It was Monday morning.

I put on American clothes, had a quart of grapefruit

juice and two bowls of Wheat Chex, and phoned Dot Fisher.

"Get your money back?"

"Oh, Don, yes, yes, I did! I'm so relieved, I can't begin to tell you. I have an appointment with Mr. Trefusis at three o'clock, and I'm going over there to Millpond and just dump the whole gosh-darn bag of money right on his desk. And, let me tell you, I've never looked forward to anything this much in all my days!"

"Mind if I tag along?"

"But you're in the hospital, aren't you? Fenton said you injured your ear fighting with those dreadful men."

"It wasn't serious," I said. "I let a doctor use my head as a darning egg for an hour last night, but now I'm practically good as new. I'll pick you up at two-thirty."

"Why, yes, as a matter of fact, that would be lovely. But I've got to run now, Don. Fenton's out back holding a press conference."

"Sorry I'm missing it, but I'll catch it on the news tonight. I'm sure he's saying something quotable."

"Oh, he is, he is."

I reached Bowman at his office.

"Whozzis?" he snarled. The man hadn't had his weekend golf fix, or sleep.

"Strachey here. Those two lovelies locked up?"

"One's in jail, the other one's over there where you are, under guard. You *just couldn't wait* last night, could you?"

"You were up in the sky. The criminals were down on the ground where I was. But I knew you were with me in spirit, Ned. As is so often the case."

"That son of a bitch should've chewed your mouth off. What a service to the community *that* would've been. You okay?"

"I'll dance again. Look, what did the Andruses tell you. They spill it all?"

"Nothing but bullshit. Duane said they'd just come out to the kennel and found McWhirter there and were about to phone the department when you guys walked in and shot their dog. And Glen won't say a goddamn thing. They've got lawyers now, and before the day's done they'll all be in bed together making up the same stories. But we've got our case. It's tight. Duane's handwriting on the ransom notes, his voice on the tapes, and McWhirter's testimony will do it."

"Did they mention who put them up to it?"

"Whaddaya mean? Why do you ask that?"

I described the telephone conversation I'd overheard at the kennel window. I did not include my own speculation about who the third party was, nor the evidence that had led me to arrive at this thought.

"Why the hell didn't you tell me this before?"

"I was unconscious. As you will recall, just as you dropped out of the sky last night, I swooned. At the sight of your descent from heaven, I guess."

"The way I heard it, you fainted when you found your ear in your pants cuff."

"Yeah, that might have been the way it happened. I forget. Did you recover all the money?"

"No. Just a hundred and a half. Tell me again about this phone conversation you heard. I want to write it down."

I recited it again.

"The third guy's got the rest of the money," I said. "That's why the Andruses are keeping mum. You've got to convince them that with kidnapping and manslaughter, even involuntary, they're going to be off the streets for a long, long time. And there's no point in their waiting to get out to collect the rest of the money. Tell them with the inflation rate what it is, by the time they're free the fifty grand will be worth about a dollar thirty-five."

"Thanks for telling me my business."

"No trouble. What else did you find out at the kennel?"

"A lot of crap, and I mean crap. Dope too. In the room up front where Duane lived we found an ounce of coke."

"Any papers, letters, addresses, phone numbers?"

"An address book with some names and numbers the department is already familiar with. The narcotic squad has been building a case against certain persons, and Andrus's list will come in handy. The boys over there are grateful to me."

"Right, Ned. You did such a bang-up job on this case. Incidentally, I ran across information that Duane Andrus was peddling his ass, and had some kind of sugar daddy who must have kept him in nose candy. Did you find any evidence to support that?"

"Andrus's room did look like some kind of fag brothel. Little bottles of that chemical you people stuff up your nose, dirty movies, and picture books full of male beaver. No offense, Strachey, but I have to tell you, it made me want to puke."

"For men, you don't say 'beaver,' Ned. If it's male you call it 'wombat.'"

"Oh."

"What else was out there?"

"Nothing incriminating or otherwise of interest. There were five bottles of Vaseline Intensive Care lotion. What the hell's that for?"

"Lotta dry skin, Ned. It's for people who work in air-conditioned places, like Albany Med."

"How long you gonna be laid up over there, anyway? Not more than six months, I hope."

"Don't know. I'm just taking it a day at a time. I'll watch the soaps, feel up the orderlies, follow doctors' orders."

"One true fact out of three. That's not bad for you, Strachey."

I gave him some improbable advice, then hung up. I was looking up an address in the phone book when the phone beside me rang.

"Yah-loo."

"Is this the . . . Donald Strachey residence?" She pronounced it "Strakey."

"Mista Strakey inna hospital. This-a his mamma."

"Uh . . . this is Annabelle Clooney at Albany Medical Center. I'm sure there's no need to be concerned, but we're having trouble locating Mr. Strakey. He has been admitted as a surgical patient here, yes, but he's . . . he's not in his room."

"Oh, that boy! I'm gonna take a strap to him! When you find 'im, you call me and I'm comin' over there and box his ears! One of 'em, anyway. The other one's still sore. You tell 'im that!"

I hung up. I looked up the address I wanted in Colonie, then took two aspirins. Timmy had brought my car back and left it in its space. Waves of heat rose off it. I could have fried an egg on the hood but wasn't hungry. I opened all the windows, placed the floor mat on the hot plastic seat, lowered myself onto it, and drove out into the midday traffic.

I picked up the Smith & Wesson at my office, as well as the lightweight jacket that covered it, then headed on out Central.

The owner of Murchison's Building Supply Company in Colonie was disinclined to answer my questions, but when I offered him the choice of talking to me or to Ned Bowman, he picked me. Bowman would have to be calling on him anyway, but I didn't mention that.

Then I drove back to Moon Road.

25.

"Hi, Jerry. Your boss says you're feeling under the weather today. Left the office early."

"Oh, hello! It's you! My boss said that?"

"Mind if I come in? I'd like to talk."

"Well . . . Sandra took Heather swimming."

"No sweat. We won't need a chaperone for this. Joey over at Freezer Fresh?"

"No, not till four. He's down mowing Mrs. Fisher's lawn. She called. That was really white of her. Very Christian. Considering."

He made no move to open the door. We spoke through the screen. The sweat ran down his pale face and splashed onto his drip-dry white dress shirt.

"Why don't you come out and we'll sit under a tree and talk?"

"What about? I'm not feeling well, actually. I was just thinking of . . . going to the doctor. Maybe another time, when I'm feeling up to it, okay?"

"Mr. Murchison says you turned over fifty thousand dollars to him this morning."

"Wh-what?"

"The fifty that was actually due last week. The second payment, including sixteen percent interest, that's restitution for the hundred and forty-one thousand you embezzled from Murchison over three years, and which he caught you at in June."

His mouth worked at speaking words. He fought to keep from collapsing, and managed it, barely. I opened the door and he backed away.

"I don't— I want— I need a drink of water," he stammered.

I followed him into the kitchen and watched him gulp

down some tap water from a plastic cup with a picture of
two Smurfs on it. He rinsed out the cup and placed it on
the drying rack. His mind was working and working.

He turned toward me with a twitchy grin. "I really
can't understand why Mr. Murchison told you that story.
That was just something between he and I. Jeez. Why
would he do that?"

"Where did you get the fifty?" I said.

He kept on grinning, his head moving back and forth,
back and forth, trying desperately to look incredulous.
"Mr. Murchison said—he told me—he'd keep that between us. I was making good. I made a mistake, but he
forgave me, and I was making good."

"If he forgave you, why did he sick Dale Overdorf on
you?"

"Who? Dale who?"

"The goon who roughed you up in June."

"Oh. Oh, jeez. He told you about *that*? You'd think
he'd be ashamed." The panic in him was rising and he
kept swallowing, but it wouldn't go back down.

"Murchison didn't strike me as being either ashamed
or forgiving," I said. "I think he had his reasons for string-
ing you along and not calling in the cops, and leaning on
you at the same time. But you didn't answer my question.
Where did you get the fifty that you paid Murchison this
morning?"

"I borrowed it," he said weakly, not much conviction
left in his voice. Then his face reddened and he slammed
his fist at the air. "Anyway, I don't have to tell you
anything! This is a private matter between Mr. Murchison
and I. Who do you think you are coming in here and delv-
ing into my private affairs! Mr. Murchison said he was
going to treat the whole thing like a loan, so as far as anybody else is concerned, it's none of your darn business!
You come in here and start questioning my integrity

and . . . and you don't have any right! I want you to . . . to leave my house right this minute!"

I said, "What did you do with the money you embezzled? There's no evidence of it around here. No steak for supper at the Deem house, just hot dogs. Where did it all go?"

The anger drained out of him in an instant, as if someone had opened an artery. He stood by the sink whitefaced and trembling now, dumb with shock, watching me, trying to prepare himself for the moment he'd been terrified of all his adult life. I despised the moment too. But I saw no point in putting it off, so I said the words.

"You spent a hundred and forty-one thousand dollars feeding Duane Andrus's coke habit. That's a lot of money for low-grade sex."

He gawked at me in hot panic for a long couple of seconds. And then he broke. Deem slid to the floor, quaking and weeping, his heaving back banging against the sink cabinet, his face in his hands. Between great racking sobs, Jerry Deem shook his head and keened, "I'm *not* a homo! I'm *not* a homo!"

I seated myself on a kitchen chair and gazed out the window at the immobilized T-bird. Not looking at Deem, I said, "The kidnapping wasn't your idea, was it?"

"No, no, I wouldn't have done *that*."

"But Andrus told you about it as soon as he'd done it. And you didn't turn him in. If you had, you might have saved Peter Greco from drowning in a sea of cat fur."

He sobbed and nodded and shook his head.

"Andrus wanted you as an involuntary accomplice to gain a further hold on you, because he thought that Dot Fisher would sell out to Millpond to raise the ransom money and make everybody on Moon Road rich. When Dot threw a crimp into that plan by raising the hundred grand through other means, Andrus decided to kidnap

McWhirter too—none of us knew yet that Greco was dead—and put additional pressure on Dot to sell. That way, Andrus would end up with the ransom money *and* whatever he could extort from you after the sale of your property went through.

"One reason you went along with it was—besides your fear of Andrus's exposing your relationship with him—the other reason was, *you* wanted part of the ransom money to pay off Murchison, who was pressing hard for his August installment and threatened to send Dale Overdorf around again to break your collarbone. Two busted collarbones in one summer would have been hard to explain to your family and friends."

He sobbed and nodded, nodded and sobbed. I looked down at him. My head hurt. I felt sick.

"Why, Jerry? I understand the two-life syndrome. Like a lot of people, I once lived that way myself. I understand the terror that drives men to it. But why Duane Andrus? Why some violent punk like him? There are two billion men on the face of the earth. Why Andrus?"

He peered up at me now, still shaking, his face awash with sweat and tears. After a long, tense moment, he said angrily, "Because he was *evil*. I am an abomination unto the Lord! Duane Andrus is what I *deserved*."

We sat gazing at each other. If Fenton McWhirter had been there he would have attempted to explain a few things to Deem. But I had neither the stomach for it nor any hope that it would make a difference to anyone living.

Breathing more easily now, Deem said, "I think— I guess I better have a Valium. I need to calm down."

I nodded.

He managed to stand and wobble into the living room, then staggered left into the rear part of the house.

After a moment, I stood and walked quickly in the direction Deem had gone. The bedrooms were empty. A door in the short hallway was shut. I knocked. He didn't answer. I tried the knob. Locked.

In an instant, I made a decision I sometimes later regretted. I lifted a leg and sent my shoe crashing hard against the flimsy plywood door. It exploded inward, knocking Deem against the sink, the battery of pills flying out of his mouth and pinging against the mirror like buckshot. He flailed about, grabbing for the pills, but I had him by the collar and dragged him into the living room backwards.

Then to the kitchen, where I bent him over the table and held him there with one hand while I dialed the phone with the other. I glanced at my watch while I dialed. Five after two. There was just enough time. I had another appointment to keep.

26.

As I drove Dot Fisher up Moon Road, we passed two Albany police cruisers and Bowman's blue Dodge parked in front of the Deem house. She asked if I knew what was going on there, and I told her. She was silent for a long time. Then she said, "I'll drop in on Sandra later. She'll probably be needing some help."

We met Dot's attorney in the refrigerated lobby of the Millpond building and rode up together to Crane Trefusis's office. Marlene Compton ushered us into Trefusis's aerie of cool brown sunlight at exactly three o'clock. Dot was wearing electric blue slacks that clashed with the buffs and rusts. Trefusis removed his shades and greeted us with the bemused serenity of a man who knew that, overall, he would get what he wanted.

"Nice of you to drive all the way over here," he said. "I would have been more than happy, of course, to send one of our people out to Moon Road to pick it up."

Dot opened a Price Chopper paper bag and dumped the dollars on Trefusis's desk. "I wanted to present this to you myself," she said. "Please count it."

Trefusis laughed lightly. "No need for that. I know an honest woman when I meet one."

The lawyer produced a document canceling Millpond's option on Dot's property. Dot and Trefusis signed copies of it. Then Trefusis handed over a receipt for the hundred thousand.

"Nice doing business with you, Mrs. Fisher," he said. "Even under these sad and unproductive circumstances."

Dot mumbled something, started to leave the office, then turned and looked back at Trefusis. "I feel sorry for your mother, if she's living," she said. "You're going to make a lot of money, Mr. Trefusis. But otherwise you're not going to amount to much."

The lawyer looked embarrassed and followed Dot out the door. I yelled after them, "I'll meet you in the lobby in ten minutes."

When the door closed, Trefusis said, "Funny old gal. I guess their minds go after a while."

I said, "The reward money. Ten grand. It's mine."

He stuck the stem of his shades in the corner of his mouth and studied me. He said, "That was for bringing Peter Greco back alive. You failed."

He was right. I didn't argue. My impulse was to break his nose, but my head hurt. I now owed Whitney Tarkington a hundred and ten thousand dollars. Fifty thousand had been recovered from Duane Andrus, and Trefusis's fee for catching the graffiti vandal would cover another ten. I still had to come up with an additional fifty thousand dollars by the next afternoon. Timmy was good for five, and my bank would, at 15 percent interest, make up the rest. Quite a weekend.

Trefusis was blathering on about how tragic the whole affair had been, but how Dot at least was going to be able to keep her beloved farm, and Trefusis had his eye on some acreage being offered for sale at the Christian Brothers retreat area, and in the end everything was going to work out all right for everyone concerned.

"Except for Peter Greco," I said. "And Fenton McWhirter, who's alone now."

"It's unfortunate," he mused. "But it's no one's fault. Not you, not I. A tragic, tragic accident. None of us is to blame."

I told him about Jerry Deem. He went white.

I said, "You knew."

"That's absurd!" he blurted, with no conviction whatever.

"Your pal Murchison, a Millpond partner and chief supplier of construction materials for Millpond projects, mentioned to you in June that he had an accountant with his hand in the till and the authorities were going to have to be called in. When you found out the financial sleight-of-hand artist was the one and only Jerry Deem, you suggested to Murchison that there were other ways of handling it. In fact, you insisted on it. You offered Murchison Dale Overdorf "

His cheek twitched.

"You didn't want to unleash Overdorf on Dot Fisher directly," I said. "You knew how stubborn she was and how much public sympathy would be aroused by the beating of an old lady. If it ever somehow got traced back to you, Millpond would suffer bad PR, bad enough maybe to fatally unravel the deals you had with the planning boards and environmental agencies. But Jerry Deem was another matter, wasn't he?"

Twitch, twitch.

"You could put all the pressure you wanted on Deem without having to worry about his blowing the whistle, and then hope that he would come up with the means, of whatever gruesome sort, for persuading Dot to sell. It nearly worked. Deem, by way of his alternating threats and promises to his family, inadvertently, or advertently, triggered his son Joey into menacing Dot with the graffiti and threatening letters and phone calls. And by Deem's holding out lurid promises of vast wealth to Duane Andrus as soon as Dot Fisher folded and Deem sold his property to you, the kidnapping and death of Peter Greco were set in motion."

His jaw was so tight I thought it might shatter if I touched it. But I'd decided to deal with Trefusis's jaw later, whenever my head stopped throbbing.

"You didn't count, of course, on matters becoming quite so messy as they did," I said. "When you brought me in, the only sacrificial lamb in all of this was supposed to have been Joey Deem. You must have guessed that he was the graffiti artist, and I was to nab him and earn Millpond's goodwill from Dot, who would gratefully relent and sell out, and Joey Deem would get a slap on the wrist as a juvenile offender.

"Except, you blew it, Crane. There was a side of Jerry Deem's life you didn't know about. You didn't check him out well enough and find out just how damaged and volatile a human being you were lighting a fuse under. Deem was more canny and driven in his efforts to cover up certain of his ongoing socially embarrassing affairs than you'll ever dream of being. You found out he was unstable and vulnerable, but not *how* unstable he was, and that he was beholden to people who were absolutely batty. Murderously so, as it happened. You fucked up, Crane. Royally. As befits your position in what passes for aristocracy in Albany."

He studied me for a long moment, his face frozen in

white rage. Then he spoke. "You're going to the D.A. with this bullshit story?"

"Yep."

A tight little grin. "It'll be laughed out of court. I'll deny it. Murchison will deny there'd ever been an embezzlement. Deem will be certified insane. The judge will chastise you and your faggot friends for wasting the taxpayers' money."

"Could be," I said, getting up. "But you'll get your name in the papers, Crane. Every day for six months. You and your company. So, if you're going to build a shopping mall on the Christian Brothers' land, you'd better do it in the next forty minutes."

He twitched some more as I walked out.

Marlene Compton chirped, "Have a nice day."

In the ways that counted, I did.

EPILOGUE

Crane Trefusis survived five months in Albany before being dismissed by Millpond and fleeing to Wichita, his wife's hometown, where he became manager of a J. C. Penney's store. Just before his departure, I walked into La Briquet and knocked him across his table into a chocolate walnut soufflé being served to the speaker of the New York State Assembly. Trefusis's jaw collided with a silver bowl and shattered. He pressed charges. I was fined five hundred dollars, put on six months' probation, and just barely kept my license. Bowman loved it.

As a result of the outrage generated by Peter Greco's death, Fenton McWhirter signed up eleven additional men and women for the gay national strike before moving up to Burlington, Vermont, for a recruiting effort there. Greco was cremated and his remains carried across the nation in McWhirter's backpack, and later scattered over the Pacific, like Harvey Milk's. At a memorial service in the Albany Gay Community Center, Dot Fisher talked about Peter's resiliently gentle ways; Edith was at her side, though she'd worn a veil over her face while entering the building.

No shopping mall was built on Moon Road. A small commercial establishment did, however, spring up at the corner of Moon and Central. On Labor Day weekend I stopped at the spot, where Dot Fisher and Kay Wilson were helping Heather Deem run a refreshment stand. The sign read, MOON ROAD PLAZA ASSOCIATES —KOOL-AID 25 CENTS.

One unseasonably warm September night, Timmy and I put Lyle Barner on a bus for San Francisco, armed with a citation of merit for his role in the capture of the Andruses. I heard later that he was living in Daly City, California, and was married to a forty-six-year-old divorced woman with six children—though this might have been gossip spread by Ned Bowman hoping that it would reach me and set an example. If so, it was an example I did not consider following.

Three days after Lyle left town, Timmy and I joined Dot and Edith for a feast of roast duck and Dot's famous elderberry cheesecake to celebrate Edith's seventy-sixth birthday. Afterwards, on the way back to the apartment, Timmy said, "Dot and Edith are quite a pair. All that love, devotion, emotional simplicity, repose. It leaves an impression."

"On me too."

"That's us, thirty years from now," he said. "With luck."

"It's what I want," I made myself say.

We were heading across Washington Park, which smelled moist and hot and alive.

"In the meantime," Timmy said, "why don't you swing down by the lake? Maybe we can pick up a couple of humpy SUNY students and take them over to our place for a wild foursome."

I swerved, straightened out, then glanced over at him to see if he was grinning and shaking with mirth. He was. As we continued on across the park and out onto Madison, I glanced at him a couple more times.

"Just testing you," he said brightly.

I said, "I'll bet," taking a quick look back toward the park, and he laughed again.

It was going to be a stimulating thirty years.